About the Author

Robert Brown was born in London in 1968. He left school with no qualifications to speak of, and has worked most of his life in the engineering industry. He first had the idea for this novel well over a decade ago but only started writing it at the end of 2015. He has since completed work on a second book and is currently working on a third. When not writing, he enjoys listening to music, running and tries to avoid being too serious! He lives on his own in Poole, Dorset, and has two children.

A Song for The Silence

Robert Brown

A Song for The Silence

Olympia Publishers

London

www.olympiapublishers.com
OLYMPIA PAPERBACK EDITION
Copyright © Robert Brown 2017

The right of Robert Brown to be identified as author of
this work has been asserted in accordance with sections 77 and 78 of the
Copyright, Designs and Patents Act 1988.

All Rights Reserved
No reproduction, copy or transmission of this publication
may be made without written permission.
No paragraph of this publication may be reproduced,
copied or transmitted save with the written permission of the publisher,
or in accordance with the provisions
of the Copyright Act 1956 (as amended).

Any person who commits any unauthorised act in relation to
this publication may be liable to criminal
prosecution and civil claims for damage.
A CIP catalogue record for this title is
available from the British Library.

ISBN: 978-1-84897-945-1

This is a work of fiction.
Names, characters, places and incidents originate from the writer's
imagination. Any resemblance to actual persons, living or dead, is purely
coincidental.

First Published in 2017

Olympia Publishers
60 Cannon Street
London
EC4N 6NP
Printed in Great Britain

Dedication

Dedicated to anyone who has ever tried to make a comeback!

Acknowledgments

I would like to thank the many people whom I have bored senseless, constantly banging on about this novel. Geoff, Jane, Clare, MBG who inspired one of the characters, Peter and Karen, Skippy, Emma, and Laura. I also owe a great deal of thanks to the internet, particularly Google maps! Also, it would be wrong of me not to mention the great singers, songwriters and musicians, real and fictional, mentioned in the story. Lastly (but not least) my family, who have been involved in the process from start to finish, especially my children, Nick and Aimee. Thanks all!

Introduction

All good songs have a great intro don't they? Not necessarily, of course, but it does help if the first few bars gain your attention and make you want to hear the rest. The song needs to have a catchy tune and lyrics that make you feel a sense of empathy with the performer. There is no magic formula to reproducing this, but some gifted songwriters achieve it time and time again. There are others who must be content with being a one-hit wonder. They probably toiled long and hard, touring round a succession of seedy looking pubs and clubs, trying to be heard. During this process they slowly gain themselves a reputation for decent tunes. They are spotted and get signed to a record label where they are handed an advance and told to produce hits. These days, unless they have something extremely special about them, they only get one album to impress. Let's just say that they have a hit single, they are expected to come up with similar quality tunes, time and time again. It's very rare that they consistently sell vast amounts. This would probably explain why so many artists these days don't write their own material as the pressure to be successful is immense.

So, what else makes a song a huge seller? The answer is that there is no magic formula involved, despite what people will have you believe. There is more to it than a good melody, strong beat and clever words. There are many considerations these days, such as getting across the right message on social media. Generally, creating an image that is going to make you interesting and intriguing enough, is paramount. Something that has always fascinated me with music is that what appeals to one person can be truly abysmal to another and why you can never really judge music on sales. How is it then that a simply brilliant song can struggle to get anywhere near the top forty? You must agree that we have had quite a few dreadful number one singles over the years.

Have you ever wondered how a song starts its life and what happens to it, in between being written and being played on your favorite radio station? The answer is: anything can happen and probably will do. Some artists work very slowly and can take four or five years in between albums, carefully honing their sound. Others, are very prolific and can bring out album after album within a short space of time, relying on spontaneity as their inspiration.

This is a story about a song, not just *any* old song, but one song in particular. It's a tune with an interesting history, sung by a performer with an intriguing past. It's also a story about human beings and their struggle to be successful, and also about their relationships with each other.

As you read the story, you will come across many song titles that are mentioned along the way. Most of them are real songs, some better known that others, and these can be looked up on YouTube, Spotify or any other online player. I would like to think that they could be put on a playlist and listened to in the background whilst you are reading. Some of the titles, however, are completely fictional and have been invented for the purposes of this tale.

Whatever your musical preference, I hope that you find in here some music that you will enjoy. I also hope that you enjoy the characters in the book as much as I have enjoyed writing about them and watching them grow and progress as the story goes on. At the end of the book, I have listed the songs relating to the chapter titles and their significance to the story. As a rule of thumb, the songs from the chapter titles are real songs, as are the songs mentioned where I have linked them with a act. Remember, that every song that you hear, whether it's an international best-seller or a debut song by an unknown act, there's always a story behind it.

1. START!

The traffic on the A31 was horrendous. An accident in the New Forest had brought the traffic to a standstill and both cars and lorries stood bumper to bumper. Max Chilton looked at the face of his smartphone and pressed the speed dial number one, reserved for his wife Charlotte, or Lottie as everyone called her.

'Hiya,' she answered.

'Hi Lottie! I'm stuck in traffic, yet again. I might not get back until about seven,' said Max

'Oh god, really? Alright, well I'll feed the kids and we can worry about food when you get here. How was your day?'

'Busy! The world of manufacturing never stops as you know and I have to go to a big conference at the N.E.C at the end of next month. It's a two-day thing, so I'll have to stay up there in Birmingham.' Max did his best Brummie accent and Lottie chuckled. Their children, Arthur and Maisie, were four and two, and Lottie was still a full-time Mum. It was a decision that they both believed in wholeheartedly, but often made them struggle financially. Lottie had been an auxiliary nurse before the children were born and was seriously thinking of going back to work to relieve their monetary worries.

They had moved into an old house in a small Dorset village seven years ago. The house was in disrepair and frankly a money trap. Max and Lottie had been lovingly restoring the place when time and money allowed, even though there were times when it all seemed like a huge burden to them. Max worked for a large Japanese Corporation called I.M.C. which stood for Imperial Mining Company. They were a huge player in the global market and had many divisions. Max worked for the Hardmetal Division, selling small engineering cutting tools to production, manufacturing and aerospace companies. It was the means to an end for Max; he dreamed of the day he could afford to give it up and do something more creative with his time.

'Oh, Max, could you stop off for bread and milk on your way through, please?' said Lottie.

'Yep, no problem. I'll stop at the Tesco Express in the Village. The traffic's moving now, I'm going to hang up, love you, byeeee!'

Max put the car into drive on his automatic transmission, and moved off slowly. After ten minutes, he passed an old Ford Fiesta that was on fire. 'So, *that* was the cause of the hold up,' he thought. The traffic sped up as he approached Ringwood.

In half an hour, Max had driven his company Toyota Avensis through Wimborne, turned onto the road to Blandford Forum, and driven into the small village of Tarrant Marshall where they lived. He approached the local shop and was lucky enough to be able to pull up right outside. He jumped out and went straight to the cashpoint and checked his balance; £800 in debit! It was only £100 away from their overdraft limit and ten days from payday. His heart sank and he put his card back in his wallet without withdrawing cash. He then went into the local shop, bought the cheapest bread and milk he could find, paying on his debit card and then drove home.

Max and Lottie had met back in 2006. Max, who was now forty-five, was ten years older than Lottie. Max was then thirty-six and just out of a long term relationship with a previous girlfriend. Lottie was nursing at Poole Hospital, and was working there when Max was wheeled into the ward after undergoing an emergency appendectomy. They had hit it off immediately and began dating very soon after Max had been discharged. To the shock of their friends and family, they got married on a long weekend in New York, in front of two witnesses, in a small registry office on the edge of Central Park. It all happened not long after they met. They lived in Max's two-up-two-down terraced house for a couple of years, and decided to take the plunge and buy the house they now inhabited in Tarrant Marshall. It was a big financial gamble, and after spending seven years on renovating and decorating, the house still had some major flaws and was not getting any better. They had recently spent a thousand pounds on treating some damp and could not afford any more expenses. They had already agreed that the family's health, happiness and sanity came before anything else. If they needed to downsize in order for this to be a reality, then that is what they would do. It seemed to Max that this is was a necessary evil, although he knew it would break Lottie's heart. Their relationship had coped well with everything so far, but there had been a few uncharacteristic rows, and the inevitable strain was starting to show.

Lottie was sat in the kitchen when Max returned, watching Arthur and Maisie eat the Bolognese that she had made.

'No, not up your *nose,* Arthur, yuck!' There was more food on Arthur's face than on the plate!

'I'm back!' Max greeted his wife. She stood up and gave him a kiss and a hug,

'And how are you guys?' Max asked his children.

Maisie blew bubbles and clapped her Dad. Arthur cheered, 'Hi Daddy!'

'I'm glad to be back,' he said.

'Have you checked the bank balance today?' said Max with a painful grimace. Lottie returned a rather sheepish response.

'Hmmm,' she said. 'I don't know how were going to carry on like this. The hospital called today and offered me one day a week. It's not a lot but it will help. I know it was me who said I wanted to stay at home until both the kids were at school, but I've got to face it, it's not going to happen! I'll take up her offer, and now that Arthur's at school, Mum has offered to have Maisie for the day that I work. Hopefully, it'll take some of the pressure off you.'

Max nodded and smiled. He walked over to his wife and hugged her. Whilst he balanced his chin on the top of her head, he spun her thick locks of dark curly hair through his fingers and thought about the stress he'd been under. Yes, it would help. A little, anyway, but if only there was something else he could do. A lottery win was out of the question and he couldn't put any *more* hours in! There were always his parents he could borrow money from, but he was very reluctant. After they had tidied up and put the children to bed, they watched the Friday Night comedy on BBC1. There was nothing like an episode of 'Not Going Out' to make Max & Lottie laugh and generally relax. They drank the bottle of red wine that Lottie's friend, Ali had bought them for babysitting her daughter last weekend. They lived to fight another day, but for how long? They went to bed just after eleven o' clock and vowed to enjoy the weekend, and not think about their dire financial state until Monday. The rain had started outside; the forecast had predicted a stormy night and the wind could be heard blowing through the row of conifers at the back of the house.

It was 2.10a.m. according to the clock radio on Max's bedside table. The wind had turned into a gale and the rain lashed hard against the windows of the Chilton's bedroom. Max was fast asleep as was Lottie until… drip! A small drop of water hit her on the nose. It was enough to wake her up and she sat bolt upright as another drop of water hit her on the top of her head.

'Max! Switch the light on! We've sprung a leak,' said Lottie.

Max reluctantly woke, turned over and switched on the small bedside light. They looked up and saw the wet patch on the artexed ceiling above them. They jumped out of bed and Max moved towards the loft hatch, which was situated on the landing. He began to pull down the loft ladder that he and his Dad had fitted last year. He clambered up and fumbled around for the light switch. He soon found it, illuminated the attic and climbed up inside. He looked around searching for a reason for the disturbance, and there it was. The gale had dislodged one of the tiles and some water was trickling through a small hole in the felt. He would need to improvise for now, fix it up temporarily and then have a look in the morning. He moved across to the other side of the loft and found an old black builder's bucket that he had used for the plastering he'd done in the lounge. He placed it under the gap in the roof and water started to drip slowly into it. He then found a very old roll of gaffer tape and fixed up the gap in the felt. 'That would have to do for now,' he thought. He walked slowly back towards the loft hatch and edged past some boxes which were balanced carefully along some rafters. As he moved past them, he lost his balance slightly and grabbed the top of the rafter to stop himself from falling. While he was doing this, his elbow knocked the top box off the pile and it fell open on the insulating material about ten feet away. The contents of the box scattered around and Max wondered what it was; it could have been books or old DVDs? He would look in the morning. For now, he headed back down the loft ladder where Lottie had moved their bed slightly so that any residual drops of water did not affect them, and they went back to sleep.

  The next morning, the rain had subsided over the village of Tarrant Marshall. It was Saturday and the weekend slowly began. A local running club paced themselves through the village. They were training for a big local 10k and wanted to score points in the road race league against all their rivals. The last, rather rotund looking runner, puffed past the Green Dragon pub and just opposite was the late 1950s house which belonged to Max & Lottie. It was one of three houses that was built at the same time in the village and looked rather at odds with the pretty thatched cottages that lined Wimborne Road, the main thoroughfare through Tarrant Marshall. Planning laws in the 1950s weren't what they are now, and the design of the houses wasn't seen to be out of place; it probably wasn't even considered that they weren't aesthetically sympathetic to the area.

Tarrant Marshall was a small village of around seven hundred people situated in the Stour Valley, equidistant of Poole and Blandford Forum. The population consisted of farmers; a few local families who had lived there for generations and whose grown up children had moved away to find more affordable housing. There were also people who had moved there from London and more affluent parts of the country, like Max, who had grown up in East Berkshire. The Chiltons had made a huge effort to be a big part of the village community, attending all the local events that centered around the village hall, the last one being for the harvest festival. They had been regulars at the Green Dragon whenever they could get a babysitter and made friends with their neighbours.

Max and the family had discussed what they would like to do today; a walk on the beach at nearby Poole was discussed and they decided to go in the afternoon. Max needed to go up into the loft again to inspect the damage. Luckily, his mate Will worked as a roofer, and he could probably fix it as a favour. Unfortunately, he was away on holiday in Tenerife until Wednesday. Max had decided to check it was secure and dry until then, and so he climbed up the ladder once again and clambered into the rather low attic space, crouching so as not to hit his head. He walked over to where the damage was. The gaffer tape had held firm much to his relief and he checked the bucket; it was about half full so he quickly carried down to the bathroom and emptied it into the bath. Back inside the loft he replaced the bucket into its position, stood up and walked back towards the loft hatch. It was then he remembered the box that had dropped and emptied. In the half-light, he could make out that it was an old Clark's shoe box, which had once probably contained a pair of his old school shoes. He remembered it well; in his teenage years he filled it with his cherished boyhood memorabilia. It lay half empty on the insulation and still contained a medal he had won with his old school football team, some badges, one which was enamelled in blue and said 'We all follow Chelsea.' He chuckled as he sorted through the items. Another badge which was in the colour of a target and said, 'The Jam.' It all came flooding back to him! There were some old 1980s coins, a ten pence piece and an old half penny. Over to the left of the box were some old football programmes, some photos of him with his first girlfriend, 'better keep that hidden,' he thought to himself and grinned. He placed them carefully back into the box and replaced it on the top of the other boxes. Just as he stood up, he noticed out of the corner of his eye a small rectangular black and transparent plastic box with a cardboard inlay. It was unmistakably an old cassette, although anyone younger than thirty probably wouldn't have a clue what it was! The cardboard inlay said in bold print, 'BASF LH90.' The cassette inside had an orange label and had the handwritten words, 'Songs 23/7/1990.' Max knew what it was straight way, he grinned and laughed in disbelief, he hadn't seen this for years. The cardboard listing contained more handwriting. He stood and carefully read what had been written on the sleeve:

    1.Never Bring Me Down

2.Citybeat
3.The James Dean of Your Own Generation
4.Cut The Love
5.My Blue Heaven
6.Rainfall
7.September
8.Love Like This
9.Forever and a Day.

It was a track listing; Max had been in a band in his late teens called The Silence. They never hit the big time but were a very popular band in the East Berkshire town where he grew up. These songs were written by Max and meant for that band but the songs had never seen the light of day. The band had split up by the time he had recorded them on his four track Tascam Porta Studio. They sat in the box ever since. He placed the cassette in his pocket, switched off the loft light, climbed back down the ladder and replaced the loft hatch. He went back downstairs to find the family.

That afternoon they drove down to Poole and spent the afternoon, as promised, on the beach at Sandbanks. Arthur propelled himself along on his Teenage Mutant Ninja Turtles Scooter along the promenade, whilst Mum and Dad walked behind with Maisie in her pushchair.

'What are we going to do, Max, I mean about money?' asked Lottie.

'I think there's only one thing we can do,' he replied 'We will have to give it until January and then put the house on the market.'

Lottie had tried to fight it, but a small tear fell from her right eye, and then the floodgates opened. They had discussed moving on several occasions; somewhere closer to town where properties were cheaper. Once there, they could get away with just the one car. With everything a little bit closer, they could find a modern house, with a modern roof and modern wiring! Something that didn't need constant updating, then perhaps they could enjoy life a little more, and maybe take a holiday or two. It was a tempting option, but on the other hand, they loved that house and the village. Their children had known nothing else and Arthur had just started at the local school and was starting to make friends. They had a lot to think about but were completely unaware of what was about to unfold.

2. Real Wild Child

Tommy was fifty-two years old. You wouldn't have thought it, but he was. He looked sixty-six but mentally he was still nineteen! He hadn't grown up, even after everything life had taught him. He was still one of the boys crawling home from the pub at 2.30a.m., and last night had been no exception! It was the morning after and Tommy opened one eye, looked around him, uttered the phrase, 'Oh Fuck no!' and closed his eyes again. He would have to get up and appear today; there were people who he needed to see, people who could maybe get him back to somewhere near his former self. They were people who would give up on him if he didn't make the effort, he knew this. It was about the only thing that would get him out of bed before two! It was ten thirty. He would get up at eleven, have something to eat and head out the door. That would give him at least half an hour to snooze.

Thomas Francis McNeill was born in Derby to a Scottish family on the third of February 1963. His father was a journalist and worked for the local newspaper, The Derby Telegraph. The family moved to Surrey in 1970 when Willie McNeill was offered a job with The Sutton Guardian. It was hardly the national press, but closer to Fleet Street, which was his dream. Unfortunately, Willie died of a heart attack in 1976 when Tommy was thirteen. The young Tommy had a gift for singing and was a chorister at his local church. At school, he was always singled out to sing in school plays and performances. He was on holiday at Butlin's in Bognor Regis with his parents at the age of nine when his Mother entered him into the talent competition. He won hands down, singing Donny Osmond's 'Puppy Love' which had been a hit earlier in the year. First prize was a free weekend for his family at the resort. He had always been small and didn't look anything like the handsome star he would grow into and always endured a fair amount of stick at school for his vocal abilities. Tommy was an only child and his Mother Miriam seemed to neglect him a little as she searched for someone to replace her husband. She eventually met Malcolm, an upstanding local bank manager. He and Tommy immediately disliked each other and continually fought and argued until Malcolm died in 2003. The young Tommy formed a band with his classmates called, The Clowns, named after legendary Singer/Songwriter Smokey Robinson's song 'Tears of a Clown', of which they were all big fans. They honed their sound, a blue-eyed soul with attitude around the Surrey pubs & clubs, eventually graduating to venues like The Marquee, The 100 Club and the Mean Fiddler in Harlesden, North-West London. At this time, they were signed by RCA Records and were given a three album recording contract. After a couple of minor hits, three number one singles followed and their cover version of Smokey Robinson's classic, 'Tracks of My Tears,' found its way onto the soundtrack of a blockbusting Tom Cruise film. This song turned them into mega-stars on both sides of the Atlantic. They ended up playing huge venues, culminating in a headlining performance at The Pasadena Rose Bowl in 1986. With around 85,000 people in attendance, this was the peak of their career. At about this time, Tommy had developed stage fright, or performance anxiety as it's also known. He would cope the only way he knew how; alcohol, tobacco and prescription drugs. Yes, there was Heroin and Cocaine around but Tommy had enough on his plate with the addictions he already had. It all took its toll in 1987. The band had been invited onto Wogan, the early evening chat show featuring the genial, late Irish presenter Terry Wogan. Tommy, who had turned up completely smashed on Jack Daniels and Lorazepam, turned away from the audience during the saxophone break, pulled his trousers down, bared his naked backside to the audience and walked off stage. It was a live show that evening and this was in the days before a seven second delay was introduced. Knowing the backlash would be catastrophic, he jumped into a taxi, travelled down to Roehampton, and checked himself into The Priory, where he stayed for the next three weeks. He was in effect, out of harm's way, leaving his bandmates to deal with the fallout. Of course, that was the end of The Clowns, and the end of Tommy's career for a few years. Tommy had started a solo career in the early Nineties with mixed results; a good start with a couple of hits soon faded, and Tommy's battles with drinking, drugs and stage fright continued. After being dropped by a couple of record labels, he found himself in the early noughties mainly restricted to the nostalgia tours. These had become popular with artists like Kim Wilde, Nick Heyward, The Human League and Mari Wilson playing mid-sized venues around the UK to enthusiastic but restrained middle-aged, middle-class audiences. It was work, but didn't pay enough. The last of Tommy's remaining properties had been repossessed in 2012 and he now lived back with his rather elderly Mum in Sutton. It was a humiliating situation for Tommy but he'd managed to kick the prescription drugs and tobacco, leaving alcohol as his only vice. His twice-weekly visits to the gym had provided him with some self-respect and he now had an agent who was trying to get him work. He mainly found him after dinner speaking about work, and bizarrely about some motivational speech work, although to be fair, this mainly consisted of a 'don't do what I did' type of rhetoric.

    After prizing himself out of bed, Tommy headed on foot into town and climbed up the stairs to the offices above Carphone Warehouse on Sutton High Street. Whilst there, he saw his agent, Peter Banister, who had found some work for him. Again, it was a motivational speech at a machine tool conference at the N.E.C in Birmingham. Tommy was to make a speech; it would be written for him and would be a humorous send-up of his infamous Wogan performance. The message of the speech was basically telling people how to keep calm under pressure, and not do things the way he did. He was to be paid £1000, plus expenses and free accommodation at The Hilton. The hotel was within walking distance of the venue. He couldn't turn down that type of work, it wasn't music, but he'd purposely avoided music recently as he wanted to avoid another meltdown. He went home via The Cock & Bull pub feeling pleased with his morning's 'work.' He downed a quick glass of single malt before arriving back at the house. He switched on the television and got his usual fix of daytime quizzes and antiques programmes. Tommy looked up at the pictures on the mantelpiece. His father, Willie, stared at him and just to the right was a picture of a younger Tommy with a young girl next to him. She couldn't have been more than three or four years old in this shot; it was his daughter, Lauren. He didn't know where she was now. Her mother had made it very difficult for them to maintain any sort of normal relationship; she would be twenty-two now. He blew a kiss towards the photo and then cast his gaze back towards 'Cash in the Attic.' Sometimes, at moments like this, he drifted off back to thinking about his music career. Could he come back? Who knows! He'd tried, heaven knows he'd tried, but he'd never been able to find the songs that would take him where he needed to go. There were so many good songs and so many good songwriters, but not all of them suited. It was all in the song. He was a soul singer and it needed to be delivered with conviction. He needed to feel it!

3. Don't Look Back in Anger

It was November 1986. Eighteen-year-old Max Chilton reclined on his single bed in his bedroom at his parent's home in the Thames Valley. He carefully held his Bass Guitar, a pearl white Fender Jazz Special, and played along to the album 'Rattlesnakes' by Lloyd Cole and the Commotions. The disc was a perennial favourite of his and spent a lot of time on his record player. He particularly loved the track 'Forest Fire' with its quiet acapella beginning, building up slowly to a crescendo of searing guitars. His music taste basically rotated around the British post-punk bands of the eighties, but the band he had helped form had a different sound. He was trying to adapt, and maybe make the band perhaps crossover to his tastes, not entirely, but the fusion might have worked. He had formed the band with his old schoolmates: Mike Dean on Vocals, Jimmy Cunningham on Guitar and Miles Houghton on Tenor Sax. They had been joined by random friends and work colleagues; Simon Jones on Keyboards, Tony Willis on Drums and they had recently acquired Lindsay Patterson on backing vocals. Lindsay was Simon's girlfriend, and as Simon was four years older than the others, he was the natural leader of the band. He also was the manager and main songwriter. Max was trying to change that by introducing some of his own songs to the band. Most of his songs were roundly rejected by the band, but encouraged by his girlfriend Kate, he carried on writing and he felt his efforts were improving. He was no guitarist but would sketch out basic chords and work melodies in over the top. Of course, because he was a bass player, they all had a strong bass riff, something for him to get his teeth into!

The band's sound was verging on a modern Tamla Motown sound and this showed in the cover versions they sprinkled in amongst their own material. Wilson Pickett's 'In the Midnight Hour' was always a crowd pleaser and The Isley Brother's 'This Old Heart of Mine' was Max's personal favorite. Max had also instigated that the band played Martha & The Muffins 'Echo Beach,' which would have been a departure had they been able to make it sound right. Unfortunately, this never made the set-list. They had called the band, 'The Silence.' The name was short, to the point, and maybe slightly ironic. Most importantly, it looked good on a poster. The band's singer, Mike, was a graphic designer by trade and had created a stunning logo which they used on promotional posters.

Tonight, they had their last rehearsal before their biggest and most exciting gig yet. They had managed to secure a support slot at the 100 Club in London's west end. This venue had started off at 100 Oxford Street as a Jazz club in the 1940s but had had a resurgence in the 1970s as the home of some of the best-known punk acts of the time: The Sex Pistols, Siouxsie & The Banshees, The Clash & The Jam. The Rolling Stones had even played there in 1982 as a warm up gig for one of their tours. They were lucky because their local gigging venue, The Coach & Horses in Slough had the same promoter, Micky Leach, and through him, Simon had managed to secure a support slot. They would be supporting The Blues Experience, a popular live act who performed covers of blues and pub-rock classics. Their closing number, 'Everybody Needs Somebody to Love,' which was originally performed by Solomon Burke but best known as a Blues Brothers song. They would need to put on a tight performance though because The Blues Experience consisted of top class local musicians and were all in their thirties and forties, they'd been gigging a long time and knew how to draw an audience. The Silence could only hope that the crowd would be kind to them.

Max had learned to play at the same time as his best mate, and now band mate, Jimmy. They had originally started about two years ago; the friends had attended a course of basic starter lessons held in the home of a German lady called Birgit. There were four or five people in the class, Max and Jimmy, being the youngest, had progressed the quickest. Birgit was exotic to the boys; she wore leather trousers, which they considered very rock n' roll for the small Berkshire town they lived in. She smoked menthol cigarettes whilst they were playing, although Max & Jimmy both joked that she probably smoked something a lot stronger once they had gone. After the lessons had finished, Jimmy and Max purchased electric guitars. Jimmy bought a Washburn Les Paul copy and Max, who had decided to play bass, bought a second-hand Fender Precision off the older brother of a schoolmate. They would set up in Max's lounge whilst his parents were out and trash out simple numbers like The Undertone's 'Teenage Kicks.' Max ran into

Mike who was another old schoolmate on a train to London; they discussed bands and music, and decided there and then, on the 7.45a.m. to Ealing Broadway, to form a band. They agreed with their old school caretaker that they could rehearse in a classroom on a Sunday afternoon. Mike, Max, Jimmy, Miles and the drum machine were soon joined by Simon and Tony. Simon, being older than the others, had been in bands for years and had even cut his own single, albeit unsuccessfully, but he had about twenty original songs to choose from. With those songs, plus the cover versions, they had enough for a set and soon started gigging locally. They sometimes played to a small audience of three or four and other times to a bigger audience. They also played at the odd birthday party. This soon led to support slots in bigger venues, culminating in their upcoming gig next week. Max loaded his amplifier into the back of his mark one Vauxhall Cavalier and sped off to their rehearsal rooms where some of the other lads were setting up.

'Alright Maxi!' said Simon and Mike in unison.

'Been writing hit songs again?'

Simon liked to goad Max about his songwriting ability; some of his material had been laughable and he knew it. Max had the makings of the best song he had ever written at home and he was in the process of finishing it off. It was called 'Forever and a Day' and he hoped to have a rough copy on tape by the first band rehearsal after the 100 Club gig. He'd show them what he was capable of even if it killed him!

'Will Micky Leach be there on Thursday, Si?' asked Max.

'Yeah,' replied Simon. 'I'm hoping to tap the old wanker up for a headline slot if it goes well, but you know what he's like!'

'Oh, I know Leachy alright. He'll probably make us play about another ten gigs at The Coach & Horses before we get anywhere near. I'd love to know how much he pockets from our gigs,' Max replied.

The band was now fully set up, ready to go and as they launched into their set, began with the evergreen 'In the Midnight Hour.' They rattled through their set in forty-three minutes. If they had a fault, it was that they were over enthusiastic and would play their songs far too quickly. They were trying, albeit unsuccessfully it seemed, to slow it down. They were supposed to be a soul band and not a thrash metal outfit, but they realised only experience would improve them as a live act. To help them improve further and maybe get them listened to by a wider audience. A local recording engineer, Grant Caine, had been watching the band and became a good friend of Mike's. He had offered the band studio time for free in return for the opportunity to use his production techniques and further his own career. The band had been generally enthusiastic about this and the first sessions were due to take place next month. Max was generally happy in the band but was, as was mentioned earlier, keen to evolve the band's style. They played a blue-eyed soul that was prevalent on the radio in the late eighties, but he felt they should have their own sound, one unique with its own DNA. The song was the most essential elements and the message it portrayed; it had to come from the heart. Creating a song was something that Max had started tentatively but he began to appreciate the beauty of a well-crafted tune, and in time, he began to listen to more diverse genres. This had a positive effect on his musicianship.

The band members packed away all their instruments and equipment and loaded them into their parked cars outside. They made tentative arrangements to meet up and travel up to London on Thursday in three cars and a van to save on parking. They would get all their instruments and amps in Simon's van which he used at his job as a driver for a printing company. It was handy at times like these! They drifted off and went their separate ways. Mike, Jimmy, Simon and Lindsay went to the nearby River Inn right on the banks of the Thames and enjoyed a swift pint or two. Tony and Miles went off to do their night shift at the local sorting office where they worked, and Max drove off to see Kate, his on/off girlfriend of the last couple of years. Max had left school at sixteen and went to work at his Dad's Precision Engineering company in nearby Slough. He was learning the business from the shop floor upwards and had been groomed from an early age to do this. This, unfortunately, had dire consequences for his education. Kate was privately educated and was home this weekend from University. She had recently left for Bristol and this had caused friction between the couple; they were obviously moving into different worlds. Max was both proud of his girlfriend's academic achievements – she gained two A's and a B in her A levels in the summer – and pleased that she was enjoying her time in Bristol, but equally happy with the way his life was going. They both knew it probably wasn't going to last forever but they were young and both had their whole lives in front of them. He arrived at Kate's parents' detached house just on the outskirts of the town, parked his car on the drive and clutched his Ovation copy acoustic guitar. He greeted Kate's parents, Dave and Doreen, and made his way up to Kate's room where she had her head in a textbook. She was studying Physics in a three-year BSc course and was trying to assimilate the information she had gleaned so far.

'Hi, Max.' She whispered and smiled across at him from her desk.

He walked over, bent down and kissed her. He felt rather distanced from her since she had gone to Bristol, even though they spoke most days on the telephone, and he had been up for the weekend to visit.

'I need to play you something Kate. I've brought the guitar up, it's pretty much finished, it's really not my cup of tea but it will fit the sound of the band a treat. More importantly, the band will *like* it.'

'Okay,' she answered. 'I would love to hear it Max and then we need to talk.'

'That sounded ominous,' thought Max and perched himself on one of the bright orange Habitat branded bean bag that covered the corner of Kate's bedroom. He checked his guitar was in tune and began to play the first chord, which was A Minor 7. Kate's face lit up. Truthfully, it wasn't her cup of tea either, her obsession for New Order was legendary! The song had a soft soul lilt, and to be honest, she could imagine Marti Pellow or that Hucknall bloke from Simply Red signing it rather than Mike! It definitely sounded like it could be a huge song for the band. Max would be thrilled with what she had to say about the song, which made what she had to say to *him* all the more difficult. Max reached the end of the song, his voice now struggling to convey and hold the notes that he needed to.

Kate clapped her approval and pointed out a couple of minor criticisms of the song. Max frowned but he knew what she meant, he made a mental note to modify the middle bridge section before he put it down on tape tomorrow.

Kate took the guitar off Max, stood up and began to speak. She shook a little as she knew what she had to say would hurt, she didn't mean to but it had to be done.

'It's not working is it? I mean you here, me in Bristol, it's like we are on different planets. I mean, I don't mean to be cruel Max, but what have you achieved really? Working for your Dad playing out your fantasy in your band and…'

'And what?!' gasped Max slightly aggressively.

'Well I've… you know met someone at Uni… he's called Nigel and he comes from Durham and…'

Max stormed out of Kate's bedroom, ran down the stairs and out of the house without saying goodbye. He never returned. He'd been expecting something like this but it was still a shock all the same. He arrived home and tried to blank out the conversation that had just taken place, it was not easy, and Kate's words kept rotating around his brain like a heap of clothes spinning around in a washing machine. He was ready though to put down the vocal tracks to 'Forever and a Day', the song he had just played to Kate. He decided to stick with the bridge section against Kate's advice, just in case at some point in the future, she would take some sort of credit for it when it was an international number one smash hit! He was fairly convinced it would be too. He just needed to get the vocals right and it would sound amazing. The tape started and the song went into its gently refrained intro. An acoustic guitar strummed over the drums, bass and some clean sounding picking that he had played on Jimmy's Telecaster. He had borrowed it off him last week. Max began to sing the verse, so far so good! He felt he was creating the sound that he wanted to. He felt good, better than he had for a long time. His mind was clear, free and ready to release his purest emotions as he launched into a big bombastic sounding chorus. He smiled as the song eased back into a minimal instrumental section leading into the second verse and into the rest of the song.

Later that afternoon, he copied the finished song onto a cassette and placed it in its box and into the pocket of his leather jacket. He would listen to it in the car on the way to work in the morning. His shift began at seven in the morning, so it was an early start, but he didn't mind, he needed to keep busy and keep his mind off Kate and Nigel. Little did he know, that this wouldn't be the only break up this month.

4. The End

Max's car sped into West London on the A4 along Cromwell Road. His passengers, Jimmy who was Max's best mate, and Tony, felt a little uneasy at being in the blue Vauxhall Cavalier, as it weaved in and out of the traffic. The trio were chatting nervously as they headed towards The Natural History Museum and on towards Oxford Street. Out of the stereo blasted 'Action Woman' by The Litter, an old sixties American garage band. The song really summed up Max's mood. The other band members were aware that he had split up with Kate and were keeping their eye on him. If only he would keep his eyes on the road, they might be spared! He could get away with playing stuff like this in the car with Jimmy & Tony; they were alright. Mike & Simon would be moaning and demanding Hue & Cry or something equally commercial like that. Jimmy knew Max well enough to know what the next song would be too. 'Thorn of Crowns' by Echo & The Bunnymen; Max's classic break-up song. He'd split up with Kate many times before; the song seemed to sum up his anger and frustration. Jimmy hoped that they would get through this gig without Max having a major wobble! His temperament was a lot cooler than Max's and he was a steady influence on him. The car eventually turned into Oxford Street, then turned off it again and drove into the small parking area that the venue had earmarked for unloading. Simon, Mike, Lindsay and Tony had already arrived and were drinking cups of coffee from polystyrene cups as they stood outside waiting for the rest of the band.

Later that evening, at about 8.30p.m., The Silence band members huddled together in the tiny dressing room just to the side of the stage at the 100 Club. The band was looking around the room in awe. It had been graffitied by some of the most famous bands of the punk era, and whilst punk wasn't any of the bandmate's cup of tea, the cast list was impressive. Max was particularly impressed with the Sex Pistols' logo in a central position on the back wall. He wondered who had penned the artwork; Rotten, Vicious, Cook, Matlock or just one of the entourage of punks that followed them around in their early days.

They had booked a coach for their friends, family and supporters – they wouldn't like to say fans, but people had begun to turn up to the gigs whom they weren't entirely familiar with. Max had been stopped a couple of times whilst out shopping in town, and asked by a complete stranger how the band was going. 'The price of fame,' he thought amusingly. They had been out, chatted to everyone they knew at the venue and there was a buzz in the air. There were well-informed rumours around the place that A & R men from Arista and Polydor were there to watch them tonight, and although these whispers were totally unsubstantiated, they would like to have believed they were true. All this would have been made even better by the presence of one individual, Kate, with whom Max had not communicated with since that last Sunday he stormed off. She was too busy making plans for Nigel!

Micky Leach stood by the open door of the dressing room. 'Right, you horrible fuckin' bunch! It's Showtime!' He was laughing now and the band saw a fun side to Micky Leach. Mick was, to coin a couple of well-known phrases, a ducker and a diver, a wheeler and a dealer and would deal in just about anything. He wasn't fussy. This made the band, with their fairly middle-class backgrounds, slightly nervous around him. They were quite happy to let Simon do all the negotiating with Micky. He was twenty-two and had been around a bit longer than the others, and whilst he was still twenty years younger than Micky, the agent had more respect for him.

The band walked on stage to a loud cheer from their crowd that had travelled 20 miles or so into the West End to see them. Mike adjusted his microphone stand as he wasn't comfortable with it, but he smiled and greeted the audience.

'Hello, thanks for coming tonight, we're going to kick off tonight with a song called "Like a Wheel."'

Max hit the two bars solo on his Bass Guitar and the band came in on the third bar perfectly. This was the only song in their set that had been penned by Max and although it was a fast flowing, energetic and full on number, it was never going to be anything but an opener. He had written it in about 10 minutes after coming home from the pub after a band meeting about six months ago. It was written during one of his famed break-ups with Kate; the lyrics were about the circle of events, and to some extent, karma. Max grinned at his sister and her boyfriend whom he could see in the crowd whilst he harmonised with Mike during the chorus.

Before they knew it, they had completed their set to rapturous applause and they were in the audience with their friends, dancing to The Blues Experience. Max and Jimmy were delighted with their evening's work, but Mike & Simon scowled, they weren't so happy. The sound was not what they were looking for. There *had* been A & R people at the gig, and they had made themselves known to Micky Leach beforehand, but had walked away unimpressed. If they were going to make it anywhere, something would have to change, and Simon knew it. He didn't listen to a single note of the rest of the gig, he was far too deep in his own thoughts. He was aware that at his age he had less time to be a credible pop star. If he didn't get anywhere by, say twenty-five or twenty-six, he would probably not be taken seriously in the recording industry. 'There was only one thing for it,' he thought… 'plan B!'

The band members packed everything away in their vehicles and travelled back home along the M4. Max put a compilation on the stereo; it began with The Undertones' 'My Perfect Cousin.' They listened intently whilst they thought about the gig. The elation of the performance and crowd reaction was tempered with the disappointment of the record companies' disinterest. 'Tomorrow is another day,' thought Max, and he was looking forward to the band meeting on Tuesday when he would be able to showcase his new song to his pals. He thought that they would appreciate the sound he was trying to create. 'It was a bridge builder,' he thought, a halfway house between his and Simon's tastes. He thought about Kate too and what she would have made of tonight's gig.

She was back in Bristol by now, and probably eradicated any thoughts of Max now that she had Nigel in her life. It was not the greatest thing that could have happened, but he was still optimistic as he had his whole life ahead of him. If everything else failed, he had his Dad's business to fall back on. It was *his* one day if that was what he wanted, although at times it felt like a fait accompli. The M4 stretched on in front of him as he signalled and turned off at junction seven. Max made his way to drop Jimmy and Tony off. He arrived home about twenty minutes later. It was 1.45a.m.

Tuesday arrived, and the band started to arrive at Mike's house for the band meeting. Miles & Tony were first, followed by Lindsay and Simon. Jimmy was late as usual, and after collecting Max, they were the last to arrive. They always met at Mike's mother's house. She was a widow and was always working in the evenings. Mike's older siblings had left home which gave them the run of the place. They all gathered around the dining room table, and Max clutched a cassette in his hand, which contained the song he had written. They always showcased new song ideas at these meetings, although he noticed Mike hadn't got the tape machine ready yet. Max thought that he was perhaps running late. Simon and Mike had very deliberately positioned themselves at one end of the table and looked very serious.

Simon cleared his throat and began to speak.

'Firstly, I'd like to say great gig on Thursday guys, the club was pleased and Micky has secured us another gig.'

The rest of the band grinned and whooped at the news but noticed that Mike and Simon still looked rather grim.

'But we're not taking him up on it,' he continued. 'We're dissolving the band. Mike and I have decided to record my songs with the help of Grant Caine, using other musicians. When we have recorded them, we will then form a permanent line-up. It's nothing personal guys but I'm sure you will agree there were musical differences.' He looked at Max as he said this, and Max went white with horror, but he couldn't deny the truth of this statement.

'So, that's it then?' said the normally silent Jimmy.

'No fucking way!' said the less subtle Tony.

'So essentially you're sacking the rest of us Simon!' said Max.

'Yes, you can look at it like that if you wish, but you can carry on being The Silence if you like,' added Mike

'Thanks a bunch,' quipped Jimmy sarcastically.

One by one they left Mike's house until only Simon was left. Max and Jimmy drove home via The Thames Inn, listening to The Doors greatest hits on the way there. Max and Jimmy sang along loudly to 'Riders on The Storm,' and rather ironically chuckled along to 'The End.' It was hard to believe it was the end of 'The Silence,' but that was it! They were never to be seen again. Once he got home, Max placed the cassette in an old shoe box under his bed, and there it stayed gathering dust. A couple of years later, he re-recorded all the songs because he was never satisfied with the originals. He also hoped to rekindle his hopes of playing in a band again, although it never happened. The new tape was put back in the box and not seen again until the night of the leaking roof.

As of today, Simon forged a career with a media production company. Mike continued in his chosen profession as a graphic designer. Tony and Miles spent their entire career with Royal Mail and never played an instrument again in their lives. Jimmy made a fortune out of computers and Lindsay moved to New York and became a successful fashion writer. Max continued to write songs and record them but never joined another band. Soon after his Dad retired, the family sold the engineering business out of necessity when times were tough in the late eighties. Max went to work as a Sales Engineer within the industry, he moved to Dorset with his job in 1992 and the rest is history. During the 'Friends Reunited' phenomenon of the early 2000's, the band got back in touch briefly but they soon lost touch again without meeting. Max also got back in touch with Kate, who had since married Nigel, and they remain Facebook friends up to the present day.

5. The Beginning of a Great Adventure

It wasn't the largest of offices, but at two hundred square feet, it would have to do. Let's face it, The Strand didn't come cheap, but in some professions you needed to be where you needed to be! It was 8.37a.m. on Monday, the 8th of November. Natalie Mancini unlocked the door and walked inside clutching the mail that she had collected from the reception area of the office suite. It was mostly junk; nothing important came by post these days. She hadn't been in business that long but it was a long-held ambition for her to go at it alone. Natalie was born in 1973 and educated in Halifax, Nova Scotia, where she completed her degree in Public Relations back in 1994, and after doing her masters in Toronto, she worked in PR in the Canadian Television industry. She came from a working class Italian immigrant family and was a bright student who became the first person in her family to go to university. She went to university in her home city because it was the only way she could afford it. After moving to Toronto, she met Canadian TV star Rick Turner through her job and fell for his rugged looks, and all action personality. He was the star of two of the country's most successful soap operas, and as such, attracted publicity wherever he went. Natalie found she disliked being in the public eye and was shattered when Rick's affair with co-star Julie Anderson became the hottest news in the tabloid press. It was an unbelievably difficult time for Natalie and she fled for England, with which she had no previous connection, as soon as she could. Not long after completing her PhD, she began to work for Stargazer Consultancy as a PR consultant who looked after the careers of rock stars, actors, politicians and TV presenters. She vowed to keep her private life and work separate, and although she'd had a few short-lived relationships since, she began to realise she might be commitment-phobic and generally preferred to stay single. Home was a shared flat with two girls in Belsize Park, which was just a few stops down the line on the Northern Line from Charing Cross tube station. This was an easy walk from her new office. She had started at NM Consultants six months ago and things had been going well for her. It was still very early so Natalie took whatever work would come her way, however, she was always looking for someone new and interesting to represent. This was the first time in all her forty-two years that she'd felt really in control of her own destiny, and whilst there was always the worry that the work may dry up one day, up to this point, it was non-stop.

She sat at her desk, fired up her laptop and viewed her appointments list. She had a lunchtime appointment with Yuki Akimoto, European CEO of I.M.C, the Japanese Engineering company. They were holding an enormous sales conference at the NEC in Birmingham and Natalie was arranging some entertainment and a motivational speaker for the second and last day of the event. She was leaving this task in the hands of her old friend, a showbiz agent, Peter Banister. He had never let her down before, and promised her an interesting and quirky speaker, one she knew very well. Natalie decided that she would talk to him shortly, but firstly, it was time for a coffee.

It was 11.15 that same morning. Natalie was researching Tommy McNeil on the internet; he certainly was interesting but she was concerned about his checkered past. She remembered The Clowns well, they had been big in Canada when she was in her early teens, and she had a schoolgirl crush on Tommy, as did lots of her classmates. He had that certain x-factor that could make a decent singer exude star quality. She decided at this point she would go to the conference herself to supervise Tommy. She didn't want any mishaps and he wouldn't dare mess her about! She made a note to call him after her lunch appointment and make sure that they were singing from the same hymn sheet. She felt confident that she could control him. She'd been dealing with difficult people all her life; her family was Italian after all, they were always falling out! Mr. Tommy McNeill would be no problem whatsoever. Natalie smiled to herself and walked across to the other side of the office where she looked in the mirror. She checked on her hair and make-up, her long dark locks and olive skin always made her look stunning. Tommy was going to be in for a big surprise when he met her. She walked out of the office, locked up behind her and walked down the stairs. She was meeting Mr. Akimoto at midday at The Admiralty, which was a themed pub at Charing Cross. It was themed in the style of HMS Victory. Natalie loved any venue that reminded her that she was a long way from home, and felt touristy. She made time for some window shopping on the way; she wanted to look her best for her trip to the conference.

The office door opened again at 2.35p.m.; lunch was a success. She was now on first name terms with Yuki and they agreed that they would work together on future projects, including areas concerning I.M.C.'s public profile. This could be a fantastic new client for NM consultants. Just what she needed! Natalie just needed a quick run through of what she was going to say to Tommy and by three o'clock she would be ready to call.

Tommy opened the front door of his Mum's house in Sutton. He carried all the bags of shopping through the door and put them down in the hall. He looked in the living room where he saw her sat on the sofa. She was watching whatever the television could offer, with the cordless telephone by her side.

'Oh Tommy, you're back!' she said.

'Hi Mum, yeah I'm back, it took me ages to get through the checkouts but I got everything you needed, and with change!' he replied.

'Thanks love, there was a call for you about half an hour ago, lovely girl! I thought she was American but she sounded a bit narky when I asked her, but Natalie her name was, I said you'd call her when you got back.'

Miriam McNeill was eighty-five now and was generally in good health. She was, however, afflicted with arthritis quite badly and this restricted her movement. Unfortunately, as a result she generally sat for most of the day with her phone by her side watching daytime television, whilst Tommy looked after her as best he could. He worried how she would get on when he was away at the conference in a couple of weeks, but then she always managed when he went on a two-day bender with his mates. She handed him a small yellow slip of paper with the name Natalie Mancini and a mobile number written on it.

'She didn't say what she wanted?' asked Tommy.

Miriam shook her head not flinching from the afternoon episode of 'Doctors,' and Tommy knew it was a pointless exercise trying to glean any more information out of her. He put the shopping away and went upstairs to his room. He sat on his bed and picked up his guitar. He looked down at its scratched body; he compared it to his own wiry frame and chuckled to himself thinking they'd both seen better days. He began to play a chord sequence strumming softly and slowly, and started to sing a tune along to it.

'They'll take your time, and steal your mind and say it's always something that you'll never find.'

'They'll show the way, but make you pay when you realise it just a waste of time

'And it's funny how they never really mean to hurt ya, it's funny how they never really mean to hurt you, and it's funny how you never even noticed at all.'

He stopped playing, unhappy with his efforts, and realised the song needed work, but it would have to wait! His songwriting had been sporadic over the years and it was never his forte, but the voice was still there alright! It was an unusual voice for a small white guy; baritone, warm and rounded. It had a touch of gravel at times. He'd learned that from Neil Finn of Crowded House whom he'd met at a festival in France.

They'd stayed friends for a while but lost touch over a decade ago.

'So, who was Natalie Mancini?' he wondered. He got lots of TV people ringing who were making nostalgia-trip programmes, asking him to be interviewed. He generally politely refused any of these requests. Was it someone from the past filing a paternity suit? There had been a few of those over the years! He decided he would ring though as it might be about this conference he'd signed up for. Besides, he liked the sound of her name and was a sucker for an accent!

Natalie was working on a spreadsheet when her mobile rang. She had the ringtone set as her favourite Clowns tune, 'Hooked On You.' She didn't recognise the number because Tommy had rung on his mobile.

'Hi, Natalie here,' she answered.

'Oh hi, Natalie, it's Tommy McNeill here, you rang?'

Natalie was temporarily lost for words, she had posters of this man on her wall as a teenager; this was every bit as exciting as Simon Le Bon or Tony Hadley ringing her.

'Thanks for ringing,' her voice softened. 'Sorry to intrude but I was given your number by Peter Banister, your agent? He's an old friend of mine and he said he's put you forward for this Conference in Birmingham in a couple of weeks. Anyway, could we meet for coffee? I need to go through what you will be saying on the day and make arrangements for accommodation and travel expenses.'

Tommy explained that he lived in Sutton so they arranged to meet up in Brixton - it was about halfway, at 2p.m. tomorrow afternoon.

'Okay Natalie, will see you then, by the way lovely accent. What part of the States are you from?' he charmed.

'Hmmm,' she chuckled. 'Not the greatest question to ask a Canadian....I'm from Nova Scotia, look it up! See you tomorrow!'

'Oops!' said Tommy to himself and laughed. One thing he had learned over the years was never to assume anything. He'd slipped up there alright. His attention turned back to the song. He tried to adjust the words in the song for the next hour, before giving up. He put the guitar down and went over to the other side of his room to his desk. Placed on top of it were some Ordnance Survey maps and some guide books of The Cairngorms National Park. He had just arranged to go on a walking holiday next year with two of his oldest friends. He had taken up walking as therapy for his troubles, and would always find himself out in the wilds somewhere, whenever he felt stressed. He didn't feel like he was in a bad place at the moment but he had a strange feeling, an air of foreboding. It also felt, paradoxically, like something wonderful was about to happen and he couldn't put his finger on it. He would have to just take it as it came and see. Whatever happened, tomorrow would be interesting. He continued pondering as he went downstairs. He walked into the kitchen and started to prepare the evening meal.

Natalie had left the office in plenty of time. It was only just past midday, but she could get there early and do some work on the laptop while she waited. She had planned carefully what she was going to wear, and when she wanted to, she could look stunning. Today was one of those days when she *really* made an effort! She didn't know why and she supposed it was because it was her teen idol. Natalie feared that she was going to be disappointed, and that he was going to be an old man these days. She got on the Underground at Charing Cross and took the Northern Line to Stockwell, there she changed for the Victoria Line, and after only one stop had arrived in Brixton. She found Costa in Brixton Road and bought herself an Americano. She soon found a table for two in a quiet corner. It was only 12.45; she logged into the Wi-Fi with the password they had given her at the till and studiously read her files on Tommy McNeill. At 1.45p.m. she felt fully prepared. She secretly hoped that Tommy would be dazzled by her.

Tommy had made an effort too, which didn't happen very often these days. He'd had his straggly grey hair cut a bit shorter, he'd shaved and put on the new tartan shirt he'd bought from Next. Carefully, he put on his jacket, made sure that Miriam was okay and left the house. He had a slightly more involved route than Natalie; he took a main line train which was destined for Victoria. He jumped off at Balham, where he too got onto the Victoria line, and changed at Stockwell for Brixton. He was as early as Natalie; they may have even passed each other on the tube and wouldn't have known it. He decided to go for a couple of pints to calm the nerves; it felt like a date and he had no idea why. He decided on The Crown and Anchor on Brixton Road, walked in and ordered a pint. Time to relax and gather his thoughts.

It was 2p.m., Tommy walked down Brixton Road towards Costa. He made sure that he bought some extra strong mints so he didn't smell like a brewery. He opened the door and looked around; he spotted a smart-looking, executive-type, dark-haired lady in the corner. Natalie looked across at Tommy and smiled. Tommy's heart melted immediately. Now, it really did feel like a date. He pulled himself together, walked across to Natalie and introduced himself.

'Natalie, I presume?' he said. 'Rather smoothly,' he thought.

'The very same!' Natalie retorted very coolly, she didn't want to give anything away but Tommy really looked great, she wasn't disappointed at all. They chatted away for about an hour and already knew each other's life history. They were getting on fine, and then Tommy suggested moving on to a pub 'for a proper drink.'

At that moment, Lauren Descartes had finished her shift in the tourist information office in the small French city of Arles in the Bouches-Du-Rhone region of Southern France. It was a nice afternoon for a Tuesday in November. Lauren decided to walk into town to visit the shops before returning home to her small city apartment. It was her last shift for a couple of weeks; she had leave booked and had no plans, but she knew what she wanted to do. She'd thought about Tommy a lot lately; she hadn't seen him since she was four years old, a whole eighteen years ago. Tommy McNeill was her dad and she needed to know him, despite what her mother would say. Her mum had married a wealthy wine exporter which was how they ended up living in Southern France. She could leave tomorrow morning and the Eurostar would see her into London tomorrow afternoon. All she needed to do was contact her old school friend, Isabel, who would gladly put her up for a few days. After half an hour of window shopping, she'd made up her mind. The next morning, she departed Arles station on the SNCF, changed at Avignon and was soon aboard the Eurostar. Soon enough, it moved quickly out of the station towards London St. Pancras.

Tommy arrived back at Miriam's house in Sutton. Natalie had declined the offer of a drink, but they got on well and had arranged to meet up and travel up to Birmingham together next week. Tommy, however, had sunk a few pints in Sutton, staggered home at 10.30p.m., where Miriam was already in bed. Tommy climbed onto his bed fully clothed and within five minutes was in a deep sleep.

6. Four Seasons in One Day

The autumn sun shone down on Tarrant Marshall. It was a beautiful sight from the top of the hill that overlooked the village. The rolling hills stood up in the morning mist. The mill house near the River Stour looked proud in its position at the head of the village, just near the road junction which brought traffic in and out of Tarrant Marshall. It was Sunday, November 16, and it was very mild for the time of year. The villagers were taking advantage of the kind weather. They were enjoying being outside. There were plenty of people trimming hedges, pulling up weeds and clearing out their guttering of the leaves that autumn had produced. The Chilton's were no different; Max wheeled Arthur down the garden in his wheelbarrow. He had just emptied a pile of leaves onto the large compost heap in the rear left hand corner of the north facing of the walled garden. Arthur chuckled with delight at the ride, 'anything to keep him amused,' thought Max. He peered up at the roof where Will had climbed up to look at Max's defective roofing. There was no way he would get up there; his fear of heights wouldn't have allowed him. They reached the midway point of the lawn and began raking up the assorted leaves. They had blown into the garden from the group of mixed trees to the side of the house. It was a small wooded area with an old oak tree, a couple of sycamores and a chestnut tree.

Arthur enjoyed throwing the leaves up in the air. He was making a big mess and annoying Max.

'Arthur! You're supposed to be helping!' he chided.

He grinned at Arthur and the young boy smiled back. He could never get too mad at him. They carried on working and Max hoped it would be done soon as he was feeling weary.

In the kitchen, Lottie, and Will's wife, Rhoda, were sat around the old farmhouse kitchen table drinking coffee. Maisie, and Rhoda's eighteen-month-old daughter, Tallulah, sat on the floor playing with some stickle bricks. They made sure they kept a close eye on the children in the kitchen, as they had a range that was fired up 95 percent of the time. Rhoda was showing Lottie a photo album from the time she spent travelling before she'd met Will and had Tallulah. She'd toured extensively around Asia and had a special love for Nepal. Lottie listened intently as Rhoda recounted stories of places she'd been and people she'd met. The sights, the sounds and the colours were things that Lottie could only imagine and she would love to travel one day; it seemed like a faraway prospect though. Rhoda stood up and took their empty coffee cups over to the sink, it was a lovely day and she wanted to make the most of it.

'Shall we take the boys out for a drink?' she asked.

'Yeah, we should get out there, it's beautiful today and there won't be many more days like this now until next spring.'

She took a couple of bottles of Merrydown cider from the fridge and unscrewed the lids. Rhoda picked up Tallulah and Maisie and they all wandered out of the back door and onto the paved patio area. Max and Arthur were just making their way back with the wheelbarrow, and Max grinned at the sight of the large bottle of cider being offered towards him. He grabbed a bottle and thanked Lottie. Just at that moment, Will appeared down the ladder looking rather serious.

'It's not good,' said Will. Max stared at him grimly.

'It really needs retiling, I can patch it up for the winter but it will need doing in the spring. It would be about five grand, but if I do it at mate's rates at the weekends, then maybe I could do it for two and a half.'

Max was grateful for Will's offer but had no idea where the money was coming from. They sipped their drinks in the sun, trying to enjoy their day, but Max had a horrible feeling that just wouldn't go away. It was like a summer's day with the depressing feeling of winter thrown in for good measure. Will and Rhoda had agreed to stay for lunch, so the two girls went inside to cook the lasagna that Lottie had prepared earlier. Will and Max liked to talk about music. Will had also been in a band in his younger days and they shared many similar experiences. They would often jam together and often thought about forming their own band but time hadn't allowed that to happen.

'Will, do you have an old cassette player anywhere?'

'Not sure. I might though, I'll let you know when I get home. Why do you ask?' said Will.

'I found an old tape of mine, circa 1990. It's a compilation of all the songs I wrote over the previous three or four years,

I'd really like to listen to it, see if it stands the test of time. There's a particular song on there, I always felt that it…you know, had legs, so to speak,' explained Max. 'I mean, I don't even know what I'd do about it if it *was* good enough, and actually, I've got the feeling it'll make me cringe.'

'Yeah, I know what you mean,' replied Will. 'I can't even listen to most of my stuff. I used to try all these wacky keyboard solos back in the day. I thought I was Rick Wakeman, and I played in a ska band!'

Will had spent his youth playing in Dorset's best and only ska band, The Settlers. He was a classical trained pianist, and like Max, played in a band that wasn't entirely to his taste, but it was all a valuable experience. He pursued a career as a session pianist for a while, although he eventually realised that ultimately, there was more money to be made in making sure people's houses remained leak free. He still liked to dabble though and Rhoda loved to watch him play; she had a decent singing voice and she had been known to croon along as tickled the ivories.

They eventually made their way in for lunch and enjoyed the lasagna with some roast potatoes, broccoli and carrots. The roof was discussed in detail and Will assured Max and Lottie he had patched it up enough to last the winter. The tiling would have to be done before any sale could be agreed, as it would fail a survey. Max was determined that they would find the money somehow as the spring was a long way off. The couples cleared away after lunch, and as the sun started to fade in the sky, they all moved into the lounge with a cup of tea. In the corner of the room was an upright piano that Lottie had bought with the intention of learning but never got round to. Max went and grabbed his acoustic guitar and Will sat on the stool by the piano.

'Shall we play a song, Will?' asked Max.

'Yep, let's play what we rehearsed the other week. You know the one,' Will replied. He didn't want to let on what the song was. He wanted to surprise Rhoda as it was one of her favorites.

Will played the first few chords on the piano and Max joined in and strummed some very gentle minor chords. He began to sing and Rhoda immediately recognised the opening line. It was 'My Ever Changing Moods' by The Style Council. She joined in and harmonised with Max on vocals. It sounded half decent, the smiles on the faces in the room made that very evident. The song came to an end and everyone applauded. Max then entertained the kids with his version of 'Postman Pat.' Will and Rhoda soon decided to make their way home to the neighbouring town of Wimborne, where they lived. They said their goodbyes and Max thanked Will for his work on the roof. Will then promised to look for the tape player on his return home. They waved them off as they drove away in their Land Rover Discovery. It was about 5p.m. and everything around the village was virtually pitch dark. The only thing that was illuminating the immediate proximity was the Green Dragon pub, where there was a constant stream of people going in and out. Max and Lottie reflected on what had been an amazing day, although the news about the roof was not great. Max had to go away next weekend on the sales conference; maybe that would throw up some new money making opportunities. It wouldn't be long; he would soon find out. He was, as instructed by his immediate superior, to have

Friday morning at home as a 'paperwork' day and then he would travel up to Birmingham in the afternoon. A large welcome dinner would take place in the evening. On the Saturday, there would be a review of the company's year and what was expected of the sales staff of I.M.C. would be highlighted. There would be some keynote speeches and a guest speaker in the afternoon, and then they could head home. It was intriguing to know whom exactly that would be. Last year, it had been legendary magician Paul Daniels and the whole speech had revolved around keeping calm under pressure. Although he disliked being away from Lottie and the kids, he did enjoy these types of things and in a strange way, was looking forward to it.

That evening after Arthur and Maisie had gone to bed, Max walked into the lounge to find Lottie reclining on their leather sofa. She was mending a pair of her jeans that had seen better days. He sat down beside her and flipped the television on, it was the results show of 'Strictly Come Dancing,' so his attention soon switched to his smartphone. A message notification appeared on the top of his screen, it was a text from Will, he'd found the cassette player and Max could collect it anytime he was passing.

'Great! Will's found the old cassette player, I'll be able to hear the tape,' he said enthusiastically.

'I hope it doesn't sound too ropey, I'll be really pissed off if it does!' he added sagely.

'Don't put yourself down,' Lottie replied. 'I'm sure it'll be fantastic. I thought you and Will sounded amazing today. You should go to that open mic night at The Pulse Bar in

Bournemouth. I've heard they get all sorts of people down there playing their stuff.'

It wasn't the worst idea that Max had ever heard, although the logistics of getting an upright piano in there weren't great, but he supposed that Will could take his electric keyboard. The Monday evening event attracted buskers, amateur songwriters and people who just wanted to go and belt out some cover versions. Everyone was allowed three songs. Max and Will would struggle to choose; there were so many good songs to choose from. It amazed him how the contestants on the X-Factor seemed to perform the same old tired material that they were fed by Simon Cowell and company. This was why he never watched such rot!

Max headed to Will and Rhoda's house on the way back from his last call the next day. He had been to a large CNC Machine shop in Poole. They had been having problems with one of I.M.C.'s products being used to bore out some aluminium cylinders. Luckily, Max had discovered it was the operating speed of the machine rather than his product that was at fault. He turned into their close and parked at the end of the drive. They had a modern house that they had purchased from a local builder. There was a large red brick, block paved driveway with room for two cars, plus Will's Mitsubishi truck. Max jumped out of his car and rang the doorbell. Rhoda came to the door holding Tallulah, with her other hand, she had her phone to her ear, engaged in conversation with her mother who lived in The Republic of Ireland. She beckoned Max into the kitchen where an old JVC cassette deck was placed on the table. Max hadn't seen anything like it for years. It was oblong in shape and was purely used for listening to and recording onto cassette. The device had a bright red record button and five other buttons for the other functions: play, pause, fast forward, rewind and stop. These buttons were all black in colour. There was also a grey eject button. There was a power lead attached and a jack socket for plugging in a microphone. Max was quite excited to see it; he hadn't owned anything like it since he was about twelve! He just hoped that it worked, and more importantly, that the cassette would still operate. He made a mental note to have the contents of the tape transferred onto his laptop and backed up on a disc. Rhoda finished the conversation with her mum and entered the kitchen where Max was carefully studying the contraption.

'You found it then,' she said.

'Yeah, takes me back! It looks like some sort of relic from the Victorian age,' Max replied.

Rhoda, at thirty-three years old, couldn't help but agree. She'd never seen one before and if she'd seen it first, she would have probably chucked it out!

'Do you know if it works?' Asked Max.

'Yeah, Will found an old Tears for Fears album. 'The Hurting,' I think, and it didn't sound too bad!'

Max said his goodbyes to Rhoda and Tallulah and drove back out of the close. He rejoined the main road and resolved to get home as quickly as he could. Ten minutes later, he arrived back in the village and walked back through the front door, where he was greeted by Arthur.

'Hi Arthur, what have you been doing today?'

Arthur told him all about his day at school as they walked into the kitchen. Lottie's Mum, Jo, was sat opposite her at the kitchen table. Max greeted them both and sat down at the head of the table.

'Do you mind if Mum and I go out for a drink when Arthur and Maisie are in bed? Mum's paying!' Lottie asked.

'No of course not,' said Max. He didn't mind the peace and quiet. He could have an objective listen to the tape without anyone else hearing. They all had an evening meal together around the table and discussed the roof saga. Jo suggested some ways that she may be able to help. She gave them some money and offered unlimited babysitting so that Lottie could perhaps work some more hours. They tidied up, put Maisie and Arthur to bed, and eventually wandered out of the front door and across to the Green Dragon.

Max waited until he knew that they had gone into the pub across the road, he needed privacy for this. If the tape was awful, then he didn't need his mother-in-law to hear it! He reached into the pocket of his coat where he found the cassette and plugged in the player, he pressed the eject button and the window of the player popped open. He nervously placed the cassette into the player; he had no idea why he was nervous. He pressed the cassette window down into place and pushed the play button. The first thing he heard was the hiss of tape noise and a clunk, then a drum rhythm started playing. It was produced on the small drum machine he once owned. It was exciting to hear and Max grinned to himself as a guitar riff started and he started to hear his 19-year-old-self sing. He had re-recorded all these songs long after The Silence had split just so he had them all together on one tape. He knew the quality wasn't great as he was no singer *or* guitarist. The one intention of the tape was to have the songs archived, just in case. He ploughed through the tape with mild satisfaction but what he really wanted to hear was track 9.

'Forever and a Day' had been written whilst watching Nelson Mandela's 70th birthday concert on BBC1. The song observed that people could get together and get along when they were sharing a common cause like this. 'Why couldn't it be like this all the time?' Max thought. From the opening chords, Max still thought the song sounded great, above everything else he had written. Verse 2 would need some work though, the lyrics didn't quite fit or feel relevant to today, but he could sort that out. He rewound the tape to the beginning of the song again and listened several times. Later that evening, he played it back to Lottie. She had heard Max play it on his acoustic guitar a few times, a bit like the way he first played it to Kate all those years ago, but she loved the song and was amazed by how good it sounded with a full complement of instruments.

'You really need to get that heard, maybe the X-Factor could use it,' she said already realising that Max would cringe at the thought of the TV show.

'Well maybe not that crappy show,' he retorted. 'But yes, I agree. The question is how?'

He pondered this question for the rest of the week but he felt the answer would come. He played the song to Will who also loved it and spoke to his work colleague Neil, whom he knew owned a device to transfer cassette tape recordings onto a PC. He agreed to lend it to Max and would bring it to the conference on Friday afternoon. They arranged to meet in the bar of the Hilton near the NEC, where their accommodation had been booked for the weekend.

7. Station to Station

Lauren Descartes McNeill was born in London, July 3, 1992, to Tommy McNeill and his former wife, Polly Walker McNeill. Polly was a well-known British supermodel, known for her marketability in the late eighties. She became involved with many advertising campaigns both on television and billboards. She had met Tommy at an awards ceremony in 1986, and they got married in Marylebone registry office during the height of Tommy's troubles in 1988. Polly was already struggling with Tommy's antics by then. Polly's parents disapproved of Tommy and were always encouraging her to leave him, but it took her until 1996 to do so. She met Sylvain Descartes, a wealthy French wine merchant and fled to his Provence home. Sylvain was kind to Polly, but he was a control freak as well and made sure Tommy's influence was kept to a minimum. Tommy was in no state to fight back, and with dwindling resources, couldn't fight against the best lawyers France had to offer.

    Lauren grew up bilingual and completed a degree in tourism at Angers University in Brittany. She had got herself a job in the tourist office in the City of Arles some 80 kilometers from her mother and step-father's chateau. It was far enough away for her to have her own life. She'd had boyfriends, and having inherited her Mother's model looks, had no shortage of admirers, but there was nobody serious on the horizon.

She stared out of the train window at the fields as they whizzed past her line of vision. All she could think about was Tommy. She tried to think of everything she could to find him and drew a blank. He wasn't on Facebook and although there was a fan page on that very site for him, he didn't participate. In fact, she had liked the page but there wasn't very much activity on the page. The odd post had indicated that he'd attended a couple of dinners as a guest, participating in a question and answer session about his career. These had taken place around the South London area. What she *did* know about him, was that he grew up in this area, so it made sense to start there. She had read all about the incident on Wogan, the stage fright and the drinking and drugs and wondered if he was over them now. The only vague recollections she had of Tommy was of a gentle, kind man and not the monster that the press, Polly and Sylvain had portrayed. Sylvain was a good man really, but he had been strict with Lauren growing up. He would not have stood for Tommy coming down to France to visit every second week, and Polly had been too weak to grant Lauren her wish.

The train had stopped at Lyon and more people got on the train for their journey to London. Her Samsung Galaxy mobile phone rang. It played 'London Calling' by The Clash as her ringtone. She felt that it had lacked imagination but it summed up where she was going. She saw from her screen that it was Polly.

'Hi Mum,' she answered.

'Hi darling, are you okay?' She began not allowing Lauren to answer.

'Sylvain and I were wondering what you were doing with your time off? Would you like to come down and visit for a couple of days?'

She continued. 'We'd love to see you and Sylvain is having some clients down from a top wine merchant's chain in the States. You never know, Mr. Right might be amongst them, they are all loaded!'

This is where she lost Lauren, she had been brought up in a world of wealth, but it didn't motivate her. Polly's continual insistence that she should find herself a rich man didn't sit well with Lauren who was much more cerebral than her mother. Lauren would bide her time and was prepared to wait until she met the right guy before considering his liquidity!

'Oh Mum,' she began. 'You know I'd love to but I'm on the Eurostar as we speak! I'm heading to London, I'm off to see Isabel, remember Isabel? I haven't seen her since she was in Marseille in the summer. I might do some site seeing whilst I'm there.'

Polly's happy tone immediately changed at hearing the word London. She knew what the real reason for the visit was. None of Polly's family lived there anymore. She'd gone to look for Tommy!

'How could she? He wasn't there when she needed him, Sylvain was a proper Dad to her, she was so ungrateful,' Polly thought. They said their goodbyes as the train dipped into a short tunnel. Lauren felt her ears pop as they travelled through it. She flicked through Facebook and again typed Tommy

McNeill into search on the application. Once again, it yielded several Tommy McNeills all over Britain, The USA, Australia and Canada but her Dad was nowhere to be seen. She tried searching for Thomas McNeill and the alternative spelling MacNeil, used by the Scottish clan, many of whom derived from the Island of Barra, but with similar, negative results. Little did she know that somewhere in London, someone would soon be seeking her out and the whole course of her life was about to change.

Polly cursed her daughter; what was she doing going to London? Tommy would be a huge disappointment to her if she found him. If only she knew the nights she spent in on her own without Tommy. He was probably up to his neck in booze and God knows what else! She knew he wasn't a psychopathic monster and it was just the demons which had taken him over. Maybe he had changed, maybe being out of the limelight had done him some good. She'd heard a rumour from an old and mutual friend that Tommy was now living in Miriam's place in Sutton and lived off of a carer's allowance. All in all, Polly really didn't want Lauren to find out, but inevitably she would. Polly knew that. Sylvain would be furious. He had two sons from a previous marriage, Clement and Emmanuel, whom he now employed in his business and he hadn't been nearly as strict with them. Despite the fact that she wasn't his flesh and blood, he treated her as a daughter, his only daughter, and at the age of sixty-seven, he would find it hard to cope with Lauren finding her father. Polly decided to keep the information to herself until she had to say something. Sylvain walked into the room as she clutched the phone to her chest.

'Everything okay, Cherie?' He asked. 'Was that Lauren? Is she coming to stay?'

'No, she's booked a holiday with a girlfriend in Cuba. She's just off to Paris to catch the flight,' she lied.

'This probably wasn't the best approach,' she thought. But if Sylvain knew what she was up to, he would try and stop her, and Polly really couldn't cope with the drama.

At 4.05p.m., the 09.50a.m. Eurostar service from Avignon arrived at London St Pancras International. The station always looked like something out of a Harry Potter film to Lauren who had been there several times before. Sylvain made several business trips to London every year and they always enjoyed coming by train. The service slowed down into the station and ground to a halt. People streamed from the train and Lauren joined the mass evacuation from the station. She went down the escalator and off to the arrivals at St Pancras.

She had arranged to meet Isabel outside her local tube station, Boston Manor at 5.30p.m., so she had plenty of time. She just needed to get on the underground and follow the Piccadilly line all the way to her destination. The 16.34 service to Heathrow Terminal 4 would get her to Boston Manor for about a quarter past five. She reached the platform just in time, boarded the train and was lucky enough to find a seat straight away.

Isabel Lagarde had been living and working in London since August; she had taken up a post teaching French at one of the big local comprehensive schools in the area and had found a flat to rent in the suburb of Hanwell situated just between Southall and Ealing. She had quickly immersed herself in the area and became a part of the community. She was lucky enough to still be getting an allowance from her wealthy parents as well as her salary, which meant she could afford to rent a two-bedroom flat by herself. This gave her room to put up her guests from France whenever she liked. Her mother would come and stay on what seemed like a fortnightly basis so she could go and shop in the West End. Her flat was a short walk from the station and by the time Lauren came up the escalator and out of the front entrance, Isabel was waiting. The two girls shrieked with joy at seeing each other and flung their arms around each other in a huge embrace. They had grown up together and knew pretty much everything there was to know about one another, but Lauren had kept fairly tight-lipped about the reason for her visit.

'Of course, Izzy I've come to see you, but also I've been thinking about Dad a lot lately. I'm going to try and track him down, but also, and nobody knows this yet, I want to find work here in London. It shouldn't be too hard with my tourism degree. I was hoping I could stay here until I find somewhere to live?'

'Naturellement Lauren. It'll be great to have you around and there's really no hurry, we might have to improvise a bit when people stay, but it's fine.'

Izzy rolled her eyes as she explained the regular visits of her mother, but Lauren liked Adrienne Lagarde, she was fun! This might just be what she needed. She would have to let her current employers know, of course, and she would have to go back to Arles to sort out her flat and belongings. More importantly, it was two weeks before she would have to tell Polly that she was staying in London… for good.

They walked up the steps to Izzy's first floor flat and Lauren was shown to her room. It looked welcoming. Lauren gazed around and saw a framed picture next to the mirror on the dressing table. It was an old picture of Tommy that Izzy had found on the internet and printed it off. She had carefully cut it out and placed it into a wooden frame with a cardboard inlay. Lauren was touched by the lengths that her friend had gone to, and she decided then and there that she would feel at home here.

Izzy watched Lauren from the kitchen as she made them both a cup of tea. She was pleased that her friend was happy and looked forward to having her around.

8. On The Road Again

It was Friday morning and Tommy had important business. It was the weekend of the conference in Birmingham. He felt a little nervous but had been so impressed by Natalie that he really didn't want to let her down. He caught the overground train from Sutton to Tooting, and then walked the short distance to Tooting Broadway tube station. Upon arrival, he took the Northern line and boarded the train all the way to Belsize Park, where he had agreed to meet Natalie. He had a large case which he wheeled along wherever he walked. Natalie was going to drive them up in her car, but first, he had to get to her place. She had scheduled a quick stop in for Toddington services, where she wanted to talk him through what he was to say at the conference. She knew that he had to be well prepared. He had been practising all week at home but there were several key points that she had wanted to highlight. Tommy felt that Natalie could really help him even get back to singing for a living. One thing that he knew though, was that this would be a real test for his stage fright.

Sure enough, Natalie was waiting when Tommy arrived at his destination. She smiled and hugged him warmly as they greeted. They walked the half mile or so and found Natalie's Mercedes SLK200 Auto in a sort of pearl white.

'Nice wheels!' Said Tommy. 'Shame about the colour!'

Natalie laughed and explained that she had treated herself when she had worked for Stargazer, before she was a poor self-employed girl.

'My heart bleeds!'

Tommy quipped as he put his case in her boot. She laughed as they got in the car. Tommy had not been in a car of this ilk for quite a few years and was curious about the buttons and switches that adorned the panel in front of him. Tommy pushed a button which he presumed was for the air conditioning.

'Careful! That's the ejector seat!' She joked.

'Oh, ha bloody ha!' Tommy grinned. He was beginning to feel really relaxed about the whole experience. He sat back as Natalie negotiated the streets of North London in the midday Friday traffic. It would take them a while to get to the North Circular Road, but from there it was just a stone's throw from Staples Corner and onto the M1. On the journey, they talked a lot. Tommy spoke about Lauren, his career, his marriage and Lauren again, and it was clear to Natalie that he missed her terribly. If only he could find her. She felt that she might be able to help Tommy with this. He'd never been on Facebook in his life and had shunned all types of social media. She would be surprised if he even owned a computer and she noticed his mobile phone was very basic. Natalie spoke about her career, her family in Canada and the men in her life. Tommy even felt comfortable enough to ask if she regretted not having children.

'Well, no,' she said. 'I still think, you know, that one day I will meet somebody and they will have kids, so I will become mom and granny by proxy! I'm lookin' forward to it!' She grinned.

Tommy admired her spirit. She obviously had a lot of life left to live. He could learn a thing or two from Natalie.

In forty-five minutes, they had reached Toddington Services where they parked and headed for Costa Coffee. They found themselves the nearest free table. Tommy went off and fetched two coffees whilst Natalie connected her laptop to the Wi-Fi and accessed her files on Tommy's speech. They chatted about what was to be said and Tommy assured her he was comfortable with it, – although he wasn't really – but it had to be done now that he was committed. The speech was to be a very self-mocking piece about doing very silly things when under pressure and harked back to the Wogan incident quite a bit. If nothing else, it was entertaining. Natalie had used a guy she knew who wrote scripts for television and whose company she enjoyed. She trusted him and thought that Tommy would be happy to read it. There would be an autocue in front of him so it wouldn't be too hard, and all in all, it would last about twenty minutes. Maybe it was all a little off the hoof but both of them were excited by the spontaneity.

Tommy had sat down opposite Natalie and unbeknown to him, she had logged on to Facebook. She clicked on the search bar and typed in a name, Lauren McNeill. There were loads in Britain and all the English-speaking countries. What if she'd changed her name? Natalie knew she was in France but she could have married or anything. Towards the end of the search, a few people with double-barreled surnames started to appear and just then she saw it, Lauren Descartes McNeill. 'Hmm,' she thought. 'Sounds French!' She clicked on the name and opened the page, and there she was! Lauren was a beautiful young woman. Her profile picture was of her at a music festival in France. She could see Tommy's smile both from Tommy, who was still chatting away opposite of her, and from Lauren on the PC in front of her. Natalie gained lots of information about her. Where she lived and what she liked to do; there were loads of photographs which Natalie scrolled down, and then she saw it. A photograph of Lauren with Izzy on a night out in Arles. That in itself wasn't significant but it was what she was wearing that made it so conclusive. It was a green cotton T-shirt, it looked like a retro tour T-shirt. It said in bold black lettering, 'The Clowns - World Tour 1986,' with a list of dates and venues below. 'Yes!' She thought. *This must* be her. She shut down the Facebook page and refocused on Tommy who was looking a little pensive but in good spirits. Natalie had already decided she was going to contact Lauren. As soon as she got to the hotel, she would tell Tommy she was taking a nap. She would do it then; he wouldn't have to know. 'How exciting!' She thought. She felt like she was taking part in one of those television shows, reuniting people with their estranged relatives. She thought about her own family back home in Canada and how they would feel if they had been prevented from seeing their kids. Natalie has plenty of nieces and nephews and loved them all. 'Tommy must really have had a struggle with this,' she thought.

Tommy looked across at Natalie, he had become slightly transfixed by her and wondered what she thought about him. He thought that she probably just saw him as a washed up old nobody. He probably had no chance there! He'd not had a regular girlfriend for a while. He needed to solve his issues and maybe he was getting close, but sometimes he really needed a drink and he really needed a drink now. The stage fright would always be an issue but maybe it could be managed. Tommy had attended many mindfulness meditation classes and had learned how to focus his energies on the job in hand and this would be the acid test. Similarly, Natalie pondered what Tommy made of her. He probably had got used to supermodels and had ridiculously lofty standards looks-wise. She probably wasn't his type all, as he probably preferred a younger, groupie type. It was all speculation, of course, but there was only one way to find out. This weekend was for work though, and whatever she felt would have to wait. Tommy had wandered off for a visit to the gents and was on his way back. He offered Natalie some spearmint chewing gum which she declined. He seemed much more relaxed, ready for the rest of the journey. They would be there in a couple of hours at the most. Perhaps he was beginning to enjoy this new venture. They headed back to the car and began the rest of the journey.

Max was busy singing along to The Arctic Monkeys' 'Fluorescent Adolescent' whilst driving up the M42 to the N.E.C. He had left Dorset at about one thirty in the afternoon, waving goodbye to Lottie and Maisie and he headed along the A31 and M27. He then took the M3 and A34 until he reached the M40, by 5p.m., and after a stop at Banbury along the way, he drove into the car park of the Hilton Birmingham Metropole Hotel. He parked the car and turned the engine off. He watched a couple unloading their Mercedes, a rather attractive Mediterranean looking lady with long dark hair and olive skin and a rather petite looking man with straight grey hair and a rather craggy, lived-in face. He looked rather familiar to Max, although he really couldn't think why. He followed them into the huge reception area and noticed that the couple were booked into separate rooms; he'd obviously jumped to the wrong conclusion there. He had thought that they seemed quite comfortable together and perhaps a little touchy-feely. He eventually booked in and was assigned room 683. He made his way there and sent a text to Neil; his colleague who had already arrived and arranged to meet him in the bar.

Natalie and Tommy had gone off to their own rooms. They had arranged to meet in the bar at seven for a quick drink before dinner. Natalie sat on her bed and fired up her laptop and within a couple of minutes had logged into Facebook. She went back to the search bar and brought Lauren's profile back onto the screen. Near the top right of her profile were two small buttons, one marked 'friend request' and one marked 'message.' Natalie clicked on both and began to compose.

'Hi! I'm Natalie and I'm a friend of your dad's. I'm working with him at the moment and he says he is very keen to get in touch with you again. He doesn't know I've sent this and he doesn't do Facebook. I thought it would be a nice surprise for him, please get in touch and perhaps we could arrange?

Nat xx.'

She pressed send. All she could do now was wait.

Meanwhile, Tommy had found the bar and found a couple of people who had immediately recognised him. They had bought him a drink or two. He really did feel better now and was heartily regaling anyone who would listen about his glory days as a top soul crooner. Twenty feet away, Max chatted with Neil and thanked him for the piece of hardware that he needed to transfer the cassette onto his PC; he was explaining what he needed it for when it suddenly came to him.

'Of course, Tommy McNeill! I knew I recognised him.'

'That would make sense,' said Neil. 'I heard a rumour that he was a guest speaker. I'm not sure what he's going to be talking about, and by the looks of him, he's not going to be in a fit state by tomorrow.'

Tommy had started to look decidedly merry. He ordered another round of drinks for him and his new friends. They were shots, Sambuca, by the looks of things. Max looked at his watch, 'bloody hell, it was only half-past six!' He thought. Tommy had wondered off when Max decided to go back to his room and freshen up before dinner. He wanted to ring Lottie and the kids. He said cheerio to Neil and headed back to the lift. Once there, he pressed the up button and immediately the lift doors reopened, they had only just closed. Max thought he had missed it! Inside the lift, much to Max's shock, crouching in the corner was Tommy looking worse for wear and vomiting violently. He had either been drinking all day or something had reacted badly.

'Hey, are you okay... Tommy, isn't it?' asked Max.

'Do I look fucking okay to you, kiddo?' He replied and then looked apologetic, sarcasm wasn't his style.

'Look, can you help me, please? I need to get back to my room.' He gasped and removed the key from his pocket. It was room number 839 so Max got to the right floor, put his arm around Tommy, and escorted him back to his room. He unlocked the door and Tommy immediately bolted for the bathroom where he was violently sick again. Max followed him there and poured him out some water into a glass. He handed it to Tommy who immediately drank it all.

Tommy began to apologise and explain that he had taken some pain killers before drinking and asked Max for his name.

'Well, Max, thanks again and sorry you got caught up in my antics, I should be okay now, you get along and enjoy your evening. I'm really grateful that you helped.' He moaned, his speech was slurred so it needed a couple of seconds to translate what he said.

Max began to turn and walk out of the bathroom when he heard a woman's voice calling.

'Tommy?' It sounded American. It also sounded furious. Just then the lady that he saw Tommy with earlier when they walked in, and she didn't look amused.

'Okay mister, what the fuck is going on here, I was waiting for you downstairs in the bar and then I hear people saying the words Tommy McNeill and skinful! Please don't tell me you've blown this whole damn thing. Thanks whoever you are. I can take over from here.' She scowled at Max, making him feel slightly nervous, wishing he'd never got involved in the first place.

Max edged towards the door silently and went on his way through the endless landings of the hotel. He had the feeling that Tommy was in all sorts of trouble. Natalie didn't seem to be the sort you wanted to mess with. He went off back to his room, made his telephone call to Lottie, telling her what had just happened. She had never really heard of Tommy and wasn't hugely impressed when he told her. He went off back downstairs still buzzing with the excitement. He noticed that the lift was out of service whilst it was being cleaned up. He saw Neil and joined the rest of his colleagues for the prearranged meal.

Natalie had dined alone. She was fuming with Tommy and had ordered him to sleep it off. For his part, he was full of contrition and agreed to her request without argument. He hadn't wanted to let her down purposely, it was just that sometimes he let down his guard too much. He had agreed not to drink until the weekend was over but maybe he needed to think about giving up drinking altogether. It always made him feel this way and he'd just about had enough. It was coming up to a new year; a time for new things. Natalie thought whilst she picked at her mushroom risotto. 'Could she guide Tommy and help to get back to where he once was? How much help would he need? Did he still have the voice?' The latter point she knew. He had sung in the car on the way up and she'd not heard a better voice; he still had it. His voice had a rare mesmerising quality. She would talk to some of her friends in the music industry and see what they could do. On her way back from the restaurant, she saw Max again, he was making his way back for an early night. It was a big day at the conference tomorrow. She smiled at him as they passed in the reception area outside the main restaurant.

'Hey,' said Natalie. 'I didn't get your name but thanks for helping Tommy earlier and sorry if was a bit, you know...grumpy.' Every now and then Natalie liked to throw in some typically British words so she *felt* British!

'That's okay. It's Max and no offence taken, are you his manager? I used to listen to Tommy back in the day. I mean,

I'll be honest, he wasn't totally my cup of tea, but I played in a band that had a similar sound,' said Max.

'Hi Max. I'm Natalie, I suppose you could say I'm kinda his manager, but PR is my background. I've just been looking after him on this gig! Not very well though, it seems.'

Max explained that he was employed by I.M.C and was here for the conference, his background was in engineering and he lived in Dorset. Natalie had no idea where that was.

'Well, like I say, thanks again. If there's anything I can help with or you're up in town let me know, Tommy, at least owes you a coffee!'

Natalie handed Max her card; it read Natalie Mancini, Creative Director, NM Consultants. It contained an address in The Strand, London, a mobile phone number and an email address. Max thanked her and continued up to his room. He couldn't imagine he would be in London soon but you never know. It had all been a bit surreal, like a strange dream. He put the card in his pocket, maybe Natalie might be able to help him. He was too tired to ponder very much right now. He reached his room, opened the door and went inside.

Saturday morning came along and Max headed down to breakfast nice and early. He was in plenty time for the opening of the conference which started at 9a.m. They needed to be there at 8.45a.m. the latest. They were under strict orders and needed to leave enough time to walk across to the NEC. Tommy texted Natalie and suggested they go for a walk after breakfast. He'd found a place on the map called Elmdon Park, a nature reserve nearby. After all, it was a lovely day. Tommy felt it would be a great way to calm his nerves and, at least, talk to Natalie and make amends for his behaviour the previous evening.

They parked the car and began to amble along the pathway that led from the parking area. Natalie insisted that they stick to the pathway because she didn't have the right shoes.

'Natalie, look, I'm so sorry that I wasn't very clever last night. I apologise... unreservedly,' he added. 'I've enjoyed working with you and well, would like to do so again. Maybe I can sing again, maybe I can relaunch and be a success but I need someone to help. I need somebody to rein me in when I need it, and to help me talk to people in the industry. To open doors,' said Tommy. 'Any idea where I can find such a person?'

Natalie looked sternly at him but couldn't keep a straight face any longer. Firstly, a smile appeared and then a grin.

'Yes, of course I will, Tommy, but please, please if you feel like you did yesterday again, talk to me! We don't need that happening again, you frightened the life out of me!'

Later that day, the conference was over. Max and his colleagues all headed back to the hotel to collect their belongings. They felt inspired by Tommy's speech which had been fabulous, he delivered it superbly and despite a nervous start, he really got into the role, and he was a success. He had the audience in stitches with constant references to making an arse of himself and getting to the bottom of things, he'd had to endure quite a lot in his life because of the Wogan incident, so he might as well exploit it to his advantage. He didn't mind, it was a long time ago and he felt together now, despite yesterday's blip. He felt a feeling of accomplishment, of progress and that he could build something from here. The delegates at the conference all left one by one, all ready to enjoy the rest of their weekend.

Back in London, Lauren felt her smartphone vibrate in the pocket of her jeans. It was a Facebook friend request and message from someone called Natalie Mancini. Lauren didn't know the name but opened the message and started reading. Her eyes widened with amazement as she took in Natalie's news. She'd found her dad, or rather he'd found her, a tear formed in her blue eyes. She sighed a huge sigh, like it was a massive relief. She wiped her eyes, accepted Natalie's friend request and began to reply to the message. She had been waiting for this to moment for a long time. All she had to do was now put it into words and make it happen.

9. A Sort of Homecoming

Max arrived home at about 7p.m., it was a little earlier than he had expected because the traffic had been reasonably clear along the route. He pondered the weekend as he drove. He felt optimistic about the future but he wasn't sure why. The conference had motivated him as he had expected. The company had announced a series of incentives as part of a way of pushing sales on a new major line of products they had introduced. He'd met Tommy McNeill too; his old band mates from The Silence would have been jealous. He had not really heard much about Tommy since the mid-nineties. There had been a few rumours in the press over the years about him and how he had fallen upon hard times. There were also rumours linking him with various reality TV shows and every year a tabloid would suggest that he would appear in 'I'm a Celebrity… Get Me Out of Here!' But that never happened. Max wasn't sure if Tommy had a big enough name these days, but that didn't seem to stop some so-called celebrities. He drove back into the village and turned his mind back to his home and family. At least he had the evening and tomorrow to wind down and think about everything. It would soon be

Christmas, and after the New Year, it would be decision time. Maybe they would have to leave the village for good or maybe, just maybe, something would come along which would save the day.

He walked back through the door and there was all sorts of activity going on. Lottie's mum, Jo, was playing with Arthur and Maisie in the lounge. They were playing a game that involved loud clapping and singing. It was chaos! Lottie was making something to eat using her Kitchen Aid mixer, which Jo had bought for her last Christmas.

'Hi,' said Max. 'It's like Piccadilly Circus in here today.' He stood right behind Lottie and put his arms around her waist, his hands meeting on her stomach.

'You hadn't forgotten about tonight, Max, had you?'

'Tonight?' thought Max. 'Yes, he had. Oh yes, Will and Rhoda!' They were meeting up with them for a curry.

'No, of course not.' Fibbed Max and then pulled a face as if to say, 'I've got away with that one.'

'I'll drive, you've probably had enough of that for one day. Will and Rhoda have been raving about your tape, they really want to speak to you about it tonight,' said Lottie.

'See! Fame at last,' joked Max. 'I'd better go upstairs and get myself changed, I see you're ready to go, you look amazing!'

Lottie felt a warm glow on hearing Max's words. She watched him go upstairs and tidied away the kitchen.

'Leave all that, hun,' said Jo. 'I'll clear away when these two little monkeys are in bed. You relax and enjoy yourselves tonight, it's been a tough old year.'

'Thanks Mum, and thanks for the money you gave us, it's given us a lifeline over Christmas. I don't know what we'd do without you.'

'Well,' she began, 'When your dad passed away, he left me well off and he'd want me to help you out.'

Jo had handed Lottie and Max a cheque for five hundred pounds the previous weekend. It felt like charity to Max but they couldn't turn it down. It felt *really* extravagant to go out for a curry and it seemed so ridiculous. The couple had lived out of restaurants when they first met.

Before long, Max and Lottie said goodbye to Arthur, Maisie and Jo, and stepped out through the front door. The children were more than happy to stay with their grandmother. Jo was at fifty-six and was still quite youthful. She could keep up with Arthur and Maisie with no problems at all, and as a widow, she looked forward to the time she spent with them.

Max and Lottie headed into Wimborne, a charming market town near the village. They were meeting at the Star of India, known as the town's finest curry house. Once they arrived and parked the car along the road, they walked hand in hand towards the restaurant. It was a lovely, clear but chilly November evening. Will and Rhoda were already there when they arrived, sitting at the table they had reserved earlier in the day. They walked in through the door, ambled over to the table where they greeted their friends and sat down.

'How was the conference, Max?' asked Will.

'Interesting!' he replied. 'I've got quite a story. I've told it to Lottie briefly but we didn't have a lot of time after I got home.'

Max told them the story about Tommy McNeill and the state he was in when he helped him. He also shared his conversation with Natalie and showed them her business card. They looked amazed and incredulous at the story but the business card was the proof. In fact, the business card was the only reason Max believed his own story.

'So, let me get this straight,' said Rhoda. 'You helped Tommy McNeill of The Clowns, eighties pop sensations, out of a jam. He was drunk in a lift, you helped him back to his room, met his manager and didn't mention the tape and your songs?'

'Yeah that's right,' he replied. 'You think I should have handed them the tape?'

'Why not, Max?' said Will. 'Forever and a Day is a great track. I could almost imagine Tommy McNeill crooning it himself, and I'm not just talking you up here, mate.'

Max really hadn't considered this as an option. He *had* thought that maybe Natalie could help him find someone to sing his songs, but really didn't think of Tommy. He smiled to himself and looked at Lottie; she shrugged her shoulders. It was at that point he started to allow himself to consider the possibilities.

'You know, Natalie *did* say, if I needed anything or was in town, meaning London.' She and Tommy owed him a coffee, at least. 'Maybe I *could* call.'

The friends enjoyed their Indian meal and tried to work out a pretense for Max to call Natalie. He had a meeting next week with a customer in Surrey; that would be near enough. He had to be careful as I.M.C had fitted trackers on their cars, and he would definitely have to explain to his line manager what he was doing in The Strand at 11a.m. on a Thursday. They decided he would say he was in Surrey on business and ask Tommy and Natalie if they would like to meet for a coffee. He would have to be quick or Natalie would forget the conversation. At the end of the conversation, Max was the only one who wasn't getting carried away. Will had even suggested bringing Tommy down for the open mic night in Bournemouth. Max knew he was being boring; he was hopeful but wanted to keep his feet firmly on the ground. He remembered all too well the feeling of rejection and how it plagued him in the past. He wasn't even sure he wanted Tommy to sing any of his songs; he would have hoped for a younger artist or band. He also felt that he would get very little artistic influence over how the music would be produced, although he acknowledged he wasn't exactly in a position of strength. He decided he *would* make the call tomorrow evening. He would have to carefully work out what he was going to say. He had no experience of any of this. All he had done was write a few songs twenty-five years ago. Was he going mad? What on earth was he thinking? The one thing he *did* know was that he was going to go through with it. He knew himself well and there was no way he would let this go, and the others would never let him, anyway. They paid for the meal. left the restaurant and headed back to their cars. It turned out that they had parked within two cars of each other.

'Right, will see you soon then? Thanks for this evening. It was fantastic. Just what we needed. Isn't that right, Max?' said Lottie.

Max didn't get the chance to reply when both Rhoda *and* Will simultaneously said that he should make the call, both making phone shapes with their hands. Will laughed and nodded whilst he climbed into Lottie's 2004 Ford Focus. They headed off back to Tarrant Marshall where Jo was waiting for them when they returned. She was asleep on the sofa when they got there. Lottie made up the bed in the spare room so that Jo could stay the night. This would save her a late, dark journey home back to Bournemouth, where she owned a bungalow. She woke her mother, who dozily announced she was off to bed. Lottie went upstairs at the same time to check on Arthur and Maisie. Max sat on the sofa and watched 'Match of the Day.' It was Chelsea beating Liverpool on screen, but Max wasn't watching really, there were much more pressing things on his mind.

Natalie offered to take Tommy all the way back to Sutton in her car and Tommy insisted on taking her to his favourite Italian restaurant, Franco's. He knew them there very well, and they would love the fact Natalie was of Italian descent; they would make a real fuss of her. She parked her car outside Miriam's house and was introduced to his mum briefly before they walked round to the trattoria. When they reached the restaurant, it was empty, and Tommy was greeted by Franco himself. Natalie immediately warmed to Franco; he was like her dad.

'Ah, buona sera Tommy,' he said. 'And who is the lovely lady?' enquired Franco with all the subtlety of a house brick.

'Alright Franco, this is Natalie, she's helping me with my career, or at least, I'm hoping to get it on track again,' said Tommy.

'This is fantastico, Tommy! I would love to see you singing again.'

Franco looked at Natalie and then gestured towards the signed photograph of Tommy that took pride of place above the bar area. Natalie felt at home as Franco showed them to their table.

'Tommy's special table,' he announced. 'Where he brings all his lovely ladies!'

Natalie laughed, especially when she saw the bright shade of crimson that Tommy had become. It was fun, but they had important stuff to discuss this evening. She wanted to know what direction Tommy wanted to take. They looked at their menus; Natalie ordered the spaghetti with calamari and Tommy ordered a pizza. He loved Franco's pizza. It was genuinely the best he had come across despite all his travels.

'Okay, Tommy, so where are we going with this?' Natalie asked. 'How do see your career?'

Tommy paused and thought before answering; he wanted to be clear about what he wanted to say.

'Well, I just want to sing again,' he responded. 'I'd like a new album with new songs across a broad spectrum of styles. Eclectic, you know. With maybe a bit of the old blue-eyed soul I used to do back in the day, but with some more modern tunes, in touch with now. I have some tunes of my own. I'm not sure if they'll cut the mustard though, but I would like to use new up and coming writers and perhaps some unusual covers. I want to really work with other people. To be honest, in The Clowns, it was the Tommy show all the way. I want this to be democratic. Natalie, I haven't known you long but I trust your judgement. I want you to have a big say.'

Natalie was spellbound by Tommy's speech. He'd obviously thought about it. There was more going on in his head than she realised. The project would need funding and she promised to use all her contacts to make it happen. They could produce an album more cheaply these days and they could go for a live sound. Tommy had the sort of voice that really didn't need enhancing. She could start making calls in the morning.

They finished their meal and walked back to Natalie's car. It was 10p.m. Tommy had been very well behaved, sticking to just a couple of glasses of wine. They chatted about the night sky and Tommy pointed some stars and constellations to Natalie. He loved the night sky. Whenever he went on a walking holiday, he would walk into the night just so he could observe the heavens. They reached Natalie's car and had arranged to speak again on Monday; they both had commitments tomorrow. Tommy needed to spend time with Miriam, and Natalie just needed to chill. Natalie unlocked her car and opened the door. It was then that it happened. It was inevitable. Tommy looked into Natalie's eyes and she stared back. He moved towards her, and very slowly and deliberately, he kissed her. From that point on, there was no looking back.

Natalie thought about the kiss all the way back to Belsize Park. What did it mean? She didn't know, but she *was* glad that it had happened. It was exciting not knowing what it would lead to. Tommy felt the same. Natalie was the first person in years that truly excited him and he had nothing but total respect for her. The fact she was beautiful helped. The fact that she was beautiful *and* that she really didn't know it, was even more of an attraction. He started to think about his career for the first time in a long while, and that was down to

Natalie. He hadn't known her long but he felt like he'd known her all his life.

The next day, Natalie woke to a message on Facebook from Lauren. It was probably there last night but yesterday was a full-on day, and she had just collapsed onto her bed when she arrived home.

'Hi Natalie, it was an amazing surprise to hear from you, I can't tell you how much it would mean to me to see Dad again. I've just arrived in London for two weeks, at least. I may even stay here. I would love to meet up as soon as we can. I really can't believe this is happening!

Lauren x '

Natalie gave her the address for Franco's restaurant and asked to her to meet at 1p.m. on Tuesday. She was to pose as another diner and then come over to the table upon Natalie's signal. It would all be perfect and she couldn't wait to see it happen. When they would finish eating, they could go round and visit Miriam. Natalie didn't have a family unit in the UK. She was making Tommy's family her family without even realising it. She spent the rest of her day doing some work on her laptop, making phone calls and skype-ing various family members back home in Canada. At about 4p.m. she started preparing herself something to eat when her phone started to ring.

'Hi, Natalie here,' she answered.

'Hello Natalie, this is Max. You know, from The Metropole Hotel. We met briefly? I was the one who helped Tommy,' said Max nervously.

'Uh huh! Hi Max, how are ya! Yeah, of course I remember. What can I do for ya?' She sounded more transatlantic than Max had remembered.

'Well, you know, you said if you could help with anything, then you would? Well, I was wondering if I could meet up with you and Tommy for that coffee? I have something I'd like you to hear.' Max was flowing now and his natural self-confidence had started to kick in.

They arranged to meet on Wednesday at Cobham services on the M25 in Surrey. It was on his territory and he had customers in the vicinity. His tracker wouldn't show up any activity that was out of the ordinary. They said their goodbyes and Natalie got on with cooking. She was intrigued; she should have asked what he wanted but was too taken aback by the call. She had left her card with countless people over the years in those sorts of situations but very rarely did people take her up on it, in her experience.

Lauren opened up Facebook messenger as soon as it sounded on her phone. She read the message and smiled. Her reply was simple and short.

'See you there!! :) L xx'

10. Come Together

The next day, Natalie was up early and ready for whatever Monday morning could throw at her. Her two flat mates, Tricia and Shelley had gone off on a winter break together in Cyprus. Of course, this meant she didn't have to queue for the bathroom and could get out of the house by seven; she needed to, she had a lot to get done. It didn't take long to walk to Belsize Park tube station and it was a nice enough morning, although it was still dark, made even darker by the cloud cover. She hopped on the next train and took the relatively short journey to Charing Cross. From there, she walked along The Strand. She stopped for a takeaway coffee and some breakfast along the way and reached her office just before eight. Natalie had a lot of work to catch up on before Tommy was due to arrive at eleven. I.M.C were keen to offer her more work, they were becoming a big employer around Europe with all their different divisions, and they were keen to promote a good image for themselves. There were also opportunities to get involved in some promotional work for some Television and Radio companies to be looked at, and then, of course, there was Tommy, the best opportunity of all of them. She thought about the kiss and wondered if she'd ever really lost her schoolgirl crush on him. She had to focus on the job in hand first; they had to have a master plan. Tommy wanted to make an album and they would need songs, musicians, producers and various other people that would get involved with the album. Her experience in the music industry was limited to promotional work, and when that side of it kicked in, she would be in her comfort zone. Her first thought would be that Tommy would need someone to help pull the whole thing together musically, somebody who knew all the personnel that would be required. The other question was financing the whole thing; would they get a label interested or would they have to fund the whole project themselves? Tommy didn't have any money, all he earned was his carer's allowance for looking after Miriam. Natalie had funds but after setting up the business, they were limited. Perhaps crowdfunding, or some other such scheme, would be an option. It all needed to be thought out, although she knew that with all the best projects, the right things generally fell into place one at a time. The song choices were obviously crucial, but that was down to Tommy and whomever would be in charge of production. She made a list of bullet points and printed it off ready for his arrival.

It was 10.55a.m. and Natalie had already been at work for nearly three hours. She had got a lot done and made various phone calls to prospective clients with some degree of success; it was her usual Monday morning routine. There was a buzz on the intercom and Natalie pressed a small square button on the device.

'Mr. McNeill for you Ms. Mancini,' said the chirpy voice over the speaker.

'Yup, show him up,' chimed Natalie and then immediately rushed over to the mirror to check her appearance. She moved back over to her desk and stood in front of it. There was a knock on the door and it was swiftly opened. There in front of her stood a smiling Tommy. He was clutching something in his left hand.

'Got some water for these then?' He handed Natalie the small bunch of flowers that he had bought from the small stall on the way up from Charing Cross tube. She hugged him for a minute and grabbed a small cut glass vase from a cupboard above her laser jet printer. She put some water in and arranged the flowers carefully in the vase.

'You should wait until your album is a million seller until you buy me flowers!' She winked at Tommy and laughed.

'I don't have to wait then; I know this whole thing will be a huge success. If I have doubts, it's about my own ability to keep myself on an even keel.'

'Okay then, Tommy, grab yourself a seat and make yourself comfortable,' she said. 'We have loads to get through but business first!'

Tommy raised his eyebrows, he liked the sound of the fact there might be something that came after the business bit. He shut all thoughts of impropriety out of his head and focused on the meeting, like a true professional.

They discussed, first and foremost, the concept of any comeback album that Tommy was going to put his name to. He didn't want to be some old crooner releasing an album of bland covers that would only appeal to the Christmas market and maybe Mother's Day. He wanted something relevant sounding, a very live sounding recording, with new material written by up and coming writers, maybe a couple of his own songs, if he could finish them off. If there were to be any cover versions, they should be lesser known songs that he would perhaps approach from a different angle. Perhaps he would record material that people wouldn't have associated him with previously. The one cover version he did have in mind was 'Ships,' a song from Big Country's 1991 album, 'No Place Like Home'. It was a haunting Celtic ballad and would be a fitting tribute to his friend and writer of the song, Stuart Adamson, who died in 2001. Tommy had first met him at a showbiz party in 1986. He and Tommy, with his Scottish ancestry, got along famously and kept in touch until Adamson's death. This, at least, could be a starting point, and Tommy revealed to Natalie that he had rung his old mate, Bill Terry, a session guitarist and ex sound engineer from Manor Studios in Oxford. Tommy worked with him many times and always got on well with him. They would demo the song at his home studio in Surrey on Friday, with Bill playing the acoustic guitar. All Tommy would have to do was sing the vocal tracks over the top. Natalie remembered the song and thought that it would be in keeping with the sound that Tommy had wanted to create. She also felt that if Tommy felt comfortable with Bill, then perhaps he should be brought onboard as part of the team. She didn't want to jump in too quickly though, they could see how the demo sounded first. A couple of hours went by, plans were made and Natalie made a list of people to speak to.

'Do you remember that guy from the hotel at the weekend? Max?' she enquired.

'Yeah I do…just!' he smiled.

'Well, we're meeting him for coffee on Wednesday. He seemed keen to discuss something... with both of us, he said. I'm not sure what it's all about, but seeing as he helped you out, I thought we should go.'

Tommy agreed, although he didn't like things like this, he was probably an old Clowns fan and wanted a selfie to stick on Facebook. There was a Clowns page or so he had heard.

'And tomorrow, we're having lunch at Franco's. I'll meet you there. There's someone I'd like you to meet. I'm not saying who though!'

He looked at Natalie's face, she wasn't giving anything away. She was a dab hand at a poker face. He knew she wouldn't tell.

Max rushed home from Devon, where he had been advising someone about drilling holes in marine grade stainless steel. He wanted to get the tape sorted and transferred across to the PC. He would give Natalie and Tommy a memory stick with two of the songs that he had written on it. They were the only two he felt brave enough to let them hear as the rest were awful. Once he arrived home, he went straight to his laptop, plugged in the small device to the USB port and inserted the cassette into the unit. Before long, an icon appeared on the screen and there was an option to upload. Max pressed the button and slowly the information was transferred to the computer. When it was complete, Max connected a memory stick to the same USB port and uploaded the tracks from there. Max checked that the process worked and tucked the memory stick into a zipped pocket in his work bag. He knew it would be safe there and more importantly, he wouldn't forget where it was. He felt like it was all a bit of a fantasy to hope that his songs might end up being used, but he was prepared to try, he had nothing to lose. Just at that moment, the door opened; Lottie and the kids had returned from Jo's. Lottie had completed her first day's work at the local hospital; they were sure to have lots to catch up on.

Natalie invited Tommy to come back to Belsize Park for a meal. She cooked him a stir-fry. It was her specialty. They promised to forget about career stuff for a while. Tommy found her a lot less like a career girl than he expected. She spoke about her hobbies. Ice hockey was a massive thing for her. It was huge back home in Canada and her father had been a coach. She was a big fan of The Halifax Mooseheads and she had adorned the living room wall with one of their flags, much to the bemusement of the other girls in the flat. Tommy insisted in tidying up after the meal; he was impressed with her cooking and wanted to do his bit. He insisted that Natalie have another glass of wine and relaxed on the sofa. He loaded the dishwasher and was just placing the clean wok on the draining board, when Natalie walked towards him purposely as he was drying his hands. There was a look on her face which meant only one thing, or at least as Tommy saw it. She pulled the tea towel from his hands and threw it on the floor, grabbed his hand and led him towards her bedroom.

The next day, Tommy and Natalie left Belsize Park at about eleven. Natalie wanted to leave plenty of time to get to Sutton. She wanted to go via the office on the way to drop off some papers; to also make it look like they were attending a business meeting. They were still beaming as they walked hand in hand towards the underground. They arrived at Miriam's just before midday and Tommy checked that his mum was okay. Her sister Gladys had been visiting so he knew she wouldn't be alone. When Tommy disappeared upstairs to shower and change, Natalie confided in Miriam that they would be back later with a special guest, but not to tell Tommy. Miriam didn't know who at that point but worked it out after Tommy and Natalie left for Franco's. They said their goodbyes and walked the half mile or so to the restaurant. Once they arrived, Franco showed them to their table.

'Table for four?' asked Tommy. 'So, who are we expecting then?' said Tommy. He didn't want to play anymore because he was getting nervous. Just at that point, Natalie's phone buzzed and it created a handy diversion. It was a text from Lauren.

'Just outside! Have brought Izzy along as I hoped, two minutes! :) x,' the text read.

'Two minutes.' Said Natalie holding up two digits to indicate. Tommy shuffled around nervously on his seat. The door of the restaurant opened and two young ladies stood in the doorway. One Tommy didn't recognise at all, but the other one he knew the smile straight away. His emotions crumbled in as he stood up and rushed to Lauren. The tears rained down from his eyes as they embraced. Natalie went over and said hello to Izzy. She suggested that they both sit down and left Tommy and Lauren to speak for a bit.

'Hi Dad,' said Lauren. 'It's been a long time.'

'Oh far, far too long,' whispered Tommy. His voice was quivering with surprise.

He put his arm around her shoulder and they walked over to Natalie and Izzy at the table, and then they sat down. They didn't talk much about the past; that conversation would have to come when they were on their own. They spoke about the present. Tommy, about the concept of a return to singing, and Lauren, about her leaving France and coming to live in London. Tommy was delighted. There was room at Miriam's although he thought it was too early to suggest this. At this point, it occurred to him how made up Miriam would be to see Lauren, her only grandchild, after all these years. It was something Tommy felt guilty about. If he'd not been in such a mess, then both he and Miriam would have had a normal relationship with Lauren. They could make up for it now though. They couldn't get the last eighteen years back but they could make the best of the present. During his most troubled times, Tommy had read 'The Power of Now' by Eckhart Tolle, a self-help guide he used to concentrate on valuing what was important in the present. He made a mental note to have another read as emotions would be running high with both Natalie *and* Lauren suddenly appearing in his life. A month ago, none of this would have seemed possible. He would need to keep himself level as it would be good practice for when he slipped back into the public eye.

'How well do you remember your Nana?' asked Tommy.

'Not that well. It'll be great to meet her. I can't wait. It's been strange growing up with the thought of family somewhere else in the world. You've always been there in my mind though. Sylvain, or papa as I call him, always wanted to keep me away. He's very manipulative, but to be fair, he's always been good to me. It's my wish that we all could maybe get along?'

'Fine by me,' said Tommy. 'I'm just pleased to have you back in my world. How did you and Natalie get in touch?'

'One word... Facebook!' she replied. 'Natalie said she knew it was me because of the French surname and The Clown's tour t-shirt in one of my photos. Clever of her, I'd say. You want to hang on to her dad, she's fab!' Then her face dropped. 'Oh, I didn't mean to assume... you are together, aren't you?' Tommy smiled and put his finger to his lips to stop her fretting anymore. He looked over at Natalie and she grinned.

'Yeah.' They said in unison. 'It's early days though!' added Natalie.

They paid Franco for their meal, said goodbye and thanked him, and ambled round to Miriam's house. When they got there, she was in her usual place in front of the television watching 'Countdown'.

'Hi Ma! I've got someone I'd like you to meet,' he beamed.

'Have you been drinking that Chianti again, Tommy? You sound a bit squiffy!'

She slowly climbed to her feet and walked toward the lounge door. Tommy was stood obscuring her view of the doorway where Lauren stood. Natalie and Izzy cowered behind them feeling like spare parts. Suddenly, Tommy ducked out of the way and there was Lauren grinning at her.

'Lauren, is that really you?' She sobbed but a large smile started to form.

'Yes Nana, it's little ol' me!'

They embraced, walked over to Tommy and he joined the group hug. It was clear they would have a lot to talk about. Natalie beckoned Izzy and they went off to the kitchen and put the kettle on. Lauren, Miriam and Tommy just needed a bit of time and space. It was about 10p.m. when they all realised they were getting a little bit tired. It had been a long day and there had been a lot to catch up on. Izzy and Lauren had arrived by tube and train and Izzy was just thinking they should begin the journey home. She was lucky enough to have the day off today because her school had been used as a polling station. There had been an emergency bi-election due to the death of the local MP, but it was back to work tomorrow. Tommy offered to walk them round to the station.

'Why don't you all stay?' said Miriam.

'Thanks Miriam,' said Izzy. 'But I'm at work tomorrow. Lauren, you must stay, it will be fine.' Her French accent was a beautiful sound and her voice was a worthy carrier of that magnificent language.

'There's plenty of room, and you too, Natalie! I'm sure Tommy will find you somewhere to sleep!' Tommy and Natalie, despite being fully grown adults, turned the colour of one of Sylvain's famous bottles of Chateauneuf du Pape. They felt like seventeen-year-olds all over again. Lauren decided to divert the conversation just to bail out her dad and Natalie.

'Ooh Izzy, if you'll be okay, I would love to stay Nana, thank you.'

Tommy put on his coat and walked with Izzy to the station where she would weave her way on London's transport system back to Hanwell. When he returned, a bed had been made up for Lauren in the spare room. Miriam went to bed and left Tommy, Natalie and Lauren to chat into the small hours. Eventually, at about 2a.m., the house was quiet. Three generations of McNeill's were present in the old Victorian town house in Sutton for the first time since Tommy was twelve; a whole forty years ago. The neighbourhood of Sutton, however, never slept totally and the urban sounds of ambulances, police cars and howling foxes went on into the night.

11. Magic

Bernard Jackson was a legend; not that anyone who *knew* him as Bernard Jackson would have realised. His G.P, or the checkout assistant would be forgiven for thinking he was an ordinary guy. Mr. Jackson came in for the occasional pint of milk or to have his blood pressure checked by the nurse. His friends and family knew him as Bernie; young at heart and ready for a laugh and a good time. He was also well known for his generosity. The public, however, only knew him as 'The Magician.' He had earned the moniker during his years as a top record producer and he had just come back home to the United Kingdom to live after a decade in The United States. He had married Tennessee born country singer, Carlene Taylor, in 2003 and spent the last ten years living in Nashville producing records for Carlene, and other top country and western artists. He had split from Carlene acrimoniously a year ago, decided enough was enough, and returned to UK shores. The divorce wasn't tricky financially as they were both wealthy and they had signed a prenuptial agreement, in any case. Bernie was a wealthy man and had bought himself a large New England style home close to the beach at Canford Cliffs, Poole in Dorset. He had spent the last six months having the basement fitted out as a recording studio and was eager for a return to work. He had chosen only the best state of the art equipment.

Bernie was perched on a black leather reclining chair with a built in footrest. The chair sat in his office opposite the window that faced out over the English Channel. He loved to watch the activities of people in boats and dinghies as he lounged and drank his favorite whisky. This afternoon, however, was a dull, grey November day with not much to see on the water, so he was catching up with some correspondence on his laptop.

Bernie was born in Manchester in 1960 and made his name as a keyboard player for New Romantic act, Tussaud, who had formed in 1980 and after a couple of minor hits, faded away and split up by 1982. He then spent the next three years as a session keyboard player, before starting to sit in on the mixing desk and assist various producers of the time, particularly, Steve Lillywhite and the legendary late, Arif Mardin. He learned a lot from this period, and before long, he started to produce bands under the name of The Magician. His output was prolific and groundbreaking, winning him several Brit and Grammy awards in the process. This made him *the* number one in-demand record producer of the period. He soon became a very wealthy man, but a bored wealthy man. He spread his wings and set off to learn and work in the rootsier climbs of The United States, immersing himself in folk, soul, jazz and country and western. It was then that he met Carlene and began to produce albums for her and other country and western artists.

Soon after the divorce, he started to crave Marmite, John Smith's, Manchester City and British culture generally and decided to make the move home. Bernie decided on Poole because he loved the sea and wanted to be in reasonable distance with London. He was starting to get settled in his new home and was looking for a new project. He had an interesting chat with an old mate, Bill Terry, from his days in Tussaud. Bill told him he was going to demo a track with a chap called Tommy McNeil. He remembered the name and he certainly remembered the voice. It was a peach of a voice and he liked Tommy's attitude on the couple of occasions that their paths had crossed. He remembered then that Tommy just called him 'Magic.' Perhaps he could help him. It would certainly be a challenge. If he had the right material, then there was definitely an audience for Tommy. He logged onto the internet and typed into google search: "The Clowns." Google soon responded with a host of website options. At the top of the listings, before all the information about 'The Wogan Incident,' was an entry in Wikipedia. He clicked on the link, took a quick swig of Glenlivet single malt and began to read:

The Clowns

The Clowns were an English Soul Pop band formed in 1978 in Sutton, Surrey, United Kingdom. They consisted of Singer/Guitarist Tommy McNeill, Guitarist Stuart Ebdon, Bass Player Matt Jones, Keyboardist Nick Williams and Drummer Robbie Little. They signed to RCA in 1981 after serving their apprenticeship in the pubs and clubs of London. They soon became a successful chart act in the mid-eighties before singer Tommy McNeill shocked the nation with his outrageous behaviour on a live television chat show.

Commercial Success 1983-1987

Discography: Albums

1983 - The Clowns	Highest UK Chart Position #4
1985 - Hooked On You	Highest UK Chart Position #1
1986 - The Circus	Highest UK Chart Position #1
1987 - Send in The Clowns (Live)	Highest UK Chart Position #1
1990 - Greatest Hits	Highest UK Chart Position #15

Bernie read the band's history and could see that they were a huge deal for four years, and rightly so. Tommy had the voice of an angel back then. He had huge potential and could have been a worldwide star for years, but due to his well-documented problems and poor management, it all fell to bits for him. Did he think with the right material he could be a success again? Very much so. Bill had told him that Tommy was being handled by a successful PR guru from Canada, Natalie Mancini. He'd not heard of her but he hoped she had a strong hand. Tommy had a reputation back then that he was hard to handle. He obviously didn't know the relationship between Tommy and Natalie yet, so he was quite correct to have his fears about it.

He walked across his office and went towards the wall where he kept all his awards and gold discs. The earlier ones were for some very diverse acts but for the last few years they were mostly country and western albums. He was now back in Britain and immersed in British culture again. What better way to make an impact on the British music scene than to revive one of its flawed geniuses. Tommy was a star who had waned but he could come back with a little help from Bernie and some decent songs and musicians. He hadn't made contact with anyone about any projects yet and it was probable that Tommy hadn't even considered working with 'The Magician.' Bernie however, was definitely considering *him*. He sat back down and began to look up songs by The Clowns and Tommy's rather up and down solo career, which gradually faded away. This was all part of the research, knowing what had worked, and just as importantly, *not* worked for Tommy. He would have to wait to hear the demo from Bill to know what sort of shape his voice was in. He loved the song they were going to do though, and he was trying hard not to imagine how he would make it sound. After years of using high tech electronic gadgets in the eighties and early nineties, America taught him about simplicity in music; keeping the sound clutter free, allowing both the musicians and the singer, to express themselves clearly. What better vehicle for a great song than Tommy's soulful and emotive voice. He helped himself to another glass of Glenlivet. He thought he better make the most of it. He refused to touch a drop while he was involved in recording. He found, through bitter experience, that he needed to focus totally on the music. He sat back down on his chair. It was a waiting game now. Bill would send him the recording over the weekend and only *then* would he decide. Would he approach Tommy's camp or walk away? Only time would tell.

 Bill Terry went through the introduction and first verse to 'Ships' one more time; he was certain he'd just about got it right. The chord sequence was so simple, it was ridiculous, and he reflected that so many of the greatest songs could be played and sung on an acoustic guitar with only the most rudimentary knowledge. Tommy didn't need him really. He could play and sing this simultaneously in his sleep; at least back in the old days. Tommy was a natural talent but he hadn't seen him for a long time. Who knows what the ravages of time had done to him? The alcohol and the pill popping would not have made him sound any better surely? He knew all that was in the past now and that Tommy was clean, or at least reasonably so. Largely, he was right. Tommy still enjoyed a drink or two but the blips were rare. At this stage both Bill and The Magician would find it hard to walk away. Maybe it was Tommy's time again. There was a long way to go, and a lot of work to be done, but maybe, just maybe.

12. Time for Action

There was a deluge on the anti-clockwise section of the M25 in Surrey. Max was heading past junction ten at Wisley, and he was in plenty of time. He looked at the dashboard clock, it was 10.15a.m. and they had agreed to meet at eleven. The traffic was pretty slow in the rain, but he was less than a mile away from Cobham Services where they had arranged to meet. Max already edged his way into the inside lane, and was preparing to exit as soon as the slip road appeared on the left. He'd put the two songs into mp3 format and had listened to them already three or four times on the journey, just to reassure himself. He signaled left and maneuvered off the motorway, down the chicaned road and underneath the motorway. The parking area was straight in front of him. It was a relatively new service station, having been opened in 2012. Max often came here on his travels in the area and would quite often meet clients and colleagues at this facility. He usually felt at ease here, although he felt anything but ease today. He felt a nervousness that was nearly at the point of nausea, although he felt huge excitement at the same time. He'd only really experienced this feeling at his wedding, the birth of his children and at some of his gigs with The Silence. He thought about it again. He, Max Chilton, was attending a meeting with Tommy McNeill of The Clowns and his manager, with the sole purpose of trying to get them to listen to a couple of his songs. This was completely insane!

He parked the car and walked towards the covered shopping and dining area. After a quick stop in the gents, washing his hands as he left, he walked into Starbucks. He ordered a latte and sat down at a table under the vaulted ceiling that was plenty big enough for three. He sat down on one of the high stools that were scattered around the table. It was now 10.30a.m. 'Plenty of time to spare,' he thought. He cranked up his laptop and logged into the free Wi-Fi that the service station provided. He had half an hour. He imagined he would get some work done but soon abandoned the idea. He soon embarked upon some further research on his subject... Tommy McNeill; not that he wasn't already well prepared!

It was a busy start in Sutton. They woke up just after eight but Natalie had agreed that they would drop Lauren back off in Hanwell on their way, even though they were taking a large detour. Lauren needed to go home, she hadn't brought a change of clothes like Natalie, who always seemed to be prepared for any situation that life might throw at her. Tommy had arranged to spend some time with Lauren and they made plans to meet up tomorrow in the West End to spend the day together. They dropped her off and got on to the M4 at Brentford heading west before getting on the M25 near Heathrow. They reached Cobham just a little bit late at 11.05a.m., walked into Starbucks, where they saw Max sitting down, facing them. He stood up and greeted them warmly.

Max was taller than Tommy remembered. Not that he remembered a great deal, and Natalie was more stunning than Max had remembered. Natalie could only recall being incandescent with rage and didn't really make any observations at all. Max went up to the counter and ordered drinks for the couple whilst they settled in their seats and recovered from their journey. Max returned to his seat and began his pitch.

'So, when I met you both in Birmingham, I didn't really think anything of it, you know. I'd met someone who was a star in my youth and thought very nice and went home but…I got home and thought. I was telling Natalie that I played in bands in my youth and still have an interest in music and I was wondering about something.'

'What's that then?' asked Tommy.

'Well, have you any plans or are you still actively involved in music, Tommy?'

'Well,' said Tommy, hesitantly at first. 'I'm not sure where you are headed with this but Natalie and myself have just started considering the possibility of a new album. Nothing concrete, yet, but starting to sketch out some ideas.'

'Hmm okay.' Said Max, by now becoming more and more intrigued. 'I have a couple of songs I wrote years ago, one in particular I think would suit your voice. They've been in a box in my attic since 1990 and I've just converted them onto mp3.' Max held out the memory stick to show Tommy and Natalie.

'Tell us about the songs' said Natalie.

'Well, the first song is called 'Never Bring Me Down.' It's an up-tempo slab of early nineties Britpop. Not particularly the type of tune I would imagine The Clowns would have done but it's catchy nonetheless. The *other* one is called 'Forever and a Day,' which is a soft soul ballad. I've always had a gut feeling about this song. I've always said that it has legs!'

Max paused as he took a sip of coffee and Natalie then took over.

'Okay, Max,' she said. ' I can see how you believe in them. Let me tell you, we want this comeback album of Tommy's to be all about the songs. We don't just want to do it for the money; it's about the music. Tommy would like fresh songs from new and up and coming writers. These songs would certainly have a quirky history to them. I like that!' she said enthusiastically.

'Right, well, let's play'em on your laptop kiddo,' said Tommy.

He had heard enough. What really would he want with two songs from some nobody he hadn't heard of? He didn't want to be ungrateful, but maybe if he said no now and to his face, it would be easier in the long run. Max lined up the tunes on his laptop and was about to press play when he decided to just oil the wheels a little.

'Bear in mind that these were recorded on a porta studio and I'm a bass player. My singing and guitar playing are not the greatest.' He grinned as he said this and clicked on play.

'Never Bring Me Down' started to play and a few disgruntled business types started to look over disapprovingly. To Max's delight, Natalie was smiling and Tommy tapped his toes to the rhythm. The song came and went in four minutes but neither Tommy nor Natalie said a word. 'Now, for the big guns,' thought Max. He clicked play again and the restrained soft guitar chords of 'Forever and a Day' began to sound. Tommy then did something very strange, something that wasn't new to him at least. He shut his eyes and began to concentrate on the vocals. Natalie shrugged across at Max and started the chuckle.

'Oooh, I think he might just like this,' she said.

At the end of the song, Tommy assured Max that he liked the songs but that he would need to listen a few more times before deciding if he was ever likely to use them. It might, he explained, take him a few weeks and even then, if they were recorded, there were no guarantees they would make the final cut. They started to talk about music and musicians they admired and respected. Van Morrison and Paul Weller were artists they both loved and so were The Isley Brothers. Natalie felt she was going to lapse into a coma at this point. She went off and bought some more coffee whilst Max and Tommy enthused about various tunes. They got along like a house on fire but Max still had the feeling that Tommy would not be back in touch. After an hour, a very weary looking Natalie decided to call a halt to things. Max too looked at his watch and felt he'd better do some work. He would be fine in the services for a limited amount of time but his tracker would blow the whistle on him if he was there for too long.

Max gave Natalie the memory stick and his contact details, hoping that they wouldn't lose them. She said they would be in touch and they all shook hands as they made their way back to their cars. Max jumped into his Avensis and drove away trying to look as cool as he could until he disappeared from view. He breathed a huge sigh as he got back onto the M25 towards Staines, where had his next appointment. He pressed speed dial number one on his phone.

'Hi Max, how was it?' asked Lottie bursting with excitement. Max had thought about pranking her at this point but thought better of it.

'Well, I think he liked 'Forever and a Day,' but not sure about the other one. Good news though, he *is* making an album! No timescales or anything but it's happening. They did say it could be weeks before they've decided on material though, but they want to use up and coming writers.'

Lottie excitedly finished the call so she could ring Rhoda and Jo to keep them up to date with events. Max drove on and tried to focus his mind on the job in hand. He tried to think about the aerospace company he was about to visit and what their requirements were. It was hopeless though, and he would just have to 'wing' it when he got there. Tommy liked 'Forever,' he was sure, but enough to want to record it? Enough for it to make the cut? Who knows? One thing he was sure of though was that Tommy would have known either way as soon as he heard the song. Musicians were like that!

'Oh, I don't know Nat!' Tommy was in a state of indecision. Yes, he liked the songs, but could he imagine singing them? It was a very personal relationship between the song and the singer. You either had to have written it or have a very close affinity with the subject to make it work, in his opinion. He would have to listen to it again and again and familiarise himself with the lyrics and the message.

'Well, I thought I could hear you at least sing the second tune. It would probably be the one song that harks back to the sound of The Clowns, and you will need one of them whether you like it or not.'

Tommy knew that she wasn't wrong. Natalie was good for him; she made good decisions, although Tommy would have to have the final say on what he sang. It had to be that way and Natalie understood that. There was much to ponder over the coming days. Tommy looked forward to tomorrow. He had a day planned with just him and Lauren. Just father and daughter going into London together, seeing the sights, having some lunch. Just normal things that a parent and grown up offspring might do. They would do the kind of things that both had missed out on; they had lots of time to make up. Thankfully, Tommy was only fifty-two, so there were a lot of years ahead to do so. He could still give Lauren away and make a father of the bride speech. There was so much to feel gratitude for rather than think about all the negatives. Lauren and Natalie had made a massive difference to Team McNeill and Tommy felt stronger than he had for a long time, possibly ever. Natalie dropped Tommy off in Sutton and headed back to Belsize Park to catch up on all the day's correspondence. Tommy made Miriam a cup of tea and they caught up on the previous week's developments. Tommy asked her if she would be okay if he asked Lauren to move into the spare room. Miriam, as expected, was delighted and Tommy made a plan to ask her on the day out tomorrow.

Natalie listened to the songs again on her return home. Something about the songs and their history appealed to her and there was something about the 'small man makes good' angle to the whole thing that made her want Tommy to sing them. Maybe for the first time ever, the musical gods were smiling down on Max. This would be the most amazing break he would ever had. It's sometimes a very thin line between success and failure and for Max it was clear just how thin it was. He finished his call in Staines, put his car into drive and started to travel the eighty or so miles back to Dorset. He arrived home early enough to see Arthur and Maisie going off to bed, which didn't happen every day, and enjoyed reading them a story. Max would always have fun by reading all the different character's lines in different regional accents. It always sent the kids off to sleep in a good frame of mind, he felt. He sat and chatted to Lottie about the day's events and how he was hopeful. At least they hadn't turned him down flat. They were just laughing about the ridiculousness of the whole chain of events when Max's mobile rang. It was Natalie.

'Hi Natalie, how's it going?' Said Max, trying to sound as cool, calm and collected as he could.

'Yeah, hi, Max, it's all good! Just wanted you to know that I liked the songs but you know this isn't my decision, so we'll see. I'm on your team and I'll do my best.'

Max couldn't quite believe what he was hearing; they were seriously considering his songs. Was he dreaming? He pinched himself, and quite clearly, he wasn't. This could be just the start! He ran into the small office next to the kitchen and returned with his old faithful acoustic guitar. Maybe it was time he knocked out some more tunes.

13. One Day Like This

Tommy had arrived early. He had arranged to meet Lauren at Piccadilly Circus by The Shaftesbury Fountain. It was agreed that this would be a good point where their respective tube lines, The Piccadilly for Lauren and The Bakerloo for Tommy, met. He had been listening on his iPod to Elbow's critically acclaimed 2008 album, 'Seldom Seen Kid,' which was one of his favourite albums of the last decade. It was during the song 'One Day Like This' that he would experience another moment of clarity regarding his upcoming recording project. He loved the sound of strings; he must get a song on the album with just him singing with a string quartet. He had a couple of songs in mind, but perhaps Bill could help him with that. He'd also send Bill the files with Max's two songs to see what he thought. They could run through them on Friday at Bill's place just outside Leatherhead. Bill had his own small commercial recording studio; it was used a lot for TV dubbing work, radio adverts and jingles. It was good enough for demos and Bill was kind enough to offer him a day's free studio time. He wasn't going to turn that down! Bill would already have a backing track for 'Ships' laid down, so all he would have to do was sing. Natalie was going to start the ball rolling today with her contacts, to see what interest there was in a Tommy McNeill comeback and would talk to A & R men, promoters and some producers. It would be a tough gig but Tommy was under no illusions.

It was 10.08a.m. when Tommy spotted Lauren making her way towards him. She was smiling broadly at him and greeted him with a warm embrace.

'Hi Dad, sorry I'm a bit late. I was a bit slow getting up this morning and it all went downhill from there!'

'That's okay, you're here now. That's all that matters.'

Tommy was going to take Lauren on a grand tour of the sights and sounds of London, starting here at Piccadilly Circus. Lauren had done this all before and so had Tommy but never had they done this *together*. He didn't mind coming to London so much now. The autograph hunters didn't bother him so much these days. The odd time that they did approach Tommy, he was much better able to cope. It was mainly selfies on mobile phones these days anyway.

'The tour starts at Madame Tussauds.' He declared and marched Lauren back on the Underground for the short journey to Baker Street tube. Whilst they travelled along together, Tommy noticed that Lauren was gently and quietly singing a Taylor Swift tune. He didn't know which one, he wasn't too knowledgeable of her material but her voice sounded amazing. 'Chip off the old block,' he thought to himself. They disembarked from the tube and joined in the queue for Madame Tussauds. It was quiet in November; all the crowds had converged on Oxford Street for the annual run up to Christmas. They paid their entry fee and wandered around the museum. There used to be a waxwork there of Tommy until 1987.

'They melted me down and replaced me with Marti Pellow!' He probably wasn't joking.

The planetarium followed, and then they moved on to Buckingham Palace where they watched the changing of the guard. It was getting near lunchtime and Tommy decided he would find somewhere to buy Lauren lunch. They settled for Pizza Express in Victoria Street where they found a table and sat down. Tommy looked serious for a minute as he started to speak.

'I'm sorry I haven't been the greatest dad, Lauren. I can't really blame your mum. I was out of it most of the time, to be fair. The music industry had welcomed me in and then spat me out. Sylvain stopped me from seeing you. He thought he was protecting you and I suppose, in a weird way, I'm grateful for that. I couldn't challenge him in court, because by that time, I had nothing left. It wasn't cos I didn't want to see you, I've thought about you every single day over the last eighteen years. It's been really tough.'

'Dad,' said Lauren clutching the menu. 'It was tough for me too. Sometimes mum doesn't stand up to Sylvain and he's used to getting exactly what he wants. I always knew I would come here to find you though. It was just a matter of when.'

Lauren grabbed Tommy's hand and squeezed it tightly as she spoke. They seemed to have formed a very strong bond already. Lauren felt like she had finally found her family after all these years. Their conversation was soon interrupted by the arrival of their pizzas. Lauren chose the Calabrese and Tommy, who it seemed lived on pizza, had the Pollo Forza. He was good at keeping himself in shape with his gym work, so felt he could get away with it. Lauren ate very slowly and rather picked at her food. Tommy could tell she wasn't a big eater, a bit like her mum. In fact, she reminded him of Polly in lots of ways and that wasn't a bad thing really. Polly had many good qualities and he was realistic enough to know that he had been the one that had ruined their marriage.

'So!' said Tommy excitedly. 'More sightseeing this afternoon and then this evening we're off to Selhurst Park!'

Tommy had been an avid Crystal Palace fan since his childhood and had bought tickets to see The Eagles play Tottenham Hotspur. It would be her first experience of a football match. Sylvain and his sons often went to watch Olympique Marseille but had not even asked Lauren to join. Tommy, however, had longed to take his daughter to football. Tommy handed her a small present he had been hiding in a bag. She grinned as he handed it to her. She soon rifled the small gift open and found inside a Crystal Palace home shirt. On the back he even had it customised with a number 22 for her age and had her name emblazoned across the back. She promised to wear it for the match this evening and she placed it in the overnight bag she was carrying. Miriam had made up the spare bed again so they she didn't have to go all the way back to Hanwell after the match.

They arrived back at Sutton at about 5.30p.m. Miriam seemed to have a new energy about her since the arrival of her granddaughter and sat them both down for a cup of tea and some apple cake which she had made that afternoon. They sat and discussed everything that had happened that day and soon the focus of the conversation turned to Lauren.

'So, what are your plans Lauren? You're at Izzy's now, but I presume you'll have to return to France at some point?' asked Tommy.

'Yeah, I will. I'm going to give up my flat and job and come over to London. Izzy will let me stay as long as I like. I will have to find work here, of course, but that should be no problem in a place like London with a degree in tourism.'

Tommy thought for a moment whilst she spoke. Should he ask her now or was it too soon? 'Ah what the hell!' he thought. He got on with it.

'So Lauren, your Nana and I were talking just yesterday evening, how would you like to move in here? We could get to know each other better. I'm not saying it'll always be perfect and I realise you're twenty-two, you'll soon want a place of your own,' he said. 'But I really, really want to make up for lost time.'

Lauren looked up at Tommy with her blue eyes fixed firmly upon him.

'Yeah, okay,' she smiled. 'Let's give it a go. I will, as you say, have to go back to France and telling mum and Sylvain won't be easy.'

'Would you like me to come with you?' he replied.

'No, no, it's probably better I do this alone.'

Miriam put her hand on her son's arm. 'Yes, I think, I agree with Lauren on this one. Best you stay here, Tommy,' she said.

They arrived at Selhurst Park at about seven that evening and took their seats in the Holmesdale Road Stand in the lower tier, towards the southern side of the ground. Lauren could hardly contain her excitement as she awaited kick off and she declared her undying love for Palace by purchasing a red and blue eagles scarf to go with the shirt. She had worn a base layer and a jumper so she could place the shirt over the top. She removed her coat and rubbed her hands together in anticipation. Tommy smiled over at her; it was great to see her so enthusiastic! Although he hoped she wouldn't be an overzealous supporter and embarrass him by being loud. He remembered taking Polly back in 1990, the year they got to the FA Cup Final. He was good friends with both Geoff Thomas and Alan Pardew back then and he could get tickets whenever he wanted. These days, it wasn't so easy. In fact, the only reason he'd got in was because his mate, Clive, had a couple of season tickets and he was away on holiday. He offered them to Tommy when he heard that he and Lauren had been reunited. Tommy gratefully accepted the tickets with glee. The teams had been warming up on the pitch as the atmosphere built and they soon disappeared off for final instructions from their coaching staff. Funnily enough, Alan Pardew was now the manager. At 19.40pm, the teams ran back onto the field to a huge roar. Lauren and Tommy sat back down on their seats for the game to begin. Two minutes into the game, Palace's Joe Ledley was brought down in the centre circle by Ryan Mason of Tottenham. Lauren was out of her seat and had to be talked into sitting down by Tommy. The first half was eventful but goalless, and the second half threatened to be exciting. Spurs were in fifth place and pushing for a champions league berth whilst Palace were struggling with relegation and badly needed a win. Their prayers were answered in the 89th minute when Yannick Bolasie headed in on the far post from a Martin

Kelly cross. Selhurst Park erupted and so did Lauren and Tommy. A perfect end to a perfect day.

'Reminds me of a line from a song I was listening to this morning, Sometimes you have a day that makes all the bad ones seem worthwhile.' Tommy told Lauren, remembering the Elbow number that was still buzzing around his brain; the string arrangement coming back strongly into his mind.

He would miss Lauren when she went back to France, but it wouldn't be for long, and then he would have her back for good. They made their way back to Sutton, catching the bus from Selhurst Park to Thornton Heath, where they walked to the railway station and boarded the train to Sutton. As they walked back, Tommy stopped at the fish and chip shop and they ate chips in the rain as they walked home. Life hadn't been this perfect for a long time and Tommy wanted to make sure it stayed that way.

The next morning, Tommy and Miriam said their goodbyes to Lauren. She was going back to Hanwell to see Izzy and tell her the news. She would keep in regular contact with her although she knew Izzy would be disappointed to see her go. The hardest part would be telling her mother and stepfather. Polly had felt a certain air of inevitability about the situation, but she would live to regret telling Sylvain that she'd gone on holiday to Cuba! He wouldn't be amused with Polly *or* Lauren. Tommy would spend the day chilling out, preparing for his studio session with Bill the next day. Whilst Lauren was away, there was someone else he needed to get to know better... Natalie! In just a few short weeks, she had changed his life in an immeasurable way and this felt like it was just the start. He would ring her later in the day. They had already arranged to spend the weekend together at Belsize Park as Natalie's flat-mates were still away until Tuesday. He began warming up his voice with some vocal techniques he had learned during his time in the limelight. He'd taken some extra tuition from a well-known singing coach, Tona Da Brett, and these exercises always stood him in good stead. He began to hum a tune and then some words came out.

'I've been waiting for the kick in my soul which I knew would be there one day,' he sang. It had a strong hook; it was familiar. He had heard it recently but couldn't quite remember where. It would come back to him though. He continued with the vocal warm up and forgot all about it. He looked forward to seeing Bill tomorrow, it had been a while, and he always gave good advice. As well as being a top sound engineer, Bill was an able guitarist, bassist and pianist. He could also turn his hand to drumming and was well known for his mastery of programming a drum machine.

Natalie looked pensive in her office in The Strand. Yuki Akimoto from I.M.C was making an unscheduled visit and had only given her an hour's notice. She had no idea what it was all about but Yuki sounded serious, and from her experience, quick-fire meetings like this usually meant there was trouble ahead. She heard the buzzer from reception and sure enough Yuki was shown into her office. Natalie greeted him and ushered him over to the sofa in the corner whilst she made him a cup of green tea. She brought it over and sat down opposite him feeling more than a little concerned by now.

'So, Yuki, to what do I owe the pleasure?' she asked.

'Firstly, Natalie thank you for seeing me at short notice but I must catch a flight to Tokyo later. Unfortunately, my father is ill and I have to go home but I *had* to see you first.'

'Sorry to hear that your father is ill, Yuki. What made you come here first?'

'Well, I had a couple of hours before getting the flight and wanted to say how we loved the conference and how we enjoyed Tommy's speech,' he replied.

'The funny thing was I couldn't quite place Tommy, so I did my research and I found he was the singer in The Clowns. I remember seeing them back in the eighties. They were great. Did you ever see them?'

Natalie nodded, smiled and let Yuki continue.

'I'll get to the point! Is he still making music? You may not know this but we have a small independent record label called Pagoda records. If Tommy's not signed to anyone and is recording, let me know, and I will use my influence. I would love to hear him sing again.

Natalie very carefully and methodically explained the situation and was very honest about the stage fright, the alcohol excesses and Tommy's general situation. She really wanted to be clear with Yuki and make sure he was in the picture.

'So, he's recording a demo tomorrow of one song and will gradually gather material together and see how it progresses, but it's all looking good for Tommy now,' said Natalie.

'Excellent, you will send me this demo when it is done?' Yuki enquired.

'Of course,' said Natalie.

They talked for a while about Yuki's family and eventually, he went off back to his hotel before leaving for Heathrow. Natalie was thrilled. This could be a major development and when she saw Tommy later, he would be ecstatic. She wasn't sure if he wanted her there at the recording tomorrow or not. She knew how sensitive some artists were about this sort of thing. She would, of course, be respectful of his wishes, whatever happened. Neither of them had any idea, but Bill Terry had not only laid down a rough backing track to 'Ships,' but had also listened to 'Forever and a Day' and 'Never Bring Me Down.' He liked them and he thought The Magician would too. He had also prepared some basic backing tracks for them. He would get Tommy to sing some vocals over the top. These were only rough demos, and it didn't matter that they weren't perfect, but he hoped that Tommy had at least some idea of the latter two songs. Although, in his experience, some degree of spontaneity was a good thing.

14. Beginning to See the Light

Tommy was getting used to being up and about on his travels early in the morning. Today, he had stepped off the bus at Great Bookham. Bill's house was just up the road. Tommy had a map drawn up but he knew he would remember the way when he got there. He hadn't caught up with him for a while but had been a frequent visitor in the past. Tommy liked Bill, he was an extremely laid back character and nothing ever seemed to be too much trouble. Bill was nothing like some of the prima donnas Tommy had come across before. He walked down the main road towards Effingham looking for the turning, and before long, there it was. To the right, there was a narrow gravel lane. 'Oh yeah, I remember!' he thought. He walked along it slowly, looking left and right. Bill's place was easily recognisable. The property was distinctive because it was the only red-brick-built bungalow amongst a row of modern, light brick mock-Georgian houses. Bill's place had the longest garden along the lane, allowing him to build a small, two-roomed studio at the end of the garden, where he worked. He was soon approaching it on the right-hand side of the lane. Bill's Range Rover was parked next to his wife's three series

BMW. Tommy walked up their tarmacked drive and rang the bell. A couple of minutes later, Bill's wife, Tala, a Filipina who Bill had met when she was his housekeeper, opened the door. She let Tommy in and smiled. They hadn't met before; she was Bill's third wife and they had only been married two years. She was stunningly beautiful and at thirty-seven, a good twenty years younger than Bill. Tommy introduced himself as Tala walked him through the house and out of the kitchen door into the garden. It was a long narrow garden and Tommy knew his way from there so he left Tala to continue her daily chores. The studio took up the whole width of the back of the garden; it was built from brick but painted white and had a pitched-tiled roof. Tommy knocked on the door and stepped inside.

There was a sound of a bass drum pulsing four beats to the bar as Tommy walked in. The first room he saw was a lounge type area with a leather sofa and armchair, an office chair and a mixing desk. Just at that moment, Bill emerged through another door that led to the live room.

'Tom!' he greeted enthusiastically. 'How are ya?' Although Bill was English, his accent had become fairly Transatlantic over the years. You could be forgiven for thinking he was American. The fact that he always wore a red bandana just added to the myth.

'Great to see you, Bill! It's been a while to say the least. I just met your new wife; you're a randy old goat!'

'Yeah, well, you know, I've obviously still got it!' Quipped Bill with a smile.

Tommy and Bill sat down to discuss the session. Bill explained that he thought Tommy would get 'Ships' down pretty quickly and he'd listened to the two songs written by Max and liked them.

'So, who is this Max Chilton guy, Tom?' asked Bill.

'I honestly don't know too much about him, really, but I met him in Birmingham at a conference. He's had these two songs in his attic for twenty-five years. It's a bit weird, really, but the songs have a story and some history, so it would be good to give them a go. In fact, I caught myself singing 'Forever and a Day' yesterday, although I didn't know it at the time,' said Tommy.

'I do know that Max does a very ordinary job in the real world. He's about mid-forties and maybe it would be good to give him a chance,' he continued.

'Well, I've done a very basic arrangement for a backing track for them and I thought we could get a rough vocal on there today and maybe judge them from there. Whaddya think?'

'Okay,' said Tommy. 'Let's give it a go, nothing to lose!'

Tommy looked over at the mixing desk and through the window to the live room. He could see a drum kit, some guitars and a very expensive condenser microphone that had been set up on a stand. He'd remembered the type that Tommy used and the position he liked it placed in. Halfway down the stand was a peg on the side. Loosely hanging from this, was a pair of headphones or 'cans' as they were called in studio-talk. Bill started playing the songs; he had put a rough vocal on what he had recorded, and then apologised to Tommy for the standard of his singing. He was never a singer and he knew it! Max had carefully rewritten the lyrics and added them to the memory stick he had brought when they met. Bill had printed them off for him. Max had rewritten verse two of 'Forever' because he was never entirely happy with it and it flowed much better now. Tommy listened carefully and started to warm up his voice by singing along. Bill smiled; it was just like old times. Tommy's voice was perfect, and if anything, it had improved with age. They listened intently, and at last, the three songs came to an end. Bill asked Tommy if he was ready for a take. He nodded decisively with a serious look on his face; he was in the zone and ready to reclaim his career. He would start with 'Never Bring Me Down.' It was almost a chant as much as it was a song and was much more flexible in its approach. Bill encouraged him to ad lib as he saw fit. Tommy was much less likely to slip up with this. He went into the live room and stood by the microphone. He placed the headphones over his ears and waited for Bill's signal. The song started in Tommy's headphones with a strong beat and a funkily played acoustic guitar. After a couple of bars, the bass guitar and an overdriven and chorused electric guitar were audible. Tommy's vocals started on the ninth bar and he came flying out of the traps. He always liked to make the first song count. Just like when he was playing live.

One hour later, 'Never Bring Me Down' was done and Bill beckoned Tommy into the studio to listen. Bill would tinker with all the tracks before they would be happy with the final demo versions, but for now, this would be fine.

Bill and Tommy took a break for a cup of tea and started to discuss other material they may be interested in. They would need about twenty songs and would whittle it down to about twelve on the final cut. Bill kept in touch with developments and presented him with options from a variety of young British writers. If they used Max's songs, 'Ships' and a couple of other cover versions, they would need another fifteen songs. Tommy told Bill that he had a couple of songs he was working on too. Maybe Bill would help him with this. Tommy felt confident and in the right place to deliver the vocals for the other two songs and was eager to get on with it. He urged Bill back into his position behind the desk and walked back into the live room.

'Right! A quick practice run and straight into a take for 'Ships.' Are you ready Tom?'

'Oh, yes.' He replied with a degree of cockiness as his eyes closed in concentration waiting for his cue. An hour and a half later, they had completed all of the vocal tracks, and just as they were about to listen to the playback, Natalie walked through the door. There was a light outside the studio door which went from red to green when access was permitted. Bill had this fitted as there was nothing worse for an artist than to be distracted mid-take. Natalie had been waiting for a couple of minutes, she smiled and Tommy introduced her to Bill.

'So, you're the famous Natalie that's got this man on the straight and narrow then?' said Bill.

'Yep, the very same! I wouldn't say that though; he's doing a pretty decent job on his own.'

Whilst Tommy appreciated Natalie's affirmation, he knew he would be an absolute mess without her. She was kind, very intelligent, supportive and not to mention, gorgeous! It was at that point, he thought of a song. It was a song that would say to her what he wanted to say. He wasn't very good at showing his feelings, but put it in a song and he could. It fitted in with his idea of a string quartet too. It was an idea for another day but he would talk to Bill about it later.

'Let's listen to the playback then,' said Bill.

They listened to the three songs one after the other two or three times. They were basic and simple but proficient and what was clear was that Tommy's voice could still cut the mustard. Bill knew there was more to come too. After a general chit chat about the music, they started talking business, and both Bill and Natalie had some great news for Tommy.

'Tom,' said Bill. 'Let's not run before we can walk but I've been talking to someone very interesting who has been asking about your comeback. Do you remember The Magician?'

'Yep, of course I do!' said Tommy. 'I thought he just produced country and western in Nashville these days. He married Carlene Taylor, didn't he?'

'Yeah, but they divorced. He's back in the UK and has spent the last six months building a studio on the south coast. He has asked to hear these. Are you happy with that?' replied Bill.

'Wow, is the Pope Catholic?' He retorted, noticing Natalie was itching to speak. He smiled and gestured to her to have her say.

'Well, I've been talking to Yuki. Remember him, from I.M.C? I'm not sure that you met him but we've talked about him... anyway, he is interested in the demos too. It transpires I.M.C own Pagoda records and he would be very keen to hear your music. He was a big Clowns fan in his youth, as was his wife.'

Tommy was stunned. His life was definitely on the up, but what if both parties hated the demos? That was a bridge that would have to be crossed at some point. Bill said that he would play around with the tracks and send them the final mixes over the weekend. If they were recording an album, this process would take far longer, but for now, they could be a bit less precise, happy and confident that Tommy's voice was in good form. Bill threw Tommy a memory-stick with all the songs on that Bill had gathered for him to listen too. Tommy offered to take Natalie, Bill and his wife Tala out to the local pub, 'The Old Thatch,' for a meal to celebrate. The offer was gleefully accepted by all parties and they walked down the road happily. The conversation turned to holidays, mutual friends and old acquaintances. Natalie and Bill had a fair few in common. It was a small world.

Tommy and Natalie stayed and chatted with Bill and Tala until about nine and decided to make a move back home. Natalie was staying in Sutton that evening so they could have a good chat when they got home. They drove off in Natalie's Mercedes, waving, as they departed. Tommy had one thought on his mind.

'Shall we ring Max then and let him know?' said Tommy. 'I don't know what it is about those two songs but they just…work!'

'We will have to use the caveat that we may not make the final cut, but yeah, let's do it!' Natalie replied.

Max and Lottie were relaxing after a hard day. BBC1 was showing 'Love Actually' for the umpteenth time but there was something about Bill Nighy's performance as an ageing rock star that was still a big draw. They had just reached the bit where Nighy's character Billy Mack goes on a kid's TV show and says, 'Kids don't buy drugs. Become a pop star and they give you them for free.'

The couple burst out laughing and just at that point Max's phone rang. It was Tommy. Lottie urged him to answer it as he fumbled with the screen.

'Tommy! How's it going,' Max answered.

'Max! Not bad. Listen, we've just demoed 'Forever and a Day' and 'Never Bring Me Down.' Basically, they sound great! We're really pleased. The mix will be done at the weekend and I'll send you an email with a file so you can have a listen. Anyway, cutting to the chase, we'd like to record them properly, if it's alright with you?'

Max couldn't believe his ears; he hadn't believed in fate up until that point. That leaky roof must have happened for a reason! His songs were going to be recorded by Tommy McNeill. He couldn't have imagined that as little as a month ago.

'Well, yeah, of course...I'd be thrilled.' Max was slightly lost for words. Lottie beamed. It really didn't take too much working out even if she couldn't hear what Tommy was saying. Max finished the call and they celebrated. Tommy had also warned them that they may not even make the album. Obviously, they would have to make choices but Max and Lottie could worry about that another day. This was a huge victory for Max, and it could yet mean that they could stay in the house in Tarrant Marshall. There was new hope and maybe this was a turning point in their lives. Tommy had explained that it could be a long time before the album was out, but that they had interest from both a producer and a record label. Hopefully, it was just a matter of time to watch this space!

Three days later and ten miles away in a New England-style house overlooking the sea, The Magician was working his spell. The three songs had been played, analysed and broken down into musical components. This was how he worked; everything was stripped back and rebuilt. He started with the rhythm and built everything up from there. It was like building a house from the foundations. He was a perfectionist, and Tommy, despite his shortcomings, had the near perfect vehicle in his voice. No one had a voice like it, in this country, at least. It was definitely a voice that needed to be heard and The Magician was the man to get it heard. He would invite Tommy to his studio to start work in the New Year, but before that, they would need to talk just to make sure they would get along. Tommy would need to realise just who was in charge. The Magician insisted on total artistic control and Tommy needed to know this. He loved the song 'Ships' and ironically, having come back to Britain to say goodbye to country and western, he could imagine this song with a definite hint of Nashville. He would get in touch with some of the lap guitar players he knew; that song was crying out for it. The other two songs, he wasn't sure about. He had heard worse, but then again, he'd heard better. Crucially though, they suited Tommy down to the ground. If Max had written them for Tommy's voice, he wouldn't be at all surprised, and if he could do that, then he was a good songwriter. The Magician knew nothing about Max personally but saw that he knew a good tune when he heard it. He could definitely work with this and was close to making a decision. In fact, he *had* already made a decision.

He would contact Bill and make all the necessary arrangements. This was going to happen; not until the new year, but it *was* going to happen. He raised his glass of single malt. He had lived like a recluse since his return to England but he was now ready to spread his wings. It was time to reinvent The Magician and propel himself back into a world where he belonged. He thought about Tommy and how he considered that they must be on a similar journey. They would probably have totally fallen out by the end of the project but that didn't matter. As far as Bernie was concerned, it was the destination and not necessarily the journey that was important. If he could make this venture with Tommy successful, who knows what it would lead to. He had a list of people he would love to work with and Tommy was just the start. He would love to work with Adele and with Paul Weller and maybe even Van Morrison. All interesting characters with a unique sound. He would love to see how far he could push them. The Magician was back and he wanted everyone to know. He still had loads of mates in the industry in this country, some well-known, some not so. He picked up his phone, looked through his contacts and began to make some calls.

15. Do They Know It's Christmas?

It was certainly Christmas in the McNeill household. Lauren had returned from France and moved into Miriam's house; both Miriam and Tommy were delighted. Lauren had been there for two weeks now and felt happy and very much at home. Things hadn't gone very well with Sylvain and Polly, who were heartbroken at her decision not only to find Tommy, but to move into his house. She would go back in the spring to make her peace when everything had settled down. It would be easier then. Firstly, she would need to find a job and she could focus on that in the New Year. She also wanted to help Tommy as much as she could with the new album project; it wouldn't be long now and recording would start soon. This was her first Christmas with her dad since she was four and it was to be cherished. It was the first Christmas she had felt excited about for ages. They had agreed on a £20 ceiling on presents as no one had much money to spend, apart from Natalie, who hadn't gone back to Canada as she usually would. She wanted to spend the festive season in Britain for the first time and go back to Nova Scotia and spend New Year with friends and family. It was a bit soon to introduce them all to

Tommy. Maybe next year! He was happy to stay at home and concentrate on preparations and rehearsals. He had already agreed to travel to Dorset for some preliminary work and had also arranged to meet up with Max whilst he was down there.

They spent the morning opening presents and preparing food for a huge Christmas dinner. Natalie had provided the turkey, which was part of a huge hamper delivered to her by Yuki, as a way of thanking her for her work during the year. In some ways, she felt that it should be her buying the hamper for Yuki; he had been instrumental in Tommy's record deal after all. Tommy had been up to the offices of Pagoda Records in West London just last week and signed a deal, which was for one album, but with the option of a further two. They would require four singles from the album which would have to be radio friendly. Tommy had been given a small advance and a deal was made with The Magician to produce the album. Recording was due to commence on Monday, January 12 at his studio in Poole. All the songs had been chosen and about fourteen tracks would be used for the album. The remaining tracks would be used as extra bonus tracks for various releases. Lauren had been helping Tommy rehearse by accompanying him on the guitar and offering some harmonies. Tommy thought that Lauren sounded fantastic, although he could be a little biased.

They eventually sat around the table in the dining room to eat their Christmas turkey; all the food had been prepared by Tommy and Lauren. Natalie had appointed herself as sommelier for the day, and so, this left Miriam to just relax and enjoy herself. She was eighty-five; it was only right. She tapped her fork on the table, lifted her glass and began to speak.

'Ahem,' she said clearing her throat. 'Firstly, I'd like to thank my son, Tommy, for looking after me these last few years, for making lunch today and I'd like to wish you luck with your new record. I hope it's a huge hit and you'll be back where you belong. But this time, with no funny business please, Mister!'

Tommy blushed sheepishly. He knew exactly what she meant.

'Lauren,' she continued. 'I can't tell you how wonderful it is to have you back in our lives.' Her voice was cracking now as she realised Lauren, Tommy and Natalie all had tears forming in their eyes. 'And we hope you'll be happy here. We're your family and we love you. You are welcome here for as long as you like.' Lauren sobbed as she reached over and hugged Miriam and then Tommy. She sat back down and dried her eyes with a tissue.

'As for you Natalie, what can I say but thank you. Thank you for bringing my family together, thank you for what you've done for Tommy and I know you've not known him for too long, but welcome to our family.'

That was it! Natalie was gone; streaming with tears. She was not the only one. Even Tommy was having a good cry.

'Anyway,' she said in a matter of fact way. 'Tuck in before it goes cold.' And so they sat, ate and drank wine. It was one of the best Christmas meals Tommy had ever had. Tommy wanted to say his bit although he decided to leave it until the end of the meal. He wasn't very good at this but felt he needed to say something. He refilled everyone's glass with the Chateau Coufran 2004 Haut-Medoc that Lauren had brought back from France. Despite his sadness at Lauren's move to England, Sylvain always had some decent wine to recommend and had given this to Lauren to try. He was not wrong in recommending it. With its soft plummy tones, it went down rather easily, especially for Tommy who, as we know, has a weakness for fine wine. He too tapped his cutlery on the table and started to speak.

'Okay, so here it goes! Mum thanks for putting up with me all these years, through the good and bad, probably more bad but I'm back in form now, hopefully, so anyway… thanks, and perhaps next year, we'll have Christmas somewhere more exotic. Maybe Lauren can recommend somewhere on the French Riviera or something like that!' Lauren shrugged. Her dad was rambling a bit now and she could tell he'd probably had one glass too many.

'Lauren, what can I say,' he continued. 'My baby has come home. Love ya and it's great to have you back, and please, let's not become strangers again.' She stood up and locked into a warm embrace with Tommy. They said nothing for at least two minutes, and eventually, he went back to his speech whilst still clinging on to Lauren.

'Finally, Natalie, what can I say to you? This lady has come into my life and in such a short space of time, transformed it for the better. I hope we can be together for a long time, love you, kiddo.'

For the second time that day, they all collapsed into tears. Even Tommy, who wasn't good at public displays of emotion. Tommy wanted to celebrate this year like it was his last Christmas on the planet. God knows there had been some miserable ones over the last few years but this made up for it. He had a new girlfriend, Lauren was back and his career seemed to be back on the right track. He seemed to have made a new friend in Max; they would talk and text all the time mainly about music. To his surprise, Tommy had found that Max had some very similar ideas about how music should be approached. He would ring the Chilton's later and was looking forward to seeing them in January. Max had persuaded him to go to the open mic night with him in Bournemouth, along with Will, so they would need to rehearse a couple of numbers. Max wanted to perform 'Forever and a Day', 'Ships' and 'My Ever-Changing Moods' by The Style Council. It was Max's gig so he'd go along with it. Tommy had a few run ins with Paul Weller back in the day but couldn't deny his songwriting prowess. He decided it was time to lift the mood a little.

'Right! Who's up for scrabble?'

They all groaned and stared back at him; all they wanted to do was snooze their way through the Queen's speech and whatever film happened to be on that afternoon.

Max was in his element; he was a vegetarian so had agreed to cook everything except the turkey. There were potatoes, sprouts, carrots, braised cabbage and parsnips. He had gone to town a little bit, considering it was only himself, Lottie, Jo and the kids. He prepared enough to feed a small army and it was all nearly ready. Lottie and Jo had decked the house in lots of homemade decorations. It would be a fairly spartan Christmas this year, but next year hopefully, it would all be different. Who knows where it could all lead if the songs were a success. Maybe he could write more. He had cobbled together a couple of new tunes in the last month but wasn't entirely happy with them. It had been a long time though since he last tried. It would take time to get back into the swing of it.

Max couldn't believe they had got Tommy to agree to visiting open mic night at The Pulse in Bournemouth. They arranged it for January 5, as this was when Tommy was coming down to have a week of rehearsals, giving his voice some exercise before recording could start. It wasn't a precise process and the final vocals would be one of the very last things to be recorded, although a rough vocal track would be put down in the first instance as a guide. The Magician would then get all the instrumental parts recorded before all the vocal parts. Finally, he would add any enhancements, effects and mix it. Bernie liked to work quickly, however, and wanted everything done by the end of March, with early May as a tentative release date.

The Chilton's were having a great Christmas but Max was restless. He loved having time with the kids and wasn't back to work until early January but he was also itching to get it out of the way. Everything was about to take off in the new year and he was absorbed with excitement and anticipation. Lottie had to keep pulling him up on this, telling him to just enjoy Christmas, but he was far too distracted. He spoke with Tommy for a good half an hour on the phone, and had given him a good idea for another final last minute cover version. It was to remain a secret between them, at least for now. Tommy wanted to record a song specifically with Natalie in mind and he now had the perfect song in mind. All he needed for this was a string quartet and his voice.

Everyone in the McNeill house was dozing in front of 'Jurassic Park' after the excess of Christmas dinner. Tommy was sporting a crepe paper crown he had got from a Christmas Cracker; Natalie had refused to wear one as had Miriam.

Tommy was snoring but they were all oblivious to the noise he was making. There was one person still awake, however. Lauren was sat in her room; she had a paper and pen and was strumming away on Tommy's guitar making notes as she played.

'Hey, sounds good!' she said to herself.

She had written some chords and some lyrics down. She had sung before and had some basic guitar playing skills, but this was the first time she had written and it was starting to flow. The song had the working title 'The Great Adventure.' It was all about her journey, moving from France to England and all the new faces she had come across. Her voice was not unlike a young Dusty Springfield, although nowhere near in the same league, yet. She would have to get a job for now but maybe this was a way forward for her. She knew the right people; all she needed was enough material, and they would all help. 'Dad, Natalie, even Max may have some ideas' she thought. She didn't know it yet but she would get her opportunity sooner than she thought.

Tommy, who had now woken up and had walked upstairs to use the bathroom, was listening outside quietly and not letting Lauren know that he was there. He smiled and crept back downstairs. Natalie and Miriam jumped as they were woken by the sound of a creaking door. Tommy laughed as they looked at him bleary-eyed and slightly grumpy.

'Anyone for a cup of tea?' he chuckled.

They both nodded because that was all they could do having just woken up. Tommy went to the kitchen and put the kettle on. He smiled to himself as he waited for it to boil.

16. With a Little Help from My Friends

Tommy looked out of the window as the train pulled out of Bournemouth Station; the next stop was where he would be getting off. Bernie or 'Magic,' as Tommy liked to call him, had arranged to meet him at Parkstone station at 11.35a.m. This was when the train was due, and it was pretty much on time, give or take a couple of minutes. He was going to meet all the other musicians tomorrow; the plan being to record all the tracks live in the first instance. The musicians would then all go back separately and record their parts one by one, culminating in the vocals at the end. The musicians would rehearse together for the week just to get the sound right and then they could record the songs pretty quickly next week. That would free up Tommy to go back home for a while before he came back to lay down the final vocals. Natalie was still away in Canada and Lauren had agreed to stay in Sutton to keep an eye on Miriam. Tommy thought it would be great for them to get to know each other better whilst he was away. The train whizzed through Branksome station and it began to start slowing down, stopping at Parkstone, in another couple of minutes. Tommy stood up, grabbed his suitcase from the rack above his head, and made his way along the carriage towards the exit. He waited behind a young mother with her two children as she negotiated with the door handle and hopped out of the train with the two boys following her. Tommy followed them, showed his ticket to the inspector and walked through the ticket office. He couldn't see any sign of Magic. He walked out of the ticket office and stood outside in a small parking area. Still no sign of him. He checked his phone, and sure enough, there was a text from Bernie.

'Sorry, running ten minutes late,' it said.

Tommy found a bench and sat down whilst he waited. His thoughts soon turned to the album. He still had to pinch himself to believe it was happening. The first new album since the last effort in 1997, which was a complete flop. Hopefully, with this one, they could generate enough interest to warrant a follow up. Natalie promised to arrange some promotional gigs after the album was complete. She was hoping that the guys he was recording with could be formed into a touring band. She considered that maybe they could even play at some festivals in the summer. Tommy knew he could rely on Bill but he didn't know the other musicians yet. They had been recruited by Bill and The Magician, and of course, Tommy had trusted their recruitment skills. Besides, if Tommy didn't like any of them, he could always find replacements. All the musicians would have now been given all the arrangements for the songs and recording the live tracks would just be a formality. It was while he was pondering this that he heard a loud car horn about twenty feet away.

'Tommy, you old bastard! Long time, no see!' It was Bernie, he was a larger than life character, and was wearing a yellow Hawaiian shirt in the middle of winter. He'd come to collect Tommy in the least practical car he owned. His red 1966 MGC hardtop. It was a beautiful car and had been restored by a specialist and then sold via auction to Bernie for £15000 a couple of months ago.

'Magic! You haven't changed then, I see. How the bloody hell are you?' aid Tommy.

'Better for being back in the UK. I couldn't wait to get back to the shit weather and the constant darkness at this time of year. Anyway, welcome to Poole, let's go and make a hit album!'

Tommy just about fitted his case into the small boot and jumped into the passenger seat. Magic indicated to turn right, checked both ways and turned out of the car park on their way to nearby Canford Cliffs.

They arrived at the house ten minutes later. Magic pressed a button on his key fob and two large white steel gates began to open. The property was magnificent. It nestled grandly on the cliff top and had views over Poole Harbour on one side and Bournemouth Bay on the other. There was a path which led from the garden of the property down some steps to the beach at the bottom of the cliff. Magic had liked it because it had a basement area which was easily converted to a state-of-the-art modern recording studio. He had consulted various acoustic specialists to get the right sound in the studio and so it would be well sound-proofed. He didn't want to upset the neighbours. He had become quite friendly with them in the last six months.

Magic showed Tommy to his room and instructed the housekeeper to make them some lunch. She obliged with a mixed platter with salad, cheeses, cold meats and various dips.

'I think I'm going to like it here.' Said Tommy as he tucked in.

Magic began to discuss the album as they ate. He had retained his passion for music, and by changing direction, he awoke his musical sensitivities. He was never one to work on a formula and churn the hits out, he always liked to change direction, and try out new things. It was ironic that he could hear one of the tracks played in a traditional country and western style.

'So, Tommy, for 'Ships.' I know it sounds weird because I came back from England to escape country music but I could see that song being played in a traditional country style with a lap guitar. I have one thing I'm just not getting with that song... yet!'

'What's that then?' asked Tommy.

'Well, I think it needs an accompanying female vocal, almost to the point of it being a duet. I've been racking my brains who could do it. My first thought was Bonnie Raitt, but no disrespect Tommy, I don't think we'd get her. My next thought was Jacqui Abbott, a bit more realistic, but I'm not sure yet.'

Tommy thought about who he would like to sing with him but he kept his thoughts to himself as they finished lunch. He had a more immediate challenge this evening. Max and his mate, Will, were taking Tommy off to open mic night. Bernie was going with them too; they were going to completely wing it as they wouldn't get time to rehearse after all. It would be a fun night and he was looking forward to seeing Max again.

The Pulse Bar stood just a stone's throw from the beach, halfway up Bournemouth's West Cliff. It was part of the split-level Mayfly Hotel and occupied the lowest floor of the building. It was an intimate venue but it needed to be that way.

The phrase 'open mic' was a very loose term, and in fact, no microphones were allowed. All musical instruments were to be played acoustically. Max and Will were worried about this because they weren't sure they would be able to use Will's electric keyboard, but after discussing it with Rick, the bar's owner, they discovered that he kept an old upright piano which was mounted on castors in a back office. This could easily be wheeled out if anyone showed interest. No one had, up until tonight, and Rick was pleased it was going to get an airing. The open mic nights had gone well. He started them when he bought the bar eighteen months ago and it quickly became the most profitable night of the week. Word spread quickly amongst the students at Bournemouth University and the evening became an almost 'must do' experience if you were a student there.

Max, Will, Bernie and Tommy were joined by Lottie and Rhoda, as Jo had agreed to babysit all their respective children for the evening. They were easily the oldest people in the bar; even Rick was only twenty-eight. He adorned the walls with tour posters of various bands including, Led Zeppelin, Jimmy Hendrix and The Who, amongst others. They looked quite authentic but in truth, Rick bought them as cheap copies online and put them in weathered frames so they didn't look like they were made last year. The music would start at 9p.m. and Rick had given the trio a slot for 10p.m., although the times were flexible. It wasn't a precise science, music never was. The acts before 'The McNeill Clan' as they called themselves, were interesting. Firstly, there was a folk trio consisting of a cello, a ukulele and a singer/guitarist who put a folk twist on modern pop songs, including Katy Perry's, 'Firework'. Following them, a father and his son and daughter played a selection of Bob Dylan, Peter, Paul and Mary and Neil Young covers. Later, a young man with an acoustic guitar playing his own material. He reminded Tommy of a poor man's Ed Sheeran, and unfortunately, the crowd was also unimpressed. Tommy felt very relaxed. This was just for fun and he felt no pressure. Significantly, he was drinking cola and he hadn't had a drop of alcohol since Christmas. Bernie knew all about Tommy's history with stage fright and thought this was a great way to loosen him up for the job in hand. Second Rate Sheeran, as Tommy had now dubbed him, left the stage to a mild applause and Rick walked onto the stage area and began to speak.

'Okay, you lucky people!' he hollered. 'We have a real treat for you now. They feature two local guys and an eighties soul legend. Put your hands together for The McNeill Clan!'

Rick left the stage and Max, Will and Tommy walked up. Max clutched his acoustic guitar and Will sat ready behind the piano. The crowd hushed as Tommy put his finger up to his lips hoping he would be heard above the ambient noise.

'Hi, I'm Tommy McNeill,' he began. 'I had some hits in the eighties with my band The Clowns, if any of you remember us?' The crowd remained silent and Tommy chuckled. 'Nah thought so,' he said. 'You're all too young! That's your trouble!' he continued. 'Anyway, this is a new song written by my good friend, Max here, and it's called Forever and a Day.'

Max counted them in and they began, tentatively at first, but gaining confidence by the end of the second chorus. Bernie grinned; he liked what he was hearing. He was going to enjoy working with Tommy. He had worked with many people over the years but Tommy just had star quality. He had the x factor.

Tommy definitely had the charisma to hold an audience. Bernie looked around the crowd of no more than twenty-five people and they were all transfixed by this returning eighties legend; the myth that was Tommy McNeill.

They brought 'Forever and a Day' to an end and received a rapturous applause, if that was possible with so few people, and then Tommy called Rhoda on stage to sing backing vocals for the last two songs. This was the first time she had sung in front of anyone other than Will, Max and Lottie, and she was thrilled to be there. She was so thrilled that she had forgotten to be nervous. They belted out 'Ships' and 'Ever Changing Moods.' Bernie liked 'Moods' so much that he instantly decided they should record it with just Tommy and a pianist. If he was up for it, of course! They were soon leaving the stage to probably the best reception that Rick had heard for a quiet night at The Pulse.

The night soon came to an end and Rick shook their hands as they left the bar.

'Come back anytime,' said Rick.

'Cheers Rick, that was amazing,' said Will.

They walked to the car park, went their separate ways and agreed to keep in touch. Bernie invited Max to have a listen to the recordings when they reached a convenient point.

Tommy and Bernie drove back to Canford Cliffs discussing their thoughts on the evening.

'Hey Tommy, I thought 'Ever Changing Moods' really suited your voice. Maybe we should try it out as an extra track. Just you and a piano, like the original album version?'

'I'll give it a go for sure, Magic!' He replied as they turned left onto the A35 back towards Bernie's house.

Max was on a high after *that* evening. It was only a small venue but Tommy McNeill had just sung his song and made it sound amazing! How was he going to calm down and get to sleep after that? He had appointments in Exeter tomorrow which meant an early start. If only he didn't have to work for a living! Maybe it wouldn't be for too much longer.

The next morning, as Max was making his way down to Devon to visit a customer that needed his help, people began to gather in The Magician's lair. They had assembled a group of lesser known, but well experienced, session musicians for the project. Bill Terry had already arrived nice and early, having left Great Bookham at five in the morning, and was asked to do all the guitar work on the album. He was a sound engineer by trade but had turned into a competent and in-demand session player over the years. Bill played with an eclectic mix of musicians over the years and could turn his hand to jazz, soul, funk, folk and had even played in some punk and heavy metal bands. He brought with him a small cache of four guitars: his trusty Fender Thinline Telecaster that he bought in the States twenty years ago, a relatively new Gibson Les Paul, a Martin standard acoustic guitar and for very occasional use, a Rickenbacker twelve string electric. He had a huge effects pedal system that he would set up on the floor in front of him. Bill's engineering experience and knowledge of production techniques would be invaluable to the whole project. What Bill didn't know about the arrangement and dynamics of a song and optimising the potential of a tune wasn't worth knowing. Perhaps Bill's greatest strength was that he had a calming influence on

Tommy and the singer felt relaxed and able to focus on the job in Bill's company.

The next person to arrive was drummer Carl Perry who was busying himself setting up his drum kit in the corner of the live room. The studio was in the basement of the property and offered no views out towards the English Channel. Magic didn't think that was bad. They had no distractions whilst they were supposed to be concentrating on the job in hand. Carl had spent the last three decades as a touring and recording session musician. He too had worked with Tommy during his unsuccessful solo efforts in the early nineties. Carl had played with artists such as, Van Morrison, Duran Duran, Donna Summer and the Bee Gees, and he had a reputation for having a big, hard hitting sound. His drum set-up was simple, and from Magic's point of view, easy to record. He liked simplicity and he liked a clear, clean sound that was uncluttered. He liked the listener to be able to hear what the singer was singing. A decade of producing country and western music had taught him that. Country and western were genres of music that told a story, and you needed to be able to listen to the story. Magic wanted to bring that quality to Tommy's music.

Last to arrive in the house was Martin Harris, the bassist. He too had a wealth of session and studio experience behind him with Simple Minds, Lou Reed and Peter Gabriel to name three artists that he had worked with. Magic was going to play all the keyboard parts on the album; something he had done on all the records he had produced. He had learned a lot from doing this. In his early days as the keyboard player with Tussaud, he was mainly an expert in the programming capability of the early iconic keyboards like the Fairlight and the Yamaha DX7, but as the years went by, he concentrated more on the musical side and had become a superb pianist. He liked to keep the sound earthy and warm. His electronic and programming prowess though came into its own when using effects to enhance the sound before finishing the final mix. Every component and instrument in every song would sound the best it could possibly sound. Magic was excited about this project, he was as excited as Tommy, Natalie and Bill, and would do everything he could to make sure it was a success.

After an hour or so, everyone was ready to go. Tommy and all the other musicians became reacquainted over a cup of tea or two whilst Magic checked the sound levels in the live room. Tommy felt a little nervous but nothing like the panic and fear that he used to feel. The incident at the hotel in Birmingham when he met Max seemed like a lifetime ago. He thought about Natalie and her contribution in this, he missed her and couldn't wait for her return in a couple of days. They discussed moving in together but the immediate plan was Natalie finding a place somewhere closer to Tommy, but also near to her office. Brixton would be a possibility. Tommy would move in part time so he could also spend time with Lauren and keep an eye on Miriam - she wasn't getting any stronger and began to look a little frail. She was eighty-five, and sooner or later, was going to need a full-time carer. He had started to look at sheltered accommodation for her; if she sold the house in Sutton it would be affordable with money to spare. Tommy's thoughts had drifted so he called on everyone to start the ball rolling.

'Right, guys,' he said. 'Let's get the ball rolling with 'Never Bring Me Down,' a nice up-tempo number.'

The musicians were by now more than familiar with the songs having each been sent the recorded demos and the sheet music a couple of weeks ago. Magic had kept himself occupied over the Christmas holidays piecing it all together. Carl clicked his drumsticks together counting them in at the same time and they began. Tommy looked around him, waited for his cue and began to sing. It was just like the old days, only now he was clean and sober, and was much more enjoyable.

17. Heart of The City

Natalie lifted her case onto the tube at Heathrow; she was tired and it had seemed a long time had passed since she boarded the plane in Halifax. Fortunately, her brother's house was only minutes from the airport and so, there was not too much travelling to be done before her flight. She was glad to be home because she always missed London when she was away. This time she had an extra special reason to long for home, and that reason was Tommy. There were plenty of free seats on the train and she gratefully grabbed one next to the door where there was room to keep her case nearby. There were quite a few stops before she had to change trains and board the Northern line at Leicester Square. It would probably be a good hour, if not longer, before she got back to Belsize Park. The flight had landed around 9.30a.m. at Terminal two and Natalie had only dozed for a couple of hours in total on the journey. All she wanted to do now was get home and sleep; she could catch up with everyone tomorrow when she felt more like a human being again! Tommy had kept in touch on a daily basis via skype, and to his amazement, had started using Facebook messenger. He had kept her well versed on how the rehearsals were going and how they had gone according to plan. Well enough that they had begun recording. Each song would be recorded first in its live form before being re-recorded instrument by instrument, track by track, until it sounded perfect. Natalie was looking forward to seeing him. These two weeks away had seemed like a long time.

Lauren spent the last couple of weeks looking after her grandmother. She was now feeling very settled in Sutton and had started at a part-time job in a local call centre. She started to make new friends and had been across London to visit Izzy a couple of times. She confided in Izzy that she now had written three or four songs and hoped to get a band together. Tommy had invited her and Natalie down to Dorset later in the week to spend a couple of days together. They could be the first to hear the new recordings and Lauren kept in touch with both Tommy and Natalie over the last couple of weeks so she knew it was sounding good.

Miriam was a cause for concern; she was finding it increasingly difficult to get around and Lauren had to help quite a bit. She complained about feeling a bit light-headed whenever she stood up; the doctor had diagnosed low blood pressure and had prescribed her medication. Lauren had arranged for Miriam's younger sister Gladys to stay whilst they went to Dorset. She had found that Miriam slept a lot leaving her a lot of free time in between shifts at work. During this time, Lauren had become intensely obsessed with singing and playing the guitar, and hoped that maybe it could be her future. She was aware that she was luckier than most with her connections in Tommy and Natalie, and thought that maybe the time had come to make them aware of her talents.

Natalie arrived home at midday. Her flat mates were at work and the place was blissfully quiet. She poured a glass of water and looked through her post. There was nothing exciting; just bills and some unsolicited junk mail from clothing companies she had used online. Here she was back in London, wondering what the New Year had in store. It was clear that Tommy and his album would be a dominating force. She was looking forward to viewing some properties in a week or two. She liked Brixton, it was warm, vibrant and very up and coming. Tommy also loved the area and was very welcome to move in whenever he felt comfortable. Six months ago, she wouldn't have dreamed that she would be thinking this way, especially when her love interest was one of her old teen idols! It was a funny old life and you could never tell what was going to happen, but towards the end of last year, she felt like fate had been in control. She didn't read her horoscope or believe in clairvoyance but this felt like it was written in the stars. Natalie put down the junk mail and ambled off towards her bedroom, she needed sleep, and lots of it. She crashed onto her bed, and quickly fell asleep, fully clothed and still wearing her jewellery. She didn't wake until about five thirty, and strangely couldn't tell if it was AM or PM, as it was dark. Natalie switched the radio on and as 'Sledgehammer' by Peter Gabriel faded to finish, the voice of Simon Mayo told her that it must be PM. He always did the drive-time slot. She could get something to eat, chat to her flat mates and catch up on any gossip, then it would soon be time to get back to bed and have a good night's sleep. Tomorrow she had to be back in the office for a day or two, and on Friday, she would pick up Lauren and drive down to Dorset for the week. She couldn't wait. It was good to be back home. She stayed still listening to the radio for a few minutes and smiled to herself as Simon Mayo played one of the old Clowns hits from the eighties.

'That was Tracks of My Tears by The Clowns, featuring the voice of the ever controversial, Tommy McNeill. Wonder what happened to him? Answers on a postcard please!' Said Mayo in a very deadpan, ironic way as was his wont.

It made Natalie think though. This was a bigger job than she had thought and one of her tasks would be to get all the radio stations playing Tommy's songs before the release of the album. It was standard practice in the music industry that in the month leading up to a release, the radio stations would be encouraged to play as much of a band or artist's back catalogue as it could. This would earn Tommy some extra money. The royalty cheques had become a little sparser in recent years. This still brought him in a small income and combined with his carer's allowance, it meant he wasn't too badly off. Certainly not as badly off as he liked to make out. She looked at her phone and there were a couple of messages; one from Tommy and one from Lauren. She opened the one from Lauren first as it would be quicker to deal with.

'Hi, welcome back! Was wondering what time we were setting off on Friday. Gladys is arriving at eleven that morning. So anytime from then on is fine by me x'

The message from Tommy was a little bit longer. 'Missed you Nat, welcome home, hope the flight was good. All going well here. Can't wait to see you on Friday. We have all the songs rehearsed and are ready to start laying down the basic songs as a starting point. Max has a day off work and is coming to watch today so we decided to start with his two songs. If we can get the bones of these two down today we have a great base to build on. Anyway, speak soon, love you x'

She plumped up her pillow, leaned back and started to type her reply. Tommy had messaged her a good three hours ago so she hoped some positive progress had been made. When she finished, she then replied to Lauren and arranged to pick her up at midday. Yuki Akimoto had personally arranged some rooms at the nearby Harbour Heights Hotel for Tommy, Natalie and Lauren. The rooms were at their disposal whenever they were needed. Yuki had interests in the hotel trade, and fortunately the CEO of FJB Hotels, who owned the establishment, was a personal friend of his. Yuki had turned out to be one of the most reliable and useful contacts that Natalie had ever made. She was secretly looking forward to the luxurious facilities at the hotel whilst reminding herself it was supposed to be a business trip! 'You only live once,' thought Natalie.

Lauren had read her reply from Natalie. She was glad to have the arrangements all sorted out. It was like going on holiday and she had been studying the website of the hotel. She was amazed by the location, sandy beaches and some top pubs and restaurants within walking distance. Lauren was certainly glad that she wasn't footing the bill! They had been told that all the spa facilities had been made available to them for the duration of their stay, and like Natalie, she had to remind herself of why they were going! Lauren was keen to meet The Magician; she had heard so much about him from Tommy and was eager for him to maybe hear one or two of her songs that she had been working on. Perhaps he would help, although this would mean her Dad knowing all about her endeavours, and she wasn't quite ready for that yet! Lauren did, however, feel that the songwriting was developing nicely and although she didn't know it, her voice was always going to open doors for her. In her school days in France, she always excelled at singing and had been a member of her school choir. She was always chosen to sing solo during their productions. She had inherited this talent from Tommy but was never encouraged by Polly and Sylvain. They would never have wanted her to follow Tommy into the music business. You only had to look at how it had affected him. She could see though that they had a point! Lauren had observed now that Tommy was a different man from the one in the eighties, he was much more relaxed, and there was no reason why Lauren couldn't have a similarly level approach.

Miriam was relaxing on the sofa as Lauren came from upstairs and walked into the lounge.

'Are you okay, Nana?' she asked. 'Would you like me to bring you anything?

Miriam looked up at Lauren and smiled.

'Oh, I'm fine, thanks love,' she replied. 'You know, you remind me so much of your dad when he was younger. I could hear you upstairs, you know, singing and playing the guitar. It sounded so professional. It was very good! You shouldn't hide your talent Lauren; it took me years to get your dad to sing in front of me. He could sing in front of an anonymous audience, but as soon as he saw the face of someone that he recognized, he would freeze. That's why he would drink and take all sorts of things before he went on stage. He said it kind of nullified his terror. It didn't do him much good, though did it? Why don't you play for me now? It might just help!'

Lauren was amazed. Firstly, she was surprised her voice had carried through the thick walls of the house, and secondly, how perceptive Miriam was to pick up on her stage fright. She was so shell-shocked that she ran straight upstairs, fetched her guitar and returned to the living room.

'Okay, let's give it a go, what the hell,' she laughed.

She sat down on the grey leather armchair - that was her favourite - and balanced the body of the acoustic guitar on her thigh. She looked at Miriam nervously and began to strum the intro to the first song. Miriam looked at her admiringly and listened carefully as her granddaughter's beautiful, angelic voice chimed out majestically. It was an even better voice than Tommy's, she observed. She was no expert and no judge, but Lauren could really go a long way. She had seen the X Factor and there were some good singers on there, but Lauren could play and write as well. Miriam clapped as Lauren finished the first song. Lauren blushed at her grandmother's praise.

'See, wasn't so bad, was it! That was amazing, you really need to play to your dad, and to Natalie too. You have your dad's talent and perhaps you could be even better. Don't tell him I said so though!'

Lauren sang the other three songs and Miriam was flabbergasted. Lots of modern music sounded the same to her, but this girl had a gift. There was, of course, the possibility that Miriam could be biased, but that was not the case.

'I tell you what, Nana, let me write a few more songs and rehearse a little and then I will arrange to play them to Dad and Natalie. Would you keep it our secret until then?... please?' she begged.

'Alright Lauren, I will, but I wouldn't be at all surprised if your dad has heard you already. He may be a little stupid but he's not deaf!' replied Miriam.

Lauren's heart sank. What if he *had* already heard and thought it was rubbish? She had to pull herself together and not think that way. She immediately decided to divert her thoughts to something completely different.

'Cup of tea, Nana?' she asked.

'Oooh, now you're talking,' replied Miriam as Lauren disappeared into the kitchen. Miriam was feeling old and weak; she really hoped that she lived long enough to hear Tommy's album, let alone anything Lauren might record. She hoped she would feel more active again soon, but at her age, every setback seemed harder to come back from. They sat drinking their tea and discussed music. Miriam revealed to Lauren that she had been a big fan of Matt Monro when she was younger. Monro had been a London born crooner whose success had mostly erupted in the sixties. He was a bit like a British Frank Sinatra and was probably best remembered for the James Bond track, 'From Russia with Love' in 1963, although it wasn't his biggest hit. He had been nicknamed 'The singing bus driver' due to his former profession. Lauren started to wonder if she could adapt any of his songs and rearrange them so that it would suit her voice. She picked up her phone, immediately logged on to her Deezer account and started to download Matt Monro's entire back catalogue. Miriam wasn't aware of what she was doing; it would be a lovely surprise for her. Lauren always felt that if you were going to perform cover versions, you had to completely change the song to make it your own. The other way was to pick a tune that had been totally forgotten. This was maybe what Lauren could do here. She didn't know if Matt Monro had ever performed a song she would like, but if she listened to his music, she may just uncover a hidden gem.

18. Down By The Sea

Max was thrilled with what he had heard. The musicians honed the songs very swiftly, as one might expect from seasoned professionals. He had no experience of session musicians, however, and all that he had previously encountered were people who played music as a hobby. Of course, with the exception of Will, and the open mic night at the beginning of the week. He obviously knew his own songs and the cover version of 'Ships.' He was now delighted to learn that Tommy enjoyed their version of 'Ever Changing Moods' so much that he was going to record it with the accompaniment of The Magician on the piano. He was due to visit again next weekend when they hoped to have all the song's 'live' takes recorded and ready to focus on each instrument individually. He always enjoyed the recording aspect of music, although once again, his experience was limited compared to Tommy, Bernie, and all the session musicians involved. He returned to Tarrant Marshall and was explaining to Lottie how everything had worked.

'So they play the songs first, over and over,' he started. 'Almost as if they were rehearsing for a live tour and then

Bernie, or The Magician… then adjust the arrangements and add little bits for all the different instruments.'

Lottie was fascinated but didn't really have a clue what he was telling her. She loved to *listen* to music but never played an instrument in her life and would never sing if she thought anyone might be listening. All she could do now was support her husband the best she could, and hope that the recording sessions would result in a positive outcome, particularly for Max. It could be the difference between them staying in the home they loved or perhaps having to downsize and live in an area that they didn't like so much. Lottie looked around the sitting room that she had decorated with a huge amount of care and attention to detail; she would hate to leave it and would feel as though she had personally failed. Jo did her best to try and support them too by giving them 'loans' on occasion. Unfortunately, however, they hadn't been able to pay anything back, but Lottie intended to return every penny when she could.

Lauren and Natalie were like two excited school children as they checked in at the Harbour Heights Hotel. Firstly, they were looking forward to seeing Tommy and hearing all the songs, but secondly, they were slightly awestruck by the hotel. It had beautiful views out across the English Channel. Natalie checked in to Tommy's suite and Lauren was allocated a fabulous room with views over Poole Harbour. The views were towards the property hotspot of Sandbanks and glimpses of Brownsea Island; famously known as the site of the first ever Boy Scout camp organised by Robert Baden-Powell in 1907. It was magnificent, and although she had been to some fairly stunning holiday locations with Sylvain and Polly over the years, she immediately loved it here. Natalie and Lauren went to their rooms to drop off all their belongings before going to visit Tommy, but after they organised a couple of spa treatments at reception. They were only there for the weekend but wouldn't be able to spend every moment in the studio, so they might as well use the facilities, and Yuki wasn't ever going to object. He would like everyone to be comfortable. He was a kind and generous man with deep pockets. He was also shrewd in business and knew how to get the best from people.

The Magician's home and studio were less than half a mile away so Natalie and Lauren made the decision to walk there. It was a nice enough day, a bit chilly being January, but it was bright and sunny. Tommy had sent Natalie directions, and after leaving the hotel entrance, they turned right into Haven Road. They chatted excitedly as they ambled along on their way. They bore right along Flaghead Road and reached a junction. Natalie looked at the map that Tommy had carefully drawn.

'Ah Cliff Drive,' she exclaimed. 'We turn right here.'

Lauren and Natalie gazed in wonder at the stunning array of houses on either side of the road. The houses got bigger as they made their way down a slight incline. Tommy said that the house was right on the cliff top. 'There must be some wealthy people that lived along here,' thought Natalie. Although these were just the *weekend* pads of the rich, successful and in some cases, very famous. They eventually reached a sharp left-hand bend and this is where the map illustrated where the house was. It was on the right-hand side and was identified by the house name, 'Madison.' Bernie had named it after the small suburb of Nashville in which he had previously lived. They saw the sign which was fixed to some very heavy duty wrought iron gates. They pressed the entry buzzer, and without saying a word, Bernie pressed a button and the gates began to slowly open. They walked along a tree-lined path and eventually saw the house behind a huge parking area. Natalie and Lauren could only stare in amazement. They had both seen some lovely properties in their life but this one really took the biscuit. The original house had been built in the 1920's by a wealthy coffee importer but had gradually been extended over the years. It had seven bedroom suites, three lounges, a cinema, a large gym, sauna and swimming pool, and of course, the recording studio. The studio was housed in the basement which was previously used as a wine cellar and general storage area. Bernie had bought all the latest state-of-the-art equipment, and the facilities were a match for any residential recording establishment in the United Kingdom. A delighted Tommy ran out of the front door waving as he lurched towards them.

'Hey, here's my girls!'

He beamed as he hugged them and then very quickly beckoned them inside. Natalie had never seen Tommy quite as delighted! He was so full of life. It was a pleasure to see. He led them into the magnificent hallway with its tall vaulted ceiling. They could see into the large dining room and noted the magnificent views from the patio doors. It was a clear day and the Isle of Wight was quite clearly visible across the other side of The Solent. Tommy ushered them through a door, which stood on the left hand side, and they walked down a small flight of stairs. There was a door in front of them and to the left of this was a small panel. The panel looked like something from a James Bond film. There was a small green

LED light which was quite clearly lit up and a similar red light below which was not illuminated. This meant it was okay for them to enter the studio. They walked inside to be greeted by a rather eccentric looking man in a loud red Hawaiian style shirt and a New York Yankees baseball cap.

'Ah, Natalie, I presume,' he said. 'And you must be Lauren. Come in, come in!'

He ushered them across to a pair of large leather sofas and urged them to take a seat. Opposite the sofas stood a mixing desk by a large window which looked across the live room. They could see all the musicians making adjustments to their tuning as they waited for Tommy to return.

'You've joined us just in time. We are about to record 'Ships;' the first take of the first track we are happy to lay down. So listen, enjoy and let us know what you think.'

The girls were glad they had come in on this song as they were both very familiar with it. Tommy went through another door and was soon to be seen taking his position behind the microphone in the live room. He put his headphones on and adjusted them so that they felt comfortable.

'Okay Magic! We're ready when you are, kiddo!' He nodded and shut his eyes, deep in concentration.

Bernie pressed a couple of buttons, one to start the recording process and another one to start what is known as a click track. The click track is like a metronome and was set to a particular speed for the musicians to play along with. This ensures that the musicians keep a constant tempo. It would then be banished from the mix later in the process. Tommy's voice sounded glorious as they reached the first chorus and The Magician then heard something that lit up the whole song.

Tommy launched into the first line of the chorus, his voice was complimented by the contralto tones, a female tone, lifting the sound and bringing the song into a whole new dimension.

It was Lauren in the control room, harmonising with Tommy, with an amazing degree of synchronicity. Bernie always had a theory about families playing music together. 'Look at the Bee Gees, the Beach Boys and the Everly Brothers,' he reasoned.

'Stop!' He hollered down a long microphone attached to the mixing desk.

'What's up? Sounded great!' There were a few rumblings of discontent from the live room.

'You didn't hear what I just heard!' he grinned.

This was why he was called The Magician; he heard the simplest things in a song and exploited them. He rushed into the live room and set up another microphone next to Tommy's and got him to start testing its sound levels as he sat back down by the mixing desk.

'Lauren!' he began. 'You know all the words to the chorus?'

'Yes, I do?' she replied quizzically.

'Then, that is exactly what I want you to do! Sing the chorus!' said Bernie, grinning from ear to ear.

Lauren looked nervously across at Natalie, who nodded to her, indicating that she should follow his instructions. She stood up and went through the door to the live room. Tommy looked mystified at being stopped in his prime and shrugged his shoulders. Then he saw who was joining them in the live room!

'Trust me on this one, boys! Let's go from the top'

Tommy winked at Lauren. He wasn't surprised she was there; he knew they would sing together from when he had heard her singing on Christmas Day. Lauren was still looking shocked but maybe this was her big chance. She tried to breathe slowly to calm herself down as the song started again. Tommy sang the verse, his eyes again closed in concentration as Lauren counted in her head the last two bars before the chorus. The result was a magnificent sound, an amazing fusion of the two voices. Natalie looked across at The Magician open mouthed, he grinned back at her.

'See!' he said. 'Sounds mind-blowing! She has one hell of a voice, chip off the old block, if you ask me.'

'I knew she was a singer but I had no idea, even when she was singing along in here, but the combination of the two of them is unbelievable,' Natalie replied.

The song went into an instrumental break after the second chorus. Bill Terry played a guitar solo which he knew wouldn't remain on the finished song.

'I'm sending the recording out to Nashville,' said The Magician. 'Where Bill is playing that guitar lick now in the instrumental break, I've got the best lap steel guitar player in Nashville to play the solo, he's called Chuck Davis and he's amazing.'

Chuck Davis was in demand in Nashville as the number one steel guitar player. He was a friend of Bernie's and was doing this purely as a favour. Bernie had been a huge help in his career, and as far as he was concerned, he was just repaying the debt. He began playing in the eighties under the tutelage of the late 'Little' Roy Wiggins, a country legend, before Wiggins died. Great steel guitar players were hard to come by.

Sadly, it was a dying art; the kids all wanted to be Dave Grohl or Lady Gaga.

The song finished and everyone trooped back into the control room to listen to the playback, amid lots of whooping and high fiving. Lauren walked back with Tommy, his arm proudly placed around her shoulder.

'That was unreal!' she said, wiping tears of joy from her eyes.

'Well, that was a take at the first time of asking!' said a thrilled Magician.

'That's great, Magic!' said Tommy. 'Can we do 'Forever and a Day' after the playback?'

'Yeah, why not, Let's make hay while the sun shines,' replied The Magician.

'Second thoughts! Let's do another song. I need to tinker with the arrangement on 'Forever' first. I'll tell you all about it at dinner tonight.'

'Okay boss!' said Tommy and did a mock salute towards The Magician.

It was 8p.m. in the evening. The day's recordings had gone well with three songs in the can ready to be worked on. A table for eight people had been booked at Giovanni's Italian Restaurant on Poole Quay. Recording was to be a civilised process on this record. There would be no recording sessions at three in the morning. They were all too long in the tooth for that, except for Lauren of course! The quay was dominated by bars on one side, restaurants, small souvenir shops and various pleasure boats moored on the opposite side. Just across the water, a large yacht manufacturer occupied a large section of the panorama. The boats on display would cost a minimum seven figure sum to purchase, and all potential buyers were vetted by the manufacturer to make sure they had the right profile. The party were shown to their table by Carlo, who would be their waiter for the evening. Yuki Akimoto had also joined them for the evening. Yuki, Natalie, Lauren, Tommy, Bill, Bernie, Carl and Martin sat down and started to peruse the menu. Yuki ordered drinks and raised a toast to everyone involved with 'Team Tommy' as he liked to call it. Bernie had sat himself near Lauren and was soon talking shop.

'So, Lauren, there will be some more backing vocals coming up. Will you be okay to stick around?' he asked.

'Well, yes, I will have to be done by Wednesday though, as I have a new shift pattern starting from then. What did you have in mind?'

'Erm, backing vocals on about four more songs and a very special role in 'Forever and a Day,' which involves very little work, for you, that is!'

Bernie explained that he recently watched a documentary on the recording of 10cc's classic hit, 'I'm Not in Love' and was amazed by how innovative they had been. They had recorded all four band members, singing a simple 'aaah' and overdubbed it hundreds of times creating an eerie choir-like sound. He intended to do pretty much the same in the fade out of 'Forever and a Day.' Lauren and Tommy's voices were to be layered to create this effect. Lauren couldn't imagine it yet, but was looking forward to hearing what Bernie had in mind. Bernie already ran the idea past Max when he visited the previous day and he had wholeheartedly given his approval to the idea. Tommy also chimed in with his own suggestion.

'Perhaps we could fade out the song in the background but have the choral sound getting louder over the top, and then when you can't hear the main song anymore, and the choir has reached its full volume, just end it really abruptly!'

This was how Bernie liked to work and this was why people liked to work with him. He encouraged democratic suggestion as long as it was feasible, and Tommy's suggestion was not only that, but it was bordering on genius. This was also why he didn't want to produce country and western anymore. He loved the genre but it was very limited in its parameters. If you listened to country, you wanted to hear the expected. There may be some unpredictable moments in the lyrics, but musically, it generally followed a standard format. Though, of course, there are exceptions to the rule.

They finished the meal and planned the next morning. Lauren agreed to go in before anyone else so they could record the voice sample that they discussed.

'Where's Dad and Natalie?' she asked Bernie.

'Oh, they're catching up, having a stroll down the quay. I can give you lift back, if you like?'

'Okay, thanks Magic!' She was taken aback by the day's events and her head hadn't stopped spinning. She could do with a good night's sleep.

Tommy and Natalie walked arm in arm and stared at the super yachts across the water.

'Which one shall we have, Nat?' he asked keeping a straight face as he did so.

'Errmm! That one there, I think.' She pointed towards a Sunseeker 130 sport yacht probably worth six million pounds.

'Okay, we'll see. Maybe we could hire one for the day!' He changed the subject back to the music. 'So, it sounds okay? I mean I'd rather you said if it was really ropey.'

'Tommy, relax! It's going to be great. In fact, you've got a couple of interviews lined up soon, and there's been a lot of interest from the music press as word has gotten out. I've been putting some feelers out and it looks like Ken Bruce would like to invite you onto 'Tracks of My Years' and Jools Holland wants you to go on 'Later…' Tommy loved 'Tracks of My Years.' It was a section of Ken Bruce's show on Radio 2, where the artist featured chose and spoke about their favourite songs.

'Wow, I've always wanted to do those two! It's all going too smoothly, I'm waiting for it all to go pear-shaped, if I'm honest!' said Tommy.

'It'll be fine… trust me!'

They walked away from the Quay, crossed the road and hailed a taxi to take them back to the hotel. They sat silently, looking out of the cab window as it made its way down Sandbanks Road. They could see the lights in the distance on the end of the peninsula. This stretch was known as one of the most expensive areas of real estate in the world. The car turned left into Haven Road and dropped them off at the hotel. Lauren was already back in her room, standing at the window, staring at the sea. It was too dark to see the English Channel but she could just make out the flickering light from a local vessel which was making its way back into the harbour after a day's fishing. It was going to be an important time over the next few days for Lauren, and she was taking it so seriously that she even refused a glass of wine with dinner. It wasn't like her to have a glass of water with a meal out. She walked away from the window, got into her bed and turned off the light. She noticed how quiet the hotel was as she drifted into a state of deep relaxation. It was indeed something that the owners had spent a great deal of money on; soundproofing the rooms so that the traffic and very windy weather conditions didn't disturb the sleep of its valued clients. Lauren fell asleep within minutes as the waves from the English Channel lapped up onto the sandy beach metres below her.

19. In Between Days

It had been two weeks since Max's visit to the studio, and it was probably the first time since then, that his feet touched the ground. It was certainly the first chance he had managed to catch up with Will. They met for a pint at their favourite watering hole 'The Albion.' It was situated in one of the little Dorset hamlets in between where Max and Will lived. Max stood patiently waiting for their pints of Guinness to settle before the barman could complete the rather delicate stout pouring process. Max thanked the barman and made his way back to the table where Will had sat down and was studying the emails on his phone. He cursed as Max took his seat; it appeared that one of his clients was refusing to pay his invoice until he sorted out a minor issue with their roof. Will knew he had done a thorough job and he was too wise and experienced not to recognise a delaying tactic when he saw it.

'Bloody cowboys! I hate this job sometimes! They put off paying if they can. It'll put some poor sod out of business before long! Anyway, sorry, rant over,' fumed Will.

'Ah, no bother,' said Max. 'I know all too well the frustrations of work, believe me. I'm hoping to give it up, remember? I've never had to be so patient waiting for this album to be released. It's only been a couple of months, I know, but it feels like a lifetime!'

It was inevitable the subject of the recording would come about sooner rather than later. It had become central to Max's life and, to some extent, dominated Will's thoughts. Max handed Will a memory stick and explained what the contents were.

'There you go!' said Max. 'The first three songs I've written in over twenty-five years. Have a listen and let me know what you think.'

'So, what are they called and what are they about?' enquired Will.

'Okay, so the first one is called 'Home' and it's about a guy I know from work. He got divorced over five years ago, had all sorts of financial difficulties and couldn't afford to buy a new home. This is about the moment he finally gets there. He said to me, 'It's good to be home,' and that's the hook line of the chorus. Then we have, 'Feel the Sunshine,' which is an idea I had on holiday in Lanzarote a couple of years ago, but never did anything with it. Finally, the last song is called, 'Sane,' and it's a bit of a play on 'You're So Vain' by Carly Simon, in the same way Robbie William's 'Supreme' is kind of nicked from 'I Will Survive,' I suppose.' Max paused for breath and let Will get a word in edgeways.

'Great! So, I've been thinking. How about we get a proper band together? I know we're both tight for time but I thought maybe Rhoda could do some of the singing and maybe Lottie could involve herself somehow in managing us. That way the girls won't feel left out. This would be just as a bit of fun mind, no lofty ambitions on this one,' said Will.

'And there you have it!' declared Max. '"No Lofty Ambitions.' What a great band name!'

'Yeah, I like it! It's decided then?' Will held his pint up.

'I'm up for that,' said Max as he clinked Will's pint glass, not considering what Lottie's reaction would be. They already spent too much time apart. They spent the rest of the evening considering cover versions for the band and then went back to the subject of Tommy and the album.

'These are funny times,' explained Max. 'I heard The Cure's song 'In Between Days' on the way here, and that's how it feels, like I'm in between one part of my life and the next.'

Tommy had completed the first part of and returned to Sutton. Life for him was also very much 'In Between Days.' He was keeping a close eye on Miriam who seemed to have less than her usual zest for life. She was complaining of feeling lethargic and tired most of the time. She would also feel faint if she tried to get up too quickly. Getting her to visit the doctor was a mammoth undertaking, and she was stubborn. Lauren was putting in plenty of hours at the call-centre and spending plenty of time out with Izzy in the West End, but really, all she had on her mind was her upcoming vocal parts on Tommy's album. Natalie was working harder than ever as her business seemed to be taking off in a big way. Yuki found her plenty of work with his connections and recommended her abilities to several of his associates in the United Kingdom. She still managed to find plenty of time for Tommy, however, and the couple had spent time fruitlessly looking for their ideal flat together, hopefully in the Brixton area. Tommy was nervous about moving out totally, not because he had any doubts about Natalie, but it wouldn't be fair to leave Lauren to care for Miriam by herself, and he also wanted to spend lots of time with Lauren too. He had only just got her back; he didn't want to lose her again. He arranged to meet Natalie at eleven that morning to view two more places, one of which they had high hopes for, it was north of Brixton, closer to The Oval but it was in a new development of apartments. The Oval tube station nearby offered Natalie a direct link to Charing Cross, and it was still close enough to Sutton for whenever Tommy returned to Miriam's house.

Lauren performed her collection of songs for Tommy. The studio sessions had made her more relaxed about singing in front of him, but she performed them in front of Tommy, Natalie and Miriam which seemed like a breakthrough. She felt it would be much easier to perform in front of an anonymous audience full of people who weren't her family or friends. She had exchanged a few messages with Max and they discussed some musical and lyrical ideas and talked about the possibility of future collaborations. It could be a situation that benefited both Max and Lauren, and Natalie spoke to them about the need to copyright their material. They were currently in touch with musical publishers negotiating deals. Natalie's contacts and knowledge were priceless which meant Tommy, Lauren and Max could just concentrate on their music.

Natalie was already stood waiting when Tommy arrived. She looked deep in conversation with the letting agent when she spotted him looking hurried and flustered. She pointed at her watch and chuckled at him, and he knew from that point, he had just about got away with it! The agent was a man called Guy who was far too slick for his own good. He showed them around the two-bedroom first floor flat in one of the back streets behind Coldharbour Lane; one of the main thoroughfares through Brixton. It had a rear view over Loughborough Park and was a pleasant, if not characterless, property with tiny rooms. The other concern they had was that it was a converted house and not purpose built. This usually meant you could hear everything that happened in the flat below. They ruled the dwelling out straight away, jumped into Natalie's Mercedes and made their way to the second viewing. The satnav took them along Loughborough Road, and when they reached the end, they turned right into Brixton Road. The route eventually took them to Bramah Road. In front of them stood a new development of modern apartments.

'Ah, this is more like it, Nat,' said Tommy excitedly. 'Who is it we are meeting?'

'She's called Irene and she comes from South London Lettings. We're meeting her at twelve.' Said Natalie who was a lot cooler about these sorts of situations.

It was a quality Tommy really admired as he was like a child in a sweet shop when looking at new things. It was a quarter to twelve, they were a bit early so spent a few minutes going through the latest developments from The Magician. The drums and the bass parts had been recorded in their entirety and Bill was currently working on the guitar parts. They should be ready for Tommy's vocals in two weeks' time, February 3, which was Tommy's fifty-third birthday. He couldn't wait. He just wanted to get the recording done so that he could go out and play it live. He was a transformed character. If anyone would have suggested this a year ago, he would have run and hid, preferably with a large bottle of single malt.

Shortly, a yellow Smart Car pulled up with 'South London Lettings' emblazoned on the side in dark green. Irene applied the handbrake and adjusted her make-up in the mirror; she had a large blond bubble perm which Tommy was quick to pick up on.

'Christ, if her hair was any bigger, she wouldn't have got it inside the car,' he joked.

Natalie smiled but then gave him a disapproving look hoping that he could be serious for a while. Irene grabbed her bag, opened the door of the Smart Car and climbed out.

'Bloody hell! If her arse was any bigger, she wouldn't have got that in either.'

At this point, Natalie couldn't help herself and she fell into uncontrollable laughter. Fortunately, Irene hadn't seen them yet, and so she managed to pull herself together as they jumped out of the car to meet her. They introduced themselves and walked over to the communal entrance. Natalie was still trying to hide the fact she was shaking with laughter. She had found that jokes were always funnier when you weren't allowed to laugh. The flat was on the third and top floor of the building. They took the small lift which looked like it had only recently been commissioned. Natalie was trying to distract her thoughts from Tommy's humour and focus on the job in hand.

'Right, here we are then. It's number fifty-nine, just over here.' Irene said as they walked towards the front door. She removed a bunch of keys from her handbag, opened the door and they walked inside. The flat was brand new and had never been lived in. It had been acquired by a capital investment firm and would net the company two thousand pounds per month in rent. They moved through a small vestibule and into the main living room which had been fitted with an oak-coloured Karndean laminate floor. There was a large pair of patio doors leading to a balcony with plenty of room to sit outside once the better weather arrived. Irene also assured them that there was a communal rooftop garden that she would show them later on. They immediately loved the place and Natalie thought how it would afford her much more space than her current digs in Belsize Park. Two grand a month was a lot of money, but with the business going well, it was affordable. When Tommy moved in fully, and would begin to pay his share, it would be even more so. She made her mind up there and then; she would take it on the initial six-month lease being offered and go from there. They had looked at so many places over the last week and this one stood out head and shoulders above all the others. Irene gave them the full guided tour and then left them to wander around by themselves, as was the protocol, whilst she made some calls.

'So, Tommy, do you like it?' asked Natalie.

'Oh yeah, this is the one alright, kiddo!' he answered vacantly as he looked around.

'Okay, so I'm going to take it!' She exclaimed and beckoned Irene, who was now off the phone, toward her.

'Could you show us the rooftop garden, please?' enquired Natalie.

Later, they followed Irene back to the offices of South London Lettings which was in nearby Stockwell. Tommy's comedy routine about Irene was in full effect and Natalie laughed until she cried. No one previously in her life had made her laugh as much as Tommy and she felt no commitment phobia where he was concerned. She had once confided in a girlfriend about a man she was dating that she wasn't sure whether he was right for her. The friend simply said, 'Does he make you laugh?' The answer was no, and Natalie soon realised that this was a crucial component in any relationship.

They made the necessary arrangements for a deposit and filled out what seemed like an endless array of forms. The flat was theirs, at least it was Natalie's, until Tommy felt comfortable about completely moving from Sutton. They made their way to Miriam's house to break the news to her and Lauren, stopping at an off-licence for a large bottle of bubbly to help them celebrate. They pulled up outside the house and walked in through the front door.

Lauren and Miriam were sat in the lounge watching an old film that they were showing on channel 5 when they arrived. They were grinning from ear to ear. Miriam's heart sunk but she smiled. She knew they were looking for somewhere and she didn't really want Tommy to move out. She had grown used to him being there and would miss him. It would only be a matter of time before Lauren met a nice chap and they moved in together.

'You two look pleased with yourselves!' She chimed, without looking up from the television. Tommy rapidly went off to the kitchen to chill the bubbly in the fridge and returned before anyone noticed.

'Yeah and we have news!' said Tommy chirpily. 'Natalie has leased a flat in Brixton and we are going to move in together, however, at first I will divide my time between there and this house, if that's okay? I want to make sure you're okay, Mum, before I move in fully.'

Miriam looked slightly relieved as he said this and managed a hearty grin. The closing titles of the film started to come up so she gave them her full attention.

'Lauren has a busy life too so I thought we could look for some sort of home to help cook and clean etcetera,' he continued. 'I know that you're very independent, Mum, and wouldn't want to compromise that, but I just want to make your life easier.'

'Tommy, I'm really made up for you and Natalie, I hope you'll be really happy together. I really couldn't be more thrilled, and Natalie, I think you're fantastic for Tommy!'

Natalie blushed slightly but recovered enough to tell Lauren and Miriam the whole story of the flat and how lovely it was. She also recounted the story of how Tommy made her laugh like she hadn't laughed for a long while. Nothing Tommy did surprised either Lauren or Miriam. His sense of fun was legendary; he was always ready to play the clown, which was ironic when you consider the name of his old band. They talked for a good hour reminiscing old times. Miriam liked to embarrass Tommy with tales on what he was like as a child, and before long, Miriam had coerced Lauren into finding the old photograph albums from her wardrobe. Tommy disappeared and came back presently with the large bottle of champagne and four glasses. He could only find wine glasses as Miriam wouldn't possess anything as decadent as champagne flutes. He filled up their glasses and they toasted to future success and happiness. Tommy had a lot of work ahead of him; he knew that and he was comfortable with it.

20. Senses Working Overtime

When Bernie was in the zone, he was in the zone, and there were never any half measures. He was an all or nothing type of guy and the album was taking up all of his concentration. It was lucky that he had a housekeeper otherwise he would have been living in a complete mess. Sunday morning was no different for him as he jogged from Flaghead Chine very close to his home and studio, down to Bournemouth Pier and back. It was almost four miles and became a daily ritual for him since he returned to England. The Magician tag that he had been saddled with was both a blessing and a curse. The blessing was that it gained him work. The curse was the pressure to deliver that it put him under, but this project was different, and it had been nothing but a pleasure. Yuki and the team at Pagoda records had been totally supportive, so Bernie felt that he was working more for the artist than the record company, and that was a huge change. This morning, Bernie was focusing his attention on one of the songs on the new album. 'Blue Sky Day' was written by a young songwriter from South Wales called Ceri Jones. Ceri was in his mid-twenties and from Ammanford in Carmarthenshire. He fronted a band called Harpattak, who were a young Indie band with critical acclaim. They had signed a three album deal with Parlophone records two years ago, and were under pressure to produce the hit records that had so far eluded them. Ceri was so prolific that he started to offer some of his songs to other artists, and Bernie had it on good authority that Elton John was keen on recording one of them. Ceri didn't help his cause with Parlophone by threatening to produce an album entirely in the Welsh language. He needed careful handling because like most talented artists, he lived close to the edge, and was resistant to whatever authority figures asked of him. Tommy loved his work and was most insistent in trying out this song. Bernie for all his years of being The Magician, really couldn't see this song working. He could imagine Liam Gallagher singing it for sure, but Tommy? It was a mid-paced song that was probably influenced by the psychedelia of the late sixties. Bill had backed Tommy up on this just because he quite fancied the guitar licks. Selfishly, as it gave him the excuse to try his new Gretsch G6115T with a Bigsby, a type of tremolo arm, giving it an amazing retro sound.

Bernie reached Bournemouth Pier and stopped for a moment to admire the view. He hadn't come out with the iPod today, he wanted to have just the one song going through his mind as he ran. He had to admit it, Tommy had been right and the song was pure genius. It worked superbly with Tommy's voice. What Tommy and indeed Bill hadn't heard yet, was that Bernie had taken some of Bill's guitar riffs from the song and played them in a backwards loop in the fade out. It was a technique he had first heard on The Beatle's Revolver album of 1966, and had been used in songs sparingly ever since. The last example of it that he could remember was on Tears for Fear's 'Sowing The Seeds of Love' but it must have been used since, as that was nearly thirty years old. Lauren had harmonised again with Tommy in the chorus to significant effect. 'Lauren's voice had many of the qualities of the late Kirsty MacColl,' thought Bernie, and that wasn't a bad voice to be compared to. He plodded his way up the hill from Flaghead Chine back up to Haven Road; close to the hotel where Tommy and his crew had stayed. Tommy was due back this evening in time for an early start tomorrow. All sorts of things helped engage Bernie's thoughts on the album. Sights, sounds and even smells. Once in Nashville he ran past a garden which had some jasmine growing at the front of the house. It immediately made him think of 'Summer Breeze' by the Isley Brothers and made him decide to use a fuzz pedal on the guitar solo of a particular track he was producing. He took his inspiration from everywhere.

He eventually made it back to the house, showered, changed and started working on getting a rough mix on 'Blue Sky Day' so that he could make some minor adjustments to the sound. The four mile run wasn't just a fitness exercise but a way of getting his brain into gear. The control room was his office, and in the last month, he had probably spent sixteen hours a day there. Anyone who thought that the music industry was a doddle needed to see Bernie at work.

Tommy was travelling down to Poole alone again on the train. Natalie was very busy up in the office in London and preparing for the forthcoming move. She had told her flat mates she was moving and they had reluctantly advertised for a third person to help with the rent. She was hoping to move to Brixton at the end of February and didn't see any hitches. Tommy would just move his things over gradually, not that he had a lot to move. Lauren would stay behind for the first week of the vocal sessions and look after Miriam. Aunt Gladys was coming to stay for the week after so Lauren could join Tommy then. Hopefully, the vocals would be finished off and the final mix could begin by the beginning of March. That was the plan anyway. Bernie didn't like a project to be too long-winded. Music, he argued, should be an act of planned spontaneity. It was a little ironic but he knew what he meant. He was looking forward to Tommy hearing what had been done and, whilst he had been informed, there was no substitute for hearing it in a studio.

The next morning, Tommy arrived at The Harbour Heights, dropped off his things and jumped back into the taxi. He arrived at Bernie's around ten and was greeted by Lucy, Bernie's housekeeper. She showed Tommy in and offered him coffee which he accepted enthusiastically. Bernie appeared from the basement studio, beaming.

'Ah! Good morning Thomas, old boy! Come on down to the studio.' Said Bernie, leading him down the stairs and into the control room.

'Now! First of all, we'll do a playback so you can hear what it sounds like with your original vocal, but with complete instrumentation.'

The music began to play loudly from the large speakers from either side of the mixing desk. Tommy thought how beefed up it sounded compared to the last time he had heard it. The Magician had been up to his tricks, and the first track they played, 'Never Bring Me Down,' sounded stupendous. He had ramped up the sound using sampling and layering of the instruments; sometimes using four and six tracks on each guitar part. What struck Tommy the most though was that it still retained a live edge and rawness. 'Never Bring Me Down' was meant to sound that way. It was a far cry from the slick, soul pop of the late eighties for which he was renowned. 'Forever and a Day' was far more representative of that. They had soon finished listening to all twenty songs that they had recorded. Tommy made notes. Ten of them stood out as being a cut above the others and Bernie more or less agreed with his selections.

'So Tom, are you ready to put down some vocals? We'll just aim for the one song today and see how we go. I don't want to dwell too much on absolute perfection. I want it to sound like you mean it! If that means the odd imperfection, then so be it. The ambient texture of the record will be enhanced. Let's start with 'Never Bring Me Down'. You look in the right mood for that!'

They did only manage to get one song completed that day and finished the session at four o' clock. Bernie invited Tommy out for dinner and Tommy was relieved that he didn't seem to know that it was his birthday. He kept very quiet about birthdays as he really didn't want the fuss and besides, the older he got, there was less reason to celebrate. They arrived at Giovanni's just before eight and were shown to their table. It was a table upstairs by the window overlooking the quay. It was a table for four and Tommy looked quizzically at Bernie.

'Is someone joining us Magic?' he asked.

'Er…possibly! You'll have to wait and see,' he replied.

He glanced over at Bernie with suspicion. Bernie just grinned knowingly. The waiter brought them across a bottle of very expensive looking French red wine specially chosen for the occasion. The fact that four glasses were on the table fueled Tommy's suspicion even more. He didn't have to wait long; coming up the stairs were two voices he recognised. Just as he suspected, Natalie and Lauren appeared and giggled their way across to the table. Tommy stood up to greet them.

'What the!... How did you get here?' he enquired.

'Teleportation!' joked Lauren mischievously.

'Do you think we would miss your birthday?' said Natalie. 'Happy Birthday Tommy!'

She kissed him and handed him two brightly decorated parcels. He smiled as they sat down and put the presents in front of him. He looked at the first one; a square box wrapped in silver paper adorned with a gold bow. It had a small tag attached and he could see it was from Lauren. He unwrapped the paper carefully. Inside it, was a box, and on the top, it was marked Ernest Jones Jewellers. Inside the box, was a watch. It was a Michael Kors Men's Rose Gold Plated Bracelet watch. She had bought it at the branch in Bond Street on her last trip to town last week.

'Wow, Lauren, that's lovely, thank you. You really shouldn't spend all your hard-earned money on me though, but thanks so much,' he beamed.

'I've only got one dad, haven't I?' She smiled back at him.

He turned his attention to the other present as he placed the watch on his left wrist, adjusting it to fit, closing the clasp. The other box was larger and was wrapped in shiny red paper with a silver ribbon and bow. Under the wrapping was a large brown box with a lid. It contained ten vinyl albums, brand new and in their original sleeves. It was Tommy's entire album back catalogue, both with The Clown's and as a solo act. There was also a small white envelope which read, 'To Tommy, enjoy! All my Love, Natalie xxx.' He looked across at Natalie as he opened the envelope. Inside the envelope, there was a photograph of a retro record player, the type Tommy hadn't seen since the eighties. It was in an orange wooden portable box and was marked 'Steepletone.'

'Oh wow, I've wanted one of those for ages!' he said.

'Well, it's all yours. Well, it will be when I get moved in to the flat in Brixton!' replied Natalie.

'Thanks, Nat!'

Natalie was due to move all her belongings into the flat at the end of February and was looking forward to getting there. Tommy was due to be away on the week she moved in, but that was fine because it would keep her busy. Tommy had arranged his walking holiday in the Cairngorms last year, before this miracle had happened. He felt guilty that he was going to be away whilst Natalie moved but she had everything arranged with a local house moving company. Consequently, there really wasn't much for him to do. Lauren would stay at home with Miriam just to keep an eye on her. He was looking forward to it but was concentrating on the job in hand.

'Right! Let's get this party started!' He declared as he started to fill people's glasses with wine. Even Bernie joined them in a small glass despite his reservations about alcohol whilst he was mid-project.

Over the next few weeks, track by track, the vocal parts on the album began to take shape. First Tommy, and then when he had finished, Lauren completed the backing vocals. On Thursday, February 23, the last note was sung in anger. It was Lauren completing the quite complex harmonies on 'Blue Sky

Day.' This quickly became Lauren's favourite song of the sessions. It was a wonderfully optimistic song with its chorus stating, 'I'm looking for the blue in the sky,' in other words, trying to see the bright side. Ceri was not known for his happy go lucky turn of phrase, but he excelled himself on this one. Most people saw him as a sort of Welsh Morrissey but Tommy had seen something in this song that he liked, and he was right. This could potentially be the first single off the album, with 'Ships' and 'Forever and a Day' also strong contenders. Tommy, Lauren and Bernie sat in the control room listening to the song they had just completed. They were more than pleased with what they heard, and it was beyond Tommy's wildest dreams, even six months ago. Everything happened so fast. Tommy was glad to have a week to get away and consider everything that had happened. Walking was Tommy's therapy and he would come home feeling happy, content and ready for the launch of the album and everything that went with it. The publicity was the bit that Tommy liked the least; the endless interviews and the publicity photos. Tommy just wanted to sing. That was what he loved. He loved writing too, that wasn't possible on this album because of the timing, but he wanted self-penned songs on the next one. This record was an album that he could be proud of. There was still the mixing to do and the track selection as the twenty songs needed to become ten or maybe twelve at a push. The artwork and promotional merchandise would need to be prepared. Natalie, however, had already set these wheels in motion.

No more than ten miles away, Max and Lottie were on tenterhooks waiting to see if Max's songs were going to be used on the album. Not only were they keen to hear them completed but keen to reap some much needed cash. Their financial plight hadn't really improved and had actually worsened since the leaky roof affair. Lottie was now working at the hospital and earning but they still didn't seem to be making inroads into the debt. Will had told them that the roof would need replacing this summer and he was eager to start, but they weren't in a position to give him the go ahead just yet. All they needed was a call, be it from Natalie, Tommy or Bernie. Just one call that could potentially change their lives, but time was running out, any more debt could force them to start defaulting on their mortgage payments. That would be the start of the slippery slope. Little did they know, Max's two songs would appear on the album although Tommy couldn't commit, at least not until he'd heard the final mix. Realistically, this could take up to at least a couple of weeks, if not a little bit more. Max and Will hadn't done much about forming their new band; life had been too hectic, although the songs were coming thick and fast. Max had now written seven new songs and Will had written five. More than enough to get them started, if they could only find the time. Maybe that would be next year's project, but they both hoped it would be sooner.

21. When The Sun Goes Down

It took about three hours on the coach from Glasgow but Tommy finally arrived in Aviemore. He was tired, but happy and relaxed. He was searching for his accommodation, a log cabin just outside Aviemore within the National Park of the Cairngorms. He was spending his holiday with Clive and Phil, two old friends from his schooldays in Sutton. They always kept in touch through the good and the bad, and although they didn't see each other *that* often, this was a yearly ritual. Phil had moved from Sutton to Nottingham in 1997. His job in education had landed him a plum position as a school's inspector for Nottinghamshire Education Authority. Clive, however, was now semi-retired. He found himself wealthy at the age of fifty, due to a rather sizeable inheritance. He usually spent six months of the year in Tenerife, and Tommy would see quite a lot of Clive when he was in town. When he wasn't, his Crystal Palace season ticket was in safe hands! Tommy and Clive went way back, right back in fact to the day that Tommy first started his new school in Sutton, in 1970. Clive could probably write a book on Tommy's life and career and was one of the few people that had stuck by him after the notorious

'Wogan' incident. He saw how Tommy had to battle his way back, overcoming his alcohol and drug excesses. Clive knew that he was still no angel but knew that he had more or less recovered. He was especially pleased when he had that heard Tommy was recording again. Clive didn't possess any musical talent; in fact, he was tone deaf but had helped out with The Clowns in any way he could.

Tommy soon arrived at the log cabin to find that Clive and Phil had already arrived.

'Hey boys!' said Tommy.

The 'three amigos' greeted each other with high fives and hugs. Phil fetched Tommy a beer from the fridge as he and Clive were already indulging in a nicely chilled Peroni. The men discussed their plans; usually they all had a different agenda during the day, but would get together in the evening to enjoy good food, drink and laugh about old times. The week was usually one of the highlights of Tommy's year. Clive would spend his days fishing for Trout on the River Spey nearby. Phil found relaxation as an amateur novelist and would spend the week writing. His latest novel was a colourful romantic story about forbidden love during the French Revolution. He only needed his laptop, Wi-Fi and decent coffee. Tommy would spend his days walking, following carefully planned routes that he had researched using travel guides. He knew it could be a dangerous game walking solo but he liked the headspace that it offered him. He generally couldn't get good signal on his phone until he was at the cabin so he had to be extra careful. Spending the night out in the subzero temperatures of late February wasn't a sensible option. It was nearly five in the afternoon and the men agreed to unpack their things, have another beer and then walk the mile or so to Aviemore to find something to eat. Tommy was already sat in the living room of the cabin, strumming his old faithful acoustic guitar when Phil and Clive returned to the room.

'Go on then, Tom, give us a sneak preview!' Said Phil to which Tommy duly obliged. Firstly, he sang a song called 'These Days Are Mine,' another song written by Ceri Jones for the new album. This was a very simple mid-tempo folk and soul hybrid. Tommy really felt the song was saying, 'Here I am, I'm back,' a message that he very much wanted to convey. He then went on to play, 'Equally Blessed and Cursed,' a new song that he had written himself. It hadn't made the sessions for the new album but he would use it on the next one for sure. Tommy wasn't the most prolific writer, he had relied on The Clowns writing team of guitarist Stuart Ebdon and keyboard player Nick Williams in the past, but he had contributed lyrics. He began writing on his own during his wilderness years and whilst his songwriting had improved, his star had waned and he wasn't big news anymore. His material during this time had been cruelly ignored. Unbeknown to Tommy, Clive had recorded both songs using the voice recorder on his phone. Tommy wouldn't have minded but Clive didn't want to put him off by telling him this. The pair were impressed with Tommy's performance and commented that his voice was on top form. It seemed to mature as he got older and there was an increased amount of gravel in his timbre. It wasn't quite as gruff as Rod Stewart or Tom Waits, but he was working on it!

The trio soon made their way into town and to Tommy's delight, found themselves in a local Indian restaurant. It had been a while since Tommy had enjoyed a curry so much, but he reflected that it was the best he had felt about anything in a long while. The men talked and reminisced for the rest of the evening, ready for whatever lay ahead.

A long way further south, The Magician was sat in his lair. The control room was only lit dimly as Bernie needed a certain type of ambience in these situations. It was the only way he could work during a mix. He had also found that he could only do this type of work late at night or early in the morning. He was armed with only black coffee made from an electric coffee maker which he had recently installed. It saved him going back up and down to the kitchen whilst he was in the middle of a creative muse. The mixing process was around about fifty percent complete at this stage and all the instrumentation had been completed. Chuck Davis had recorded the lap guitar solo on 'Ships' in Nashville. Tommy had arranged for a gospel community choir in Brixton to sing on the chorus of 'You Make Me Feel Like a King,' giving it a whole new dimension. Effects had been added to the instrumentation as and where necessary and the vocals and backing vocals had been cleverly layered and multi-tracked. Lauren's choir-like sampled voice on 'Forever and A Day' was a masterstroke and was probably one of the highlights of all the songs. Working with Tommy had been an absolute joy. He had been out of the industry for such a long time that his humility was like that of a new up and coming performer. Bernie had worked with a few prima donnas in his time and Tommy definitely wasn't one of them. The end result was that Bernie was passionate about the album, and put his heart and soul into it completely. That was what he wanted. He had produced too many albums in Nashville that he didn't care about at all; it was just a job at that stage of his career. He was currently mixing a track called 'The Mayor of Simpleton' which was very much Tommy's idea. The song was originally written by Andy Partridge of XTC and was released in January 1989 as a single from the album 'Oranges and Lemons.' It was originally a mid-Atlantic indie-pop song with jangly guitars. Tommy's idea was to record it with a string quartet and no other instruments. This was an idea going back to when Tommy first conceived the album. Bernie had recruited a string quartet from London and one of their violinists, Tim Kramer, who was an accomplished composer and had written a beautiful arrangement. To Bernie's surprise, the song worked magnificently. It was Tommy's love song to Natalie and it had a lyrical sentiment not dissimilar to Sam Cooke's, 'Wonderful World,' a song that Tommy loved. Recording the song from a technical point of view was tricky and they had spent four hours just getting the sound set up right. Bernie asked them to play it five times before using the original take. He had enhanced the sound with some multi-tracking, sampling some violins, violas and cellos. Thereby making it sound more like a full orchestra. Mixing it was a challenge but it was nearly there. Bernie had set himself a challenge of finishing the track this evening. He looked across the desk with a furrowed brow. The Magician was in his element; this was what he loved to do. When he was back in Nashville, he would regularly stay away from all the showbiz parties that were on offer with Carlene, just so he could absorb himself in studio culture. He wasn't a party animal; he was more like a mad scientist trying to build the perfect beast.

Natalie was sat in her new living room admiring the view from the balcony. Brixton was slightly more urban than Belsize Park but the property was away from the main road and felt more open. This was the beginning of a new era and she couldn't believe how quickly it had happened. She would miss the girls at the flat that she shared, but she had Tommy to look forward to. They had both conquered their demons in the process of meeting each other. Tommy still enjoyed a drink but had calmed down considerably in the last two or three months and Natalie, for her part, no longer felt commitment phobic. She presumed that was the difference in meeting the right guy. Communication with Tommy hadn't been easy whilst he was in Scotland, telephone signal in The Cairngorms was erratic, but they had agreed to Skype at about six every evening. The log cabin had an excellent Wi-Fi coverage. It was three in the afternoon. Just three more hours and they would be able to catch up. There was a knock on the door. Natalie walked to the front door and opened it; it was Irene from the lettings agency.

'Hi, Natalie, I was just showing a client round one of the other flats and just thought I would check everything was okay?' asked Irene.

'Thanks, Irene, that's sweet of you. Yes, it's all good! Thanks for dropping by.'

Natalie smiled as she went back to her cup of coffee; she remembered how Tommy had made her laugh the day they first looked round the flat. It wasn't very kind of him to mock Irene but she had a slightly naughty sense of humor. She knew she shouldn't laugh but that was what made it funny.

'Now, where was that box with all the cutlery in it?' She said to herself as she continued to unpack everything. The removal men had long gone but Lauren had agreed to come round and help, and she would be there soon. She found the correct one and began to peel off the buff parcel tape that held it together.

Tommy was starting to panic. Whilst he was walking a guided route and following a map in the guidebook, he had stopped for a rest and become slightly confused about his whereabouts. Despite being well dressed with all the right clothing to suit the situation; he was feeling the cold. It was still February and temperatures were hovering around zero degrees. Worryingly, the light was going to be fading soon. He took a sip from the hip flask he carried around with him; it contained a twenty-five-year-old Glenfiddich, and if that didn't warm him, up nothing would. He started to feel a little helpless about the situation as he appeared to be going around in circles. He looked at the map in the guidebook and it now made no sense whatsoever. This was the main hazard of walking alone. If he didn't get back soon, he would be all alone, overnight without any of the right equipment. He didn't even have a lighter to start a fire. A sense of real fear and trepidation began to engulf him. He hadn't even brought his phone along, not that he would have got any signal at all where he was. He decided to try something different and turned left at a fork in the path that he was taking. He was convinced that the right fork had been the correct route to take but it had always taken him back to the same point. He resolved to keep calm as the sun slowly started to disappear. He started to climb up a hill in an effort to find a viewpoint and reset his bearings.

It was half past five and Clive and Phil had started to worry. Tommy should be back by now. There was no way he would want to miss his six o'clock Skype with Natalie, especially as he had told them Lauren was going to be involved too. Clive noticed that Tommy had left his phone on the small table next to the sofa. He thought that it would be no use to him out there. He pressed a button on the side of his Samsung Galaxy and the screen lit up. There were messages for him on whatsapp; it was easier to use the Wi-Fi for messaging rather than the phone signal. There was a message from Natalie, one from Lauren and another one from someone called Bernie. Clive didn't recognise him but supposed he was something linked to music. He didn't like to pry on Tommy's phone but circumstances might require he do so later on if Tommy still hadn't returned. It was a cold evening, temperatures felt freezing and they could see small flurries of snow out of the window. It was starting to get very dark too. Clive had a horrible feeling at the pit of his stomach; he decided to act and call the park wardens. They would know how to contact the mountain rescue team if they were required. He picked up his own phone, went to the far corner of the room, the only place he could get signal and started to type out the number.

There was no word from the rescue team at 8p.m. Natalie and Lauren back in London were going frantic, but there was nothing they could do. Phil and Clive were in regular contact with Natalie but there wasn't much to report. Weather conditions could have been worse; there was snow on the ground but it wasn't snowing. It was the temperature that was of concern and hypothermia was the biggest worry. Natalie and Lauren had decided not to tell Miriam that Tommy was missing. It would only distress her and she was already quite frail. Natalie thought about Tommy, out there in sub-zero temperatures, how would he cope? Tommy wasn't known for his calmness in these situations. She resolved to try and keep positive about the situation. Lauren, however, wasn't quite so easily convinced, pacing around the lounge in Brixton. It was lucky that she wasn't at home with her grandmother. Miriam would have known that something was wrong.

At just after 10p.m., Clive had a call from the mountain rescue team. They were calling off the search for the night. There was nothing they could do but hope. Nobody had been spotted by helicopter or on foot and conditions were not getting any easier. Clive finished speaking, thanking them for all they had done so far. The search would resume at first light. Clive was filled with pessimism, he stood out in front of the cabin smoking one of his cigars and was feeling useless and helpless. It was at this point, he saw in the distance a small figure in the dark trudging slowly down a distant slope. The figure had started off as a tiny light on the dark horizon but was getting larger as it got closer. It looked like he could see a reflective patch on some clothing. It couldn't be, could it? Clive called Phil and they ran out to the bedraggled, hunched over figure in the distance. They stumbled along the snowy pathway with only Phil's head torch for guidance, and as they approached, they could see it was Tommy, who was shivering when they reached him and couldn't communicate coherently. His breathing was quickened and his gait was awkward and seemed uncoordinated. They managed to support him as they led him to the cabin. When they arrived, Phil quickly contacted the park management team who had been alerted and were waiting for news. They immediately called the emergency services. Clive sat Tommy down in a chair and gathered as many blankets as he could and wrapped them around Tommy who was still trying get his words out but failing. Clive then called Natalie and broke the news that he had at least been found and was safe. The ambulance arrived and after the paramedics had satisfied themselves that it was safe to move him, he was stretchered into the emergency vehicle.

Hypothermia cases were quite a regular occurrence at Raigmore Hospital in Inverness. Tommy could laugh about it all now but it had been a sobering experience for him and everyone concerned. He had been discharged and was told to take it easy for the remaining two days of the holiday. Phil and Clive promised to keep an eye on him and Natalie threatened to kill him if he went AWOL again, somewhat ironically. No sympathy there then, Tommy had joked. In fact, Tommy barely ventured out of the cabin again until he boarded the National Express coach back to Glasgow. The events of two days ago reverberated through his mind over and over. He was so lucky and he knew it. He would have to review his penchant for walking alone in places like that. He'd only found his way back by chance, after going round in circles for what seemed like hours, he came to the peak of a hill and saw some lights in the distance. He was frozen through and weak by then, becoming more and more disorientated by the minute. It was just pure chance that the lights he saw were from the holiday park, it was the only civilization for miles. If he'd been out there for another hour, that may have been the end of him. He spent his journey home partly in reflection and partly on the future. Bernie had sent him a message to say that the mix was complete and the album was ready for track selection, ordering and media and promotional material to be considered. Exciting times for Tommy, not only for him, but everyone involved in the project. Natalie had briefed him of a big meeting next week. Yuki, Bernie, Tommy and Natalie would sit down and discuss the artistic direction and the logistics of its release. Tommy had loads of ideas and couldn't wait to convey them. He sent Natalie a text from Glasgow airport just as the boarding message went up for his flight back to Gatwick. In two or three hours he would be back home.

22. 10/10

A meeting had been called for Monday, March 9. It was to be held at Pagoda Records offices in Shepherd's Bush, West London. Tommy, Natalie and Bernie were attending along with Yuki and Andy Clayton, who had recently been appointed CEO at the record company. He was an ambitious character and at thirty-five years old had come a long way in a short space of time. He had a background in A & R (Artiste and Repertoire, a glorified term for talent scout) for several record labels including Virgin and Parlophone. He was responsible for helping such artists as Bastille and Catfish and The Bottlemen to break through. When Yuki offered him the position at Pagoda, he jumped at the opportunity. Tommy's album was an interesting proposition to him. He was smart and realised the power of the middle aged audience in today's market. It wasn't all about youth, and Tommy McNeill sat right up there amongst all the old acts, Duran Duran, Spandau Ballet and Simply Red. He could make this album work and it just needed careful marketing. The meeting was called to discuss all the important factors in selling the album. Track selection, artwork and the choice of singles were all important issues, as well as, all the media and live engagements that Tommy would have to fulfill. He had heard all about Tommy's reputation from some of his older peers in the record industry and hoped he would be able to carry out his obligations. Andy was also aware just how much he could impress his boss Yuki, if the album was a success. Mr. Akimoto had seen this as his pet project. The Clowns had been big business in the Far East and particularly in Japan. Yuki had been a fan in his younger days and Yuki's wife, like Natalie, had a teenage crush on Tommy.

It was 10a.m. and people started to gather in the boardroom at Pagoda. The room was in a typical London office block with a large window that had views across London towards the BT Tower. There was a large table in the centre of the room with a large jug of water in the middle, some glasses and a huge bowl of what looked like mint imperials. They all greeted and sat down around the table, it was quite obvious from the way he sat down, and his business-like manner, that Andy was chairing the meeting. The CEO took control from the start, he cleared his throat and began to speak. The four onlookers couldn't help but be impressed by his demeanour.

'Okay, so morning people, welcome to Pagoda! I'm Andy Clayton, the CEO of Pagoda and I know the rest of you are all acquainted, so I'll spare you the introductions. We're here today to discuss your project and its forthcoming release. What I would like to establish is the overall concept of the work. We need to narrow the songs down from twenty to ten, decide on the singles and the artistic details. So, over to you... Natalie?'

Natalie looked up, she felt slightly like she was back at school being asked the answer to a complicated piece of algebra that her teacher had put on the board.

'Yes, hi, Andy,' she replied, not knowing what else to say.

'I gather you have a full programme of media and promotional activities planned so I would like a full rundown, or report, of everything you have planned by the end of the week. Is that doable?' he asked.

'I don't see why not, yeah.' She paused for a second and looked at her notes.

'I have a rough draft now. I have people plugging Tommy's old material both with The Clowns and solo as we speak. Some of the latter details towards the date of release may change, all according to how we gauge interest in the album. The feedback I'm getting so far is good and Tommy, I know, will back me up in saying that people are starting to remember him again.'

She continued watching Tommy who was nodding in agreement. His mishap in The Cairngorms had gained some column inches in the tabloids; this served to put him back in the public eye slightly. Several well-wishers had asked him about his health and wellbeing as he'd gone about his business for the last couple of weeks. He did feel fine, however, and was prepared for the next stage of events. He hadn't even thought about stage fright in the last couple of months and it no longer seemed like an issue.

'Yeah, they are remembering me again, that's for sure,' he said. 'I've been asked for a few selfies with people recently, that's a new phenomenon! It was usually autographs back then. I got to autograph all sorts of people's anatomy! But going back to one of your original points, I think between Bernie and myself, and with your blessing, we have ten very strong tracks that speak for themselves and we have a track listing for everyone's approval,' said Tommy.

Bernie nodded in agreement with Tommy, and at that moment, Yuki looked ready to interject.

'I have only one request.' Said Yuki whose demands had been minimal really considering his position. I and my wife, Hikari have listened a lot to all of the tracks and we would love 'Forever and a Day' to be the first single.'

The room stayed silent for a couple of seconds and Andy, sensing his opportunity to please his boss, smiled and nodded in approval. Tommy and Bernie looked at each other quizzically before Tommy spoke.

'Well, Bernie and I were torn between that song and 'Blue Sky Day,' so Natalie, what do you think?' he said.

Natalie grinned enthusiastically. There had only been one choice for her since the day that they met Max in the service station all those months ago.

'Well, I loved the song from day one, and I love the romance behind the song's history. It's 'Forever and A Day' for me,' she said.

'The fact that it's been in someone's attic for a couple of decades just adds weight to its marketability,' she added.

'I think that's carried then.' Said Andy who was pleased that there were none of the usual petty arguments involved with these types of meetings.

'We can make 'Blue Sky Day' the second single and then subsequent releases can be decided after we gauge the success of the album. Now, we need to decide when we are going to release them.'

The date that was decided upon for the release of the first single, 'Forever and A Day' was Tuesday, April 7. The album which was yet to be titled would be released on Monday, April 20. That only left four weeks to get it all done. In the digital age, this wasn't so much of a problem, although photo sessions, artwork and a promotional video for the first single would have to be done rapidly.

'I have an artistic director I want you to meet who can get the job done. She's great! A young up and coming director and she likes to work rapidly,' said Andy.

'Sounds like my type of girl!' chortled Bernie.

'So Tommy, any thoughts for the album title?' Natalie asked, knowing full well that he did. Sometimes Tommy needed to be pushed into speaking in these type of situations.

'Yep, the album will be called, 'The Kick in My Soul,'' he replied. It was part of the first line of 'Forever and A Day' and just sounded right. Bernie began to sing it, not as well as Tommy but Yuki's face lit up, and from that point, there was no looking back. The meeting then went on to discuss the specifics, the whys and wherefores, and the logistical arrangements involved. They didn't have long; it was a tight deadline but all parties were keen to get moving. The meeting ended around 12.30p.m. and an outside catering company brought in a buffet for everyone. The final decision that Tommy and Bernie would have to make was deciding the ten songs that would be used. They listened to the twenty tracks as they ate lunch; three tracks were in and another six or seven were obvious choices. There were two or three tracks, however, that were a sticking point. Natalie had booked a few days away in a Dorset spa hotel after the meeting, and they had planned for Tommy to spend a morning with Bernie to make these decisions. Natalie would spend the morning with Max and Lottie at their house, breaking the news to them about his song, and discussing the finer details of the publishing rights.

Tommy and Natalie arrived at their hotel at around 3.30p.m. It was a country Manor house in between Ringwood and Christchurch just on the edge of the New Forest. The meeting had gone well and they had the rest of the day to relax. Forest Lodge Spa Hotel had a gym, swimming pool, sauna and steam room. Tommy spent his afternoon flitting between all of these. Natalie joined him after going for a manicure and a hot stone massage, which was a new, and pleasant experience for her. They discussed the day ahead tomorrow and decided it would be best to combine the two duties in one fell swoop. So Natalie revised their plans. They arranged to travel to Canford Cliffs first and talk to Bernie, and then on to The Jazz Café at Sandbanks, where they would meet Max and Lottie for some lunch and a chat.

The next morning, they arrived at Bernie's house and studio bright and early at just after 9a.m. They sat in the lounge and soon started to make some decisions. It wasn't long after eleven when they finally had an agreement and wrote a track listing for 'The Kick in My Soul.' The remaining tracks were still considered good enough to be used at some point and may well see the light of day as bonus tracks on subsequent releases. They felt relieved that it was finally all over and glad to have worked together on the project. Bernie mentioned to Tommy that he thought Lauren had talent too and asked what her plans were.

'I think she plans to see if she can get in on the music scene,' said Tommy. 'I will help her all I can obviously and she's written some cracking songs. I think she has potential,' he continued.

'Send her in my direction, Tom', said Bernie. 'Maybe I can help!'

Tommy said he would do so as they climbed back into Natalie's Mercedes to drive the short journey down to Sandbanks. They both waved as they passed through the large iron gates to the front of the property and they had soon disappeared from view. Bernie went back inside the house and got changed and ready for his daily run down to the pier and back.

Max and Lottie had already arrived at The Jazz Café; they were way too early. Max sat on the low wall outside the café and looked out towards the English Channel. Lottie walked out towards the sandy beach and was staring at the sea. She turned and walked slowly back towards Max. They hadn't spoken much that morning, they were too nervous. This was decision day for them. The day they found out whether Max's songs were to be used on Tommy's album. He now realised what it was like to be a contestant on the X-Factor or The Voice; he almost felt sick with worry. Lottie had just returned to Max when she saw two familiar faces approaching from the car park in Shore Road. It was Tommy and Natalie. They *looked* happy enough as they strolled hand in hand but that was no guarantee of anything. Looks could be deceptive. Max imagined that Natalie could be a deadly assassin when needed, capable of being the bearer of bad news and thinking nothing of it.

'Hi guys! How are you?' Natalie greeted them warmly and pointed towards the entrance to the establishment. They sat at a table for four near the window with views out towards the beach. Tommy ordered some coffees whilst they looked at the food menu and he insisted on buying them lunch. He sat back down and began to speak.

'Well, you're probably wondering what's happening with the album and more specifically your songs, so I won't delay anymore, I will just spit it out.' Tommy tried to look as serious as he could, noticing how apprehensive Max and Lottie were.

'It's good news on three fronts!' He grinned. 'Firstly, both 'Never Bring Me Down' and 'Forever and a Day' are to be included on the album, but there's more…' Tommy tried to do his best impression of a game show host from the 1970s trying to build the suspense.

'Secondly, the first single off the album is to be'…Tommy made the sound of a drum roll. 'Forever and a Day!' At this point, Max had his head in his hands with disbelief and Lottie was wiping tears from her eyes with a handkerchief. Tommy paused for a second, he was grinning from ear to ear as he had one last piece of good news to deliver.

'We've named the album,' he said. 'We used a line from one of your songs, it's to be called, 'The Kick in My Soul'. I love the opening lines of 'Forever and a Day' and the words inspire me!' he continued. 'I've been waiting for the kick in my soul which I knew would be there one day.' Tommy had burst into song, rather loudly so that the occupiers of the adjacent tables looked over to see what was going on exactly.

Max didn't really know what to say. He had achieved a lifelong dream and probably earned himself some financial breathing space. Lottie could only think about their lovely house and at last felt that they may be able to stay. Tommy started to look serious again and he did have a small word of warning for the couple.

'Of course, the album could be a complete flop. There are never any guarantees but Natalie has put the publicity machine into overdrive and with the help of things like social media, we'll get the word around.' They chatted over lunch and Natalie went through the publishing deal that she had negotiated on Max's behalf. She advised him to run it past his solicitor, sign it and return it to her. Max assured her that it would be back as soon as he could get it looked at. It was around 2.30p.m. when Max & Lottie left, Arthur needed collecting from school and they would go home where Jo was babysitting Maisie for the afternoon. Max had a lot to think about over the coming days but time would tell how successful the record would be. He couldn't even guarantee that he would be able to give up his job at I.M.C, and there was no way he was going to gamble on it. He supposed he would have to stay doing exactly what he was doing, in the short term, at least. Still a small price to pay in the long run.

Tommy and Natalie had a short walk along the promenade and reflected on the meeting. It felt good to have broken *that* news to Max and Lottie. Tommy knew what it meant to experience a personal victory out of adversity. It was probably the best feeling that he had experienced. It was like telling somebody that they had won the lottery. They got back to Natalie's car and started the thirty-minute drive back to their hotel. They knew that they had the rest of the day and tomorrow to enjoy themselves but the next few months would be full on.

23. The Message

The rest of March was already booked solid. Natalie had spoken to various people in the media and arranged a multitude of promotional activities, all leading up to the release of the first single. Whilst Pagoda records had taken charge of social media activities, Natalie was adept at dealing with the press and the rest of the media. Tommy was helping the BBC who was interested in making a documentary on Tommy's rollercoaster career on BBC4. It was to include interviews with Tommy and the rest of The Clowns. He was a little nervous at what they might say as he hadn't spoken to them in nearly thirty years. There had been a lot of bitterness in the years after the Wogan incident and the band splitting. Tommy hoped it had all been forgotten but couldn't be sure. They had also planned to interview Boy George, Marti Pellow and Mick Hucknall who were amongst Tommy's contemporaries at the time. With Easter looming quickly, they only had three full weeks to get the ball rolling. Tommy was looking forward to recording the Tracks of My Years, a feature on the Ken Bruce radio show on Radio 2. It involved picking ten of his favorite songs that would then be played two at a time each day for a week, along with an interview with Tommy explaining what they meant to him. This would also involve significant airplay on Bruce's show of 'Forever and a Day.' Pagoda would get people to plug the song across a wide range of music stations anyway, but Radio 2 would be the best station for Tommy's target audience. It was going to be in the forty to sixty age range, anyone of this age group would remember Tommy, and it was proven that retro was always in fashion. Pagoda also hoped to reach a younger audience too. Tommy was due at New Broadcasting House in Portland Place on Monday, March 16, to record the feature. He had spent hours at home with Lauren, Natalie and Miriam deliberating which ten songs he should choose. It wasn't easy and he kept changing his mind right up until the day. He was careful not to be too predictable. People of his genre *always* chose Marvin Gaye, Sam Cooke and Otis Redding, so he carefully avoided those three. People made the mistake that Tommy only liked one genre of music, something that he wanted to lay to rest on this album. He arrived at his destination and was greeted by a member of the production team who escorted him to a surprisingly small hospitality area. He was given some coffee and biscuits and was told Ken Bruce would be along shortly. He didn't have to wait long when a chirpy, bald Scottish disc jockey appeared, smiling and holding his hand out to be shaken.

'Hi Tommy, it's good to see you,' Ken said. 'It's been a while, how are you?' Tommy hadn't seen Ken Bruce for years and years; they used to cross paths quite a lot in Tommy's heyday.

'Yeah, I'm good, thanks Ken. It's good to see you again too, it must be twenty-five years, at least!' he remarked.

'I would think it is. Where has the time gone?' Ken explained the procedure of what was going to happen; they would go to a studio and discuss Tommy's ten songs, and that's all that was needed, the rest could be edited in later. Tommy looked down at his list and showed it to Ken. It read:

Tracks of My Year's songs - In no particular order!

1. The Clash - Rock The Casbah
2. Jimmy Ruffin- What Becomes of the Broken Hearted?
3. Patsy Cline - Crazy
4. Roy Orbison- It's Over
5. Terence Trent D'Arby - Wishing Well
6. Prince - The Cross
7. Adele - Rolling in The Deep
8. Crowded House - Pineapple Head
9. Big Country – The Storm
10. Bob Dylan - Don't Think Twice It's Alright

It was an eclectic mix but still radio friendly and not too over-indulgent. He wanted to also get across to the audience that he wasn't just about white boy soul, and that would reflect in the new record. The dialogue with Ken that would be played on the air reflected this. It didn't attempt to make him look more musically educated than the audience. Selections eight and nine were in because not only were they great songs, but because of his friendship with the artists. Tommy had no problem discussing his choices with Ken who was very attentive and knowledgeable on his selections. He had no prior warning of the songs involved and so couldn't possibly have researched them in advance. This was a good way for Tommy to get the message across that he was back. He would have to sit through endless banal interviews with papers and magazines and he was dreading it. This, at least, was constructive in its nature, and he could trust Ken Bruce not to make non-stop references to the 'Wogan' incident. Ken thanked him for his time, they shook hands and Tommy headed off home. He was eager to get home and see Miriam before heading off to meet with Natalie. Miriam had been back and forth to the doctor's for several weeks but seemed to have lost faith in them. The arthritis and low blood pressure had taken their toll. Miriam hadn't left the house for a few days now and she was showing no signs of improvement. Tommy really didn't expect her to be doing anything too strenuous at her age anyway. It would just be nice to see her relaxed and happy. A home help had been hired which took the burden of care away from Tommy and Lauren to some extent. Lauren seemed to be spending an increasing amount of time rehearsing her songs with some new found musician friends. They had found some rehearsal rooms over towards Streatham, and according to Lauren, had enough material for an album ready to go. Bernie had shown quite an interest and had promised to go to a gig when they had some arranged. Natalie had also agreed to help with the gig situation, so it wouldn't be too long and Lauren could continue the family business!

The rest of the week was a mixture of interviews, photo sessions and general promotional activities. Tommy was at the BBC again for an interview with Jo Whiley for her evening show, and again with Sara Cox, for her late-night eighties nostalgia show. Tommy was enjoying it although he loathed to admit it. On Friday of that week there was a pre-release, press only launch party, arranged by Natalie and funded by Yuki and Pagoda Records. It was to be held at The Lanesborough Hotel at Hyde Park Corner. Twenty of the capital's top music publications were invited to hear the album and view the track listing. Tommy would be on hand for a question and answer session. The party was billed as informal as Tommy didn't want anything too heavy going. Some artwork and photos from the album were also to be put on display and were hastily being completed in time. Most album sales these days were in the digital format but the release would also be available on Vinyl and CD. The track listing had finally been concluded; it had been designed on a large self-standing cardboard poster using the same theme as the album artwork. The track listing was as follows with the songwriter's names in brackets as was the music industry tradition:

<u>Tommy McNeill – The Kick in My Soul</u>
 1. **Blue Sky Day (Jones)**
 2. **Ships (Adamson/Watson)**
 3. **Forever and A Day (Chilton)**
 4. **Don't Let It Drag You Down (Jensen/Jackson/McNeill)**
 5. **My Ever Changing Moods (Weller)**
 6. **Never Bring Me Down (Chilton)**
 7. **Strange (Jackson)**
 8. **You Make Me Feel Like a King (Thompson/Carr)**
 9. **These Days Are Mine (Jones)**
 10. **The Mayor of Simpleton (Partridge)**

Natalie had emailed a copy to Max. He had to double take at the sight of two of his songs listed on an album by Tommy

McNeill. The new material he had written was coming along nicely and he was nearly ready to start rehearsals with Will, as and when they could find the time. Other than the better-known cover versions on the album, Tommy had used songwriters like Max, Ceri Jones, Kyle Thompson and Jamie Carr from London soul/funk band Metropolis, who were just starting to gain attention worldwide. It was a mixture of styles and didn't really adhere to any one theme. It contained soul, funk, pop-rock, indie, folk and country. Bernie was certainly proud of its diversity and after all those years of pure country and western, it was a breath of fresh air to him. He was pondering over a few new projects; the most exciting being working with Lauren. Her voice had impressed him; she could easily be the next Ellie Goulding or even a British answer to Taylor Swift. With the right songs and production, she would go far. Bernie was also pleased that with Tommy's help he had used a couple of his back catalogue of songs. He started writing 'Don't Let It Drag You Down' with a Nashville guitarist called Chas Jensen who wrote the guitar riff that they had based the melody on. Bernie had worked a chord sequence around it and Tommy had written the lyrics. 'Strange' was written by Bernie when his marriage had ended but he was still in Nashville. He had felt like a stranger in a strange land and it had culminated in this eerie, haunting piece of work.

Natalie couldn't remember a time when she had been busier. Certainly since her days in PR for Canadian television. They were exciting times and she would regularly get to meet people that she had watched on screen since her childhood. Meeting Tommy though was the pinnacle for her. Working with her teenage pin up and now she was in a relationship with him; she could hardly believe it. There were no signs of the commitment phobia that had dogged her with her previous relationships. She had no doubts about Tommy, she just hoped that he felt the same. There was something she needed to talk to him about, something important. It may be nothing but it could be something very major. They never really had the chance to pause for breath these days, and they hardly spent any time alone together since Natalie moved into the flat in Brixton. She was currently putting together the arrangements for Tommy's forthcoming appearance on 'Later...with Jools Holland.' This was to be filmed and shown live on Easter Sunday, April 5. It was filmed at Maidstone Studios in Kent. Tommy would perform 'Never Bring Me Down' with Bill, Carl, Martin and Bernie on keyboards as his backing band. Tommy would then perform 'Ever Changing Moods' with just Jools on piano at the end of the show. They would only get the chance to run through it once or twice on the day so he was quite nervous about it. The show was to go out on BBC2 in the evening, two days before the release of 'Forever and a Day' as a single, and would maximise publicity for it. It was quite a coup for Natalie to have pulled off. He was to share billing on the show with Blur, Cee Lo Green, Slaves and Suzanne Vega, so he felt quite privileged to have a solo spot highlighted by Jools, close to the climax of the show. He had known Jools for quite a few years; they were both South London boys and he had provided some piano parts for several of The Clowns songs back in the eighties. Jools Holland was pleased to see Tommy making music again. He had thought about asking him to tour with his Rhythm and Blues Orchestra in the past but had heard Tommy was in no fit state to perform, which had saddened him.

Natalie was also sifting through some invitations for Tommy to play some festivals in the summer. Tommy was keen but was also aware of the logistics. He would have to put a band together and that would involve some fixed term contracts to hire them. They were unwilling to commit on this until they knew how well-received the album would be. Most of the festivals were in June, July and August, so they only had a short time to decide. The next few weeks would be crucial but if the feedback was anything to go by, interest was growing. Life was exciting but she really needed to get her life in order. There was a serious conversation that she had to have with Tommy. She didn't know how and when, but soon. The day after the Jools Holland show would be the best time. She was hoping to go along with Tommy on that day but Yuki was flying in, and she had agreed to go out to dinner with him and Mrs. Akimoto. Hikari was in town to shop in London and meet Tommy; they would arrange *that* meeting later in the week. Natalie knew in her heart that soon life would change forever. She thought Tommy was committed to their relationship but she needed to know now for sure. They hadn't met that long ago but she felt that they were destined to be together; she just wanted some affirmation. Tommy had no idea what was going on in Natalie's mind or that anything had changed. If either of them had realised the course of events to come, they would have made the time.

Everything behind the scenes was set. 'The Kick in My Soul,' the fourth solo album by Tommy McNeill, was ready for release. National and local radio stations had started to play

'Forever and a Day.' All of them claiming to be featuring 'exclusive' airplay. They couldn't all be exclusive, of course, but it sounded good. From Yuki at the top of the pyramid to the artists involved down to the most junior of office staff at Pagoda, everyone was excited about the release and wanted it to succeed. Tommy had made sure he was on good terms with everyone at Pagoda. It would help if he really needed them to pull out all the stops when it came to marketing the album. Things had changed since he last released music; downloading songs from iTunes was the new thing. The days when you would look forward to going to your local branch of HMV to buy the new release by your favourite band or artist were long gone. He had spoken about this with Max, who fondly remembers asking his local record shop for all the point of sale material for The Jam's, 'Beat Surrender' EP. It was their final single and the record shop agreed that he could have it for free, when they had finished with it, of course. It adorned his bedroom for about the next six months until his mother cruelly threw it away when he was on a school trip. He had never quite forgiven her! It was digital these days and Tommy looked forward to experiencing the record business in the twenty first century.

24. The King of Rock N' Roll

Easter Sunday had finally arrived and it was the most significant date on Tommy's calendar for a long time. Years ago, he would have considered it as just another TV appearance and very much part of his usual routine. It was completely different now, and it was on the eve of the release of his first single in nearly twenty years. The BBC had commissioned a live performance of Later...with Jools Holland to be shown between eight and ten on the evening of Easter Sunday. The corporation wanted to showcase and highlight their commitment to music by putting on this show. They had recently recruited a reformed Britpop act, Blur, to headline the show to play a couple of tracks from their forthcoming album, 'The Magic Whip,' their first new studio album since 'Think Tank' in 2003. They had also been asked to close the show with one of their biggest hits from the past. Like Tommy, they were hoping for a boost in their media coverage. The irony was not lost on Tommy, that both himself and Blur were publicising their comebacks on the day of the ultimate resurrection! The programme would also feature American Singers, Cee Lo Green and Suzanne Vega, and very local punk duo, Slaves, both from Kent where the show is recorded. Tommy's duet with Jools of 'Ever Changing Moods' was to be the penultimate song of the evening, followed by Blur performing 'Tender' from their 1999 album '13,' an anthemic and rousing climax to the show. Tommy stayed the night at Natalie's flat in Brixton and they would travel together to Maidstone early in the morning to prepare for the performance. Natalie wanted to try and watch the rehearsals but she had a busy day and had to meet Yuki and his wife as they were having dinner that evening. So even watching the rehearsal was probably not going to happen for her. This was a crucial twenty-four hours for 'The Kick in My Soul,' and there was to be no letup in proceedings afterwards, with the release of 'Forever and a Day' coming on the following Tuesday.

It was ten-thirty in the morning. Tommy sat at the kitchen table in Natalie's flat eating porridge. She had been in the bathroom for a long time that morning and she appeared looking rather pale and disheveled.

'Are you alright, Nat?' Tommy enquired on seeing her look so under the weather. 'Have you been throwing up?'

Natalie nodded whilst sipping on a large glass of water.

'Yeah, I think it must be something I ate. Don't worry, I'll be fine. I just need to eat something.' She munched on a slice of toast that Tommy had prepared. Tommy had never seen her eat so quickly. He shrugged his shoulders. Natalie was tough and Tommy knew she would be fine. The real reason for her nausea was completely lost on Tommy. He finished his breakfast and began to look around the flat to check he had everything he needed to take for the day. He was meeting with the rest of the band at Maidstone Studios, where they could rehearse and sound check before the show started. Tommy would also have the opportunity to run through 'My Ever Changing Moods' with Jools Holland. This was going to be tricky to pull off, but it was a simple arrangement, and Jools had agreed to keep it identical to the version on the album. Bernie had emailed Jools with the musical score of the piano parts he played so it would be seamless.

After about half an hour, both Tommy and Natalie were ready to leave Brixton and they jumped into Natalie's car taking the South Circular Road. Soon they reached Horn Park, where they followed the A20 and the M20 before arriving in Maidstone shortly after midday. Natalie was very quiet on the journey. She couldn't understand why Tommy hadn't worked it out. Did she have to spell it out to him? She couldn't and wouldn't say anything before tonight's performance. There was always tomorrow. She just hoped he wouldn't be frightened off by what she had to tell him. Tommy knew that Natalie wasn't right, he wondered what the problem was, but he couldn't focus on it now. Today was a huge landmark and he had to give it his all. They had booked him in at The Hilton in Maidstone. Tommy had no means of getting back to either Sutton or Brixton after the show. He would book in and the BBC would send a car round for him at 2p.m.. They stopped in the car park and Tommy retrieved his case from the boot of Natalie's Mercedes.

'Okay well, here we are,' said Natalie. 'Good luck tonight. I wish I could be there.' She hugged Tommy and he made his way off to reception. She could tell he was distracted. He was probably worrying if he would be afflicted by the stage fright that had dogged him in his younger days. He soon disappeared from Natalie's view and she drove back to London to meet Yuki and his wife. It seemed that something had changed forever; nothing could and would be the same again.

A car arrived for Tommy at 2p.m. and it took him on the short journey to the studio. It was ridiculously close and he would have been just as happy to walk. The BBC, however, wouldn't hear of it and insisted that he was treated like a VIP. He was greeted by the studio floor manager and he could hear that Suzanne Vega was already set up and rehearsing 'Marlene On the Wall' for her sound check. He was greeted by an enthusiastic Jools Holland who had seen him arrive out of the corner of his eye.

'Tommy! Great to see you back,' he beamed. 'We'll have a run through in a while of our duet, but first, we need you to play the other song you're playing tonight, the one with your band.' He noticed that Bill, Bernie, Carl and Martin had set up just to the left of Suzanne Vega.

'As soon as Suzanne has finished, you're on!' he instructed.

Suzanne Vega seemed happy enough with the sound but she was just telling the sound crew that she needed her fold back monitor, which was positioned just in front of her, to be a touch louder. They made the adjustments and the band played the song again from the last verse. She smiled and raised her right thumb up to the sound crew and then she swigged from a bottle of Evian mineral water. She put her guitar down and nodded at Tommy as he walked across to his band. Before he could pause, Carl was counting the band in and they began to play 'Never Bring Me Down.' Tommy was delighted with how it sounded; he hoped it would sound this good this evening. On the studio version of the song, Bernie had put an effect on Tommy's voice that made him sound as if he was singing through a crackly telephone line. The sound engineers at Maidstone Studios recreated it perfectly. It was done using a very flat sound, taking away as much echo and reverberation as possible. Bernie had first heard it on the song, 'The Days of Pearly Spencer,' by the late Ulsterman David McWilliams and covered twenty-five years later by Marc Almond. Bernie was a huge fan of that song and the producer of that song, Mike Leander. He had borrowed heavily from his style of production which was famed for his string arrangements. Tommy grinned at Bill as he launched into the guitar riff in the middle of the song which involved a lot of work with his wah-wah pedal, a device used to make the guitar on a very funky sound by using a foot pedal. The song ended and the band members were more than happy with their sound. The acoustics of the venue had taken it to a whole new level. The band members were ushered off to the green room where a huge buffet had been laid on, not for Tommy though, he had more rehearsing to do.

Jools Holland sat behind a Steinway grand piano as Tommy was ushered over by the floor manager, Graham.

'Okay Tommy, when we go live we'd like you to stand here just at a slight angle to Jools and the piano. That way you'll be able to see each other and the cameras will be able to pick you both up in the same shot,' Graham instructed carefully.

'No problem, boss,' replied Tommy. He nodded to Jools who looked like he was ready for a run through.

'Okay then, Tom, shall we give it a go?' Jools said.

'Yeah, let's do it.' Said Tommy assertively as they began to perform a slow intimate version of Paul Weller's 'My Ever Changing Moods.' The song was included on the album because of Max and Will's version, and their decision to play it at the open mic night. It suited Tommy's voice superbly and was arguably, even better than the original version. In just over four minutes, they had finished the song with no hitches, and whilst they had both been nervous about doing this live on television with just one rehearsal, it just seemed to click and Tommy no longer had any fears about it. The stage fright that had once crippled him as a performer was a thing of the past. At least, he hoped it was. When he thought about how it had affected him over the years, he regretted what a waste it had been, but this was a new dawn. The new Tommy McNeill was about to emerge.

In Dorset, Max and Lottie had invited Will and Rhoda around to their house for the show. It was a premiere for Max; the first time his song had been played on television. 'Forever and a Day,' however, was already picking up lots of radio airplay, particularly on Radio 2 and some of the big independent stations like Heart, Capital and Absolute Radio. The Chiltons felt a little more confident about their financial future now and Will had already started to rebuild the roof on their house. There were still no guarantees that the song would net them a fortune. Lottie and Jo had arranged a huge buffet of finger foods to help them through the evening. Max was aware of what songs Tommy was performing on the night. Natalie kept him well informed of developments and had even texted him to tell him that Tommy had arrived safely at the television studios earlier that day.

'So, are you all ready for this then, Max?' asked Rhoda.

'Well, as ready as I will ever be,' he replied. 'It's all a bit surreal to be honest, like it's all a weird dream.'

'Yeah, I can imagine,' said Will. 'I feel surreal just knowing you!' he joked.

At last, the programme started and Jools soon introduced Slaves, who launched into their song, 'Feed the Mantaray.' Everyone laughed as someone from the Slaves road crew danced with the band dressed as a manta ray. They were followed by Cee-Lo Green and Suzanne Vega. It was soon time for Tommy to take centre stage. The room was silent in anticipation as Jools orated a short biography of Tommy's career.

'Ladies and gentlemen, please welcome the one, the only, Mr. Tommy McNeill!'

They all cheered and whooped as the camera panned across to Bill and Carl who started the song with the count of four. It was a rawer sound than they expected. If anyone thought that it was going to be the Tommy McNeill of The Clowns of 1986, they were in for a surprise. He was dressed in a way that he would never have done in the past. The slick suit was replaced by a denim shirt and jeans; just the sort of stuff he would wear every day. He felt more comfortable and the whole thing seemed less regimented. The stage fright had not materialised and he didn't even have a swift beer before the show. There were signs by the end of the song that he was really starting to enjoy himself; arms flailing around playing air guitar. You would have thought he was trying to be Freddie Mercury!

Back at the Chilton's house, the party was in full swing. They roared as Tommy finished the song and it came to a shuddering halt. Jools Holland reappeared and introduced Blur with their first song of the evening, 'Lonesome Street,' a single released in the previous week from the latest album. Natalie had somewhat controversially persuaded Tommy to play 'Never Bring Me Down' rather than 'Forever and a Day' on the night as she felt it was the better live song and would demonstrate the diversity of the album. As he normally did, Tommy had agreed that she was probably right and judging by the evidence of this evening, she was spot-on once again. Max ran to the kitchen and reappeared clutching a large bottle of bubbly and four glasses and Will made a quick speech, toasting Max's success. Lottie, whilst enjoying the evening, had wondered how Arthur and Maisie had stayed asleep with all the din that was going on. The tension was now building as they all knew that Tommy's second song was coming up soon; all the artists got to perform two songs, apart from Blur, who played three. Tommy was, however, lucky enough to be highlighted by performing with Jools Holland. Max felt particularly pleased that he had a hand in Tommy performing 'My Ever Changing Moods,' and thought back to last year, when they performed it in front of the family. That was only last autumn and it seemed like a lifetime ago. What had seemed relevant then, was no longer worrying Max in the present. It just went to show what can happen if you keep plugging away. Suddenly, the room went quiet as Suzanne Vega finished a rousing rendition of 'Luka,' her 1987 song about domestic abuse. It was her biggest worldwide hit to date. Jools was sat beside his Steinway and began to interview a terrified looking Tommy about his life and career. He wasn't very good at this as he liked to keep his private life private, and one of the reasons he agreed to do this, was because he knew Jools would stick to the music. Jools was good to his word and didn't mention Tommy's checkered past, or more importantly, the Wogan incident. The song was introduced and Jools played the opening chords on the piano. Tommy began to sing. He felt strangely liberated and relieved as soon as the first line was sung. The first verse seemed to sum up how he felt. The lyrical content was a comparison between light and dark, between happy and sad and between the good and the bad times. A perfect summing up of Tommy's whole existence

This was the calm after the storm; the end of a torrid period of his life. He had Natalie, Lauren and Miriam. He had some great friends and he had his career back. What more could he ask for?

Max put his arm around Lottie's shoulder; it was the calm after the storm for them too. Max knew how Tommy felt when he sang those words. What neither of them knew was that it was the calm *before* the storm that they needed to worry about. For now, though, they would enjoy the rest of the song in blissful ignorance.

25. Road to Nowhere

Yuki and Hikari Akimoto were staying at Claridge's for a few days. It was nothing unusual because they always stayed there when they were in London. They had invited Natalie to watch 'Later' at their suite, and even arranged a room in the hotel for Natalie to stay in that night, so they could all unwind and enjoy the programme. They had been to Chisou, a nearby Japanese restaurant and had now retired back in the lounge of their suite. They opened a rather expensive bottle of bubbly to toast Tommy's success, although Natalie was drinking a soft drink. Hikari had noticed this and could guess why but said nothing, it wasn't her place. They were watching in deep concentration as Tommy finished his duet with Jools. Natalie had been apprehensive about the whole thing and felt a huge weight lift off her shoulders. The single was released in two days' time and she hoped to get a nice quiet day with Tommy tomorrow so they could have a serious talk. She wouldn't rest until it was all out in the open.

'Amazing.' Said Yuki as Tommy sang the last note of the song. They all applauded although they felt a bit silly and laughed when they realised what they were doing. Natalie looked at her phone to check it wasn't on mute. Tommy had promised to ring when he got back to the hotel. She probably wouldn't hear from him for another hour or two, but best to be prepared, it was 10.20p.m. They continued to watch carefully as Jools thanked Tommy and then started to launch into some dialogue about Damon Albarn and Blur who would be closing the show.

'That was Tommy McNeill, ladies and gentlemen. Great to see him back in such fine form. Good luck with the album, Tom!' Tommy nodded back as Jools continued.

'Now, for the finale. Coming up, is a huge name in Britpop, who have reformed to produce a new album. They close the show tonight with an old song and they are joined by the London Community Gospel Choir, with whom they originally performed this track. The song is 'Tender,' ladies and gents. Please welcome... Blur!!' The camera panned away from Jools and over to Graham Coxon, who started the opening riff of the song on his guitar.

The windscreen wipers rocked back and forth and Charlie Pike wearily watched them as he waited at the traffic lights. He didn't want to be driving his van around Maidstone at this time in the evening on Easter Sunday. He had been unlucky in the draw with his shifts. He was only two months away from retirement and he couldn't wait. He could spend all his time with his wife, Rose, indulging in their hobbies. They liked to cycle and had recently purchased a Cannondale road tandem for £3000. He would retire just in time for the better weather and lighter evenings. He took off the handbrake and moved off from the lights on this grim, wet and breezy Sunday night. He had done his last drop and was on his way back to base. He worked for Tesco, the supermarket giant, delivering people's online grocery orders. He had enjoyed the job for the last few years. He became tired of his job as a toolmaker at a local engineering company and wanted something different for his last few years of employment. He looked at the clock on the dashboard; he was running late! He put his foot down as he moved away from the traffic lights. There was nothing worse than giving his employers any more of his precious time than he had to.

Tommy sat alone backstage in his dressing room. Bill, Bernie and the others were already back at the hotel enjoying a glass or two and celebrating a successful evening. Tommy had agreed to join them but was just taking a minute. Everything in his mind was starting to clear; he began to think about Natalie and how self-absorbed *he* had become in recent weeks. Was she ill? He knew she had something to say to him but what? He thought that maybe he was in denial because he couldn't bear the thought of anything being wrong with her. Every time he heard anything on the TV or the radio about cancer or heart disease, he couldn't bring himself to listen. He looked up at the TV monitor in his dressing room as Damon Albarn began to sing 'Tender.' Tommy loved this song; it was one that he'd wished he could have written himself. The London Community Gospel Choir were beginning to make themselves heard. The rich vocals of the choir interplayed incredibly well with Albarn's distinctive voice.

Tommy was in awe of the huge sound that they were producing, immediately cutting back to Damon's solo vocal again.

There was something in the lyrics, something that made Tommy think, it was all starting to make perfect sense. Sometimes a well written lyric could tell you something, without even meaning to. Tommy stared across the room and suddenly a switch flipped. His eyes suddenly widened, his jaw dropped open and he started to mutter to himself. Just one word in the song, repeated over and over, got the message across to Tommy, at last.

'Baby? Natalie? No… it couldn't be… could it? Nat?' He reached into the pocket of his denim jacket and found his phone, looking frantically for Natalie in his contacts. He pressed dial and waited for Natalie to answer. The penny had finally dropped and Tommy had just realised he was going to be a father again.

Natalie heard her phone ring. She reached across and picked it up and went to answer, she was excited to hear from Tommy and fumbled at her mobile like a nervous schoolgirl. She accidentally hit the wrong button and rejected the call.

'Damn!' Cursed Natalie and then recovered her composure. 'I'll give it a couple of minutes and try again.' She told Yuki and Hikari and they continued discussing the single release on Tuesday.

'Hi, this is Natalie, leave a message and I'll get back to you.' Tommy heard Natalie's answer phone message and had started to become agitated. He couldn't wait anymore, he had to go and find her! He knew where she was; at Claridge's. He would get a taxi and ring her en route. It would all be fine but he *had* to see her. All thoughts of music and the album were completely forgotten, as were his possessions and friends he'd left back at the hotel as he jogged down the corridor towards the way out of the studios. He didn't really have a clue what he was doing or where he was heading but he was certain he would find a taxi outside, there would be dozens of them. He eventually found his way out of the building but there were no taxis to be seen. He saw a security gate away in the distance to his left and started to run quickly towards it. He asked the man on duty as he would know where to find a cab.

Charlie was less than half a mile from base. He'd broken a few speed limits on the way back but he knew where the police cameras were and he was perfectly safe. He knew the Vintner's Park area of Maidstone like the back of his hand. It was about five past ten as he whizzed around the roundabout. Charlie turned right off Bearsted Road and into New Cut Road heading coincidentally towards Maidstone Studios.

Tommy reached the security guard and pleaded him to help.

'Hey kiddo!' he said. 'Where can I get a taxi around here? I thought there'd be loads around!'

The security man looked rather puzzled at Tommy, wondering why one of the artists wasn't being picked up in a limo. It wasn't normal.

'Not sure.' He managed, still a little perplexed at the sight of Tommy McNeill in front of him.

'Through the gate at the end of the road is a roundabout, go straight on and you'll be in Grovewood Drive. There's a supermarket and a pub not far away, about half a mile. You're bound to see one up near there. Good luck!'

Tommy was already off and running although he shouted 'Cheers' as he went on his way. He reached the roundabout and couldn't believe his luck! A taxi was just dropping somebody off at a house on the other side of the road.

'That'll do!' He shouted to nobody as he ran out onto the roundabout not looking to see if any vehicles were in the vicinity. The only focus he had was for the taxi waiting to take him to Natalie. He felt his phone vibrating in his pocket, the ambient noise levels blocking the sound of the ringtone. He chose to ignore it as he broke into a sprint.

Natalie found a pause in the conversation and made her excuses to visit the bathroom. She walked across the lounge area of the Akimoto's suite. She selected Tommy's number; she was itching to tell him how proud she was of him and some news that she had learned today. Stevie Wonder's management had been in touch and wanted Tommy to record a duet with the Motown legend. The song was to be used on the soundtrack of an untitled Hollywood movie that was to feature Samuel L Jackson and Angelina Jolie. The movie was about an interracial relationship in the nineteen-twenties, long before such a thing was socially acceptable. Natalie immediately accepted because she knew Tommy would jump at the chance. They had so much to look forward to, so much more than Tommy would ever know.

Charlie sped along New Cut Road, the rain was now lashing against his windscreen and he put the wipers on full speed. It was a horrible night and Charlie thought whoever was out in this was mad as he passed two late night running enthusiasts to his right. He could see something had parked on his side of the road up ahead, it's hazard lights were flashing, so he started to move into the other lane. There was nothing coming the other way so it was safe. He could now see that the vehicle in question was a taxi that was just dropping somebody off. It was just at that point that something appeared in front of him, very suddenly a dark figure was looming. He only had a split second to act and hit the brakes as hard as he could, but it was too late. There was a sickening thud on the front of his van as Tommy was forced down and underneath the van. Charlie skidded as he had tried to turn to avoid hitting Tommy. He spun out of control along the road until his van at last mounted the pavement and crashed into a lamppost. There it stopped. Charlie had hit his head on the window and was now unconscious, unaware of the events that had just taken place. Tommy lay on the floor, not moving or breathing. He had reached the end of the line, all his hopes and dreams extinguished in one blow. The rain continued to fall. All was still for a few minutes until the distant sound of the emergency services got increasingly louder. They had been alerted by both the passing runners, who had stopped in their tracks, witnessing the entire course of events along with the taxi driver. The road was quickly closed off and Charlie was taken away speedily on a stretcher and transported to Maidstone Hospital. He made a full recovery physically, but was never quite the same again. Tommy was pronounced dead on the scene, and after a short investigation, his body was transferred to the local mortuary for identification and various other checks which would take place. Road traffic accident investigators were soon on the scene and conclusions would have to be reached before the delivery van could be removed.

It was two thirty in the morning. Natalie couldn't sleep. She had made her excuses and went to bed at about midnight hoping to have a long discussion with Tommy before she slept.

She had tried several times to ring but there was no response. Tommy's phone had been completely smashed to pieces in the accident and was scattered along the roadside in Kent. Natalie's imagination was working overtime and she couldn't help but wonder if Tommy had met a groupie and was back at the hotel with her. Thoughts that were paranoid and groundless. She stared out of the window, looked down at her phone again just to double check she hadn't missed anything. She had a bad feeling which she couldn't shake off, and the first tear fell from her eyes, and was followed by a deluge. The endless traffic continued to flow outside on the London streets where life went on but for Tommy there would be no tomorrow.

26. Big Sleep

Max was lying in bed thinking about the night before. It was eight in the morning. Lottie was still dozing and Max could hear Arthur and Maisie playing in Arthur's bedroom. The kids hadn't been awake too long but they'd been in Max's and Lottie's bedroom playing hide and seek without disturbing Lottie. Max was starting to feel restless and had decided that a cup of coffee was in order. He slowly climbed out of bed without disturbing Lottie. He put on his dressing gown and opened the bedroom door to be greeted by a grinning Arthur. They had a staircase on the landing to stop Maisie from attempting to climb the stairs and falling. Max let Arthur through the gate and picked Maisie up and carried her down. As Will had started work on the roof of the house, which was nearly complete, Max spied the bottom of the scaffolding out of the window as he descended. They reached the ground floor and Arthur scampered into the lounge. Maisie soon followed once Max had let her down. He went into the kitchen, filled the kettle and switched it on. Whilst he waited, Max switched on the television. It was BBC breakfast news. The reporter seemed to be talking about a tragic death on the roads in Kent.

Max thought nothing of it and went into the lounge, checking that Arthur and Maisie weren't getting into any mischief. They were playing a game involving building blocks and Arthur was helping Maisie to build a tower. Once it was built, Arthur knocked it down scattering wooden bricks all over the floor. Maisie promptly burst into tears prompting Max to get cross with Arthur.

'Arthur! What did you do that for?'

Arthur shrugged and looked sheepishly across at Maisie who was still in tears.

'Help her build it again and this time leave it standing!'

Max heard a click in the kitchen that told him that the kettle had boiled. He returned to the kitchen and smiled as the TV was showing Tommy and the video for 'Forever and a Day.' The song played out and the camera panned back onto the news presenter and he looked rather sombre. Charlie Stayt had a habit of looking serious quite a lot anyway, but this time, he looked grim.

'That was Tommy McNeill and his comeback single. He was tragically killed last night in a road accident. He is believed to have been run down by a van in Maidstone, Kent. There are not thought to be any suspicious circumstances.'

Max stood still. He stared incredulously at the screen in front of him, his jaw fixed wide open. He couldn't believe his eyes and ears. He had exchanged texts with Tommy just yesterday, wishing him all the best for the show. Tommy had thanked him and finished the message with a smiling faced emoticon. He'd kept the text, and in fact, had retained the entire history of dialogue between them. The newsreaders on BBC Breakfast had moved on swiftly and were now discussing the forthcoming general election. Max flicked through the channels to see if he could find any more coverage of events. He found that ITV's breakfast show was showing an in depth report of events. They discussed the general history of Tommy's career with The Clowns, to the 'Wogan Incident,' to his wilderness years. The world was only just getting to know Tommy McNeill again, and suddenly, he was gone. Max turned on his heels, completely forgetting about the hot drink he was making and ran up the stairs.

'Lottie!' He hollered as he reached the landing. 'Lottie, are you awake?'

'Well, I am now!' She uttered wearily, although as soon as she saw the look on Max's face, she became very alert. She had seen this look before, when Max had taken the call from Jo telling him her Dad was critically ill in hospital after a heart attack and unlikely to pull through.

'Max! What is it?'

Max sat on the bed next to Lottie, still struggling to take in the news he had just heard.

'It's Tommy,' he began. 'He's been killed in a traffic accident. It's not clear what happened but he ran out of the studios last night after the recording, ran across the road and was knocked down by a delivery van. It's all over the TV.'

Lottie looked disbelievingly at Max but his face was deadly serious. April the First had come and gone, and if it *was* a joke, then it was a pretty sick one.

'Here look,' said Max. He could tell that Lottie was struggling to take the information in. He grabbed the remote control unit and switched on the small television that they had fixed to the wall in their bedroom. He switched it on to Good

Morning Britain on ITV1 where Kate Garraway was interviewing DJ, music journalist and writer, Stuart Maconie, on Tommy McNeill and his legacy in the music industry. It was now clear to Lottie just what had happened. To a news programme, this was a welcome change in focus from the general election which was dominating the headlines up until that point. Tommy had a sort of notoriety as well that had made him very newsworthy over the years, although not in recent times.

'Poor Natalie and poor Lauren,' she said. 'They must be absolutely devastated.

Max looked at the screen of his mobile; there were several texts from various people who must have found out the news before him. The question was, what would happen now? The single was due out tomorrow; would it be withdrawn from sale or would they go ahead with it anyway? When John Lennon died, which Max could just about remember, the song '(Just Like) Starting Over' went straight to the top of the charts. Tommy, however, although still a well-known name, wasn't in the same league as the ex-Beatle. For the first time in quite a while, Max didn't really know what to do. He would have to contact Natalie at the very least to offer his condolences. That was possibly the only thing that he could do. He obviously couldn't really ask questions that related to his commercial interests, even if he wanted to. He was undoubtedly shocked and saddened at what had happened to Tommy, but a small part of him couldn't help wondering what this all meant for his songs. He had come to the end of a very long road, but now it was as if the road had become jammed up with traffic. He sat with his left arm around Lottie's shoulder as they continued to watch the news reports coming in from Kent. Eventually, Max thought he'd better check on Arthur and Maisie. He went back downstairs to find them happily watching 'Postman Pat' in the lounge. He finished making the coffee and took it back upstairs. Lottie had switched the volume down on the television and looked pensively at Max.

'You realise what this means?' She said sensing Max's uncertainty of what would happen.

'No, what does it mean?' he replied.

'It means, Max, that you have a gigantic hit song on your hands!' She barely paused for breath before continuing

'It stands to reason, I mean John Lennon, Elvis and Freddie Mercury all had huge hits just after their deaths. I know Tommy isn't really in that category but he was a huge star in the eighties. There's a general malaise in the music industry, and with the news headlines all about the general election at the moment, this could really capture the public's imagination.'

Max was impressed with Lottie's perception of events but also felt a twinge of guilt about profiting from Tommy's demise. He'd got to meet him a few times since their first fateful meeting and had always liked him. He'd had his troubles, but came across as a genuine, down to earth character. His thoughts immediately went back to Natalie and Lauren and he began to wonder if and how he would be able to help them.

Natalie had received the call at about three in the morning at Claridge's. It took her a couple of minutes to calm a distressed and sobbing Lauren down enough to relay what had happened. Naturally, she couldn't take in the news and was completely shell-shocked. She contacted Yuki via reception and he came with Hikari immediately to Natalie's side in her time of need. Yuki, despite being horrified himself, kept his calm; something that was needed in this situation. His first move was to call the press officer of Pagoda Records. He broke the news to him but gave him instructions to release a statement and to field any questions that the press or public may have. Natalie was not to be disturbed under any circumstances; she needed to grieve. This was an act which Natalie would be very grateful for. In years to come, she would always remember Yuki's kind leadership. Natalie sat on the edge of her bed. Hikari had an arm around Natalie's shoulder as she sobbed uncontrollably.

'I need to be with Lauren and Miriam,' she said. 'Could someone get me to Sutton?'

Yuki took control of the situation. He called reception who arranged a car to take her.

'Don't worry about anything, Natalie,' said Yuki. 'We will deal with it. You go and be with Tommy's family and give them my sincerest condolences.'

Natalie was now incoherent with sorrow as she tried to thank Yuki, but it didn't come out as words that he would recognise. He understood, but he would need to talk to her before the day was out. There were decisions that would need to be made. Tomorrow 'Forever and a Day' would be released on a wave of publicity following Tommy's death and his appearance on 'Later,' and Yuki would need to know just how much Natalie was now prepared to be involved given the circumstances. There was a knock at the door as one of the staff from the hotel was sent to collect Natalie. The car had arrived and was waiting downstairs. She quickly changed in the bathroom and was ready to go. Natalie followed the lady from reception as she made her way back to the McNeill's house in Sutton.

The police were still present when Natalie arrived. A trained counsellor was dispatched with the police officers that had arrived there at around two in the morning, to break the tragic news. Ciara Donnelly had been working with The Metropolitan Police for two years after coming over from Dublin. She had trained with The Garda in Ireland but after meeting her soon to be husband Matt, an officer in The Met, she made the move to London. Her role really was to help relatives of accident victims to deal with their grief. She would also help them go through what needed to be done before they would be able to organise a funeral for Tommy. The body would have to be identified by somebody and that task would probably either fall to Lauren or Miriam and someone would have to be prepared for that.

Natalie knocked on the front door which was opened by one of the police officers who had been sent with Ciara to break the news. She explained who she was and was allowed into the house. It was still only four in the morning and the streets of Sutton were still bathed in darkness. Miriam and Lauren stood up upon seeing Natalie and the three embraced silently in the middle of the room. They all visibly shook as their tears flowed, and eventually, they sat down to talk. Ciara and the other officer, who they now knew as Tim, had explained to them exactly how and what had happened. The driver of the van, who they now knew as Charlie, was not under suspicion and had very little chance of seeing Tommy before the accident happened. Tommy's death was a tragic accident. However, there would be a short investigation into any improvements that could be made to visibility on New Cut Road, Maidstone. What that meant for Miriam, Lauren and Natalie was that Tommy's body could be released and funeral could take place as soon as possible. Ciara asked whether Tommy had made a will and Miriam, who was a bit calmer now, was able to answer.

'Yes, he did make a will at a solicitor's in town,' she said. 'Blenkins Smith, I believe is their name.'

Ciara offered to contact the solicitor on their behalf. The three women all pondered that whilst Tommy possessed very little at the time of the will, potentially his estate was worth a lot of money and none of them knew if it been updated very recently. What there was in his estate at the time would have been left to Lauren. It seemed wrong to be thinking about all this, with Tommy barely cold, but it would have to be faced sooner or later. The question then came around to who was prepared to identify the body and Natalie and Miriam were surprised to see Lauren very quickly volunteer.

'He was my dad, and if I can do anything for him, then I will. The quicker I do this, the sooner he can rest.'

She wiped her eyes with a tissue and hugged Miriam. She had been warned that after a road traffic accident, bodies could look gruesome but that didn't deter her, and Ciara began to run through the arrangements for this to take place. Lauren would be accompanied by Ciara and taken to a mortuary in Kent. Once this had been done, the body could be released to an undertaker and arrangements for a burial or cremation could be made, depending on what was stated in Tommy's will, if indeed any preference was stated. The three women agreed that if Lauren dealt with this, then Miriam would deal with the solicitor and Natalie would organise the press side of things. This was another aspect of dealing with the death of someone well-known, particularly, in such terrible circumstances.

Later that morning, and after a couple more hours of reflection, Lauren and Ciara left the house. Natalie said she would stay with Miriam, and so Tim felt happier about returning to Sutton Police Station in Carshalton Road, where he was based. Natalie made a cup of tea for both herself and Miriam. She supposed they should eat something too but couldn't face it just yet. She put the tea on the table and sat back down in an armchair opposite Miriam.

'Miriam, there's something else you need to know,' she began.

'I will tell Lauren too but all in good time. The fact is I'm pregnant with Tommy's baby. I'm only about eight weeks and I wasn't even going to tell anyone yet. I thought Tommy might have worked it out but I'm not sure if he did.'

Miriam sat staring back at Natalie, not knowing whether to laugh or cry. It was so much to take in. She was an elderly woman who had brought up her only son and lost him at the age of fifty-three, only to discover on the very same day that she was to have a second grandchild, twenty-three years after the first. Tommy had pulled off some surprises in his time but this really topped them all. Suddenly, Miriam didn't feel like she knew Natalie at all and they sat in silence for a while. It was maybe ten minutes later when Miriam finally broke the silence.

'So, was it planned then?' she asked. Her voice still sounded shaky like she still couldn't comprehend what was happening.

'No, it wasn't planned, not at all. In fact, when I first realised I didn't know what to do, and then I moved into the flat in Brixton and everything became clear. I thought Tommy and I were going to be together. I think Tommy wanted that too but with everything going on with the album, I don't think he could think straight.'

Natalie began to weep again and Miriam slowly stood up and walked over to Natalie and rested her hand on her shoulder.

'Well, you're family now. We'll deal with this together, you, me and Lauren.'

Natalie smiled through her tears not knowing just how she should feel.

Lauren and Ciara walked through the sterile corridors of the mortuary in Maidstone, both dreading the experience they were about to go through, but realising that it had to be done. The walls, ceilings and floors were a shiny, clinical white. Lauren thought it looked like something out of a futuristic drama. They were led into a seated area where they were asked to wait for someone who would take them to see Tommy.

'Now, are you sure you're okay with this?'

Ciara's soft Irish lilt had a calming effect on Lauren and she felt ready to face the task in hand.

'Yeah, I'll be fine.'

They were joined in the room by a man who was all dressed in white. He was wearing latex gloves, a white cap and a white tunic with a small logo on the top left.

'Miss McNeill?' he asked.

'Yes, Lauren Descartes McNeill, that's right,' she replied.

'Follow me,' he said. He had no other conversation other than that, and he walked solemnly in front of her, never pausing to look back. She had been drilled, however, and knew exactly what was about to happen. Ciara stayed in the waiting area and would be there for her when she got back. They walked into a dark room where she could see a large table with a body upon it. The body was covered in a white sheet exactly like she had seen in police dramas that she had watched on television. She followed him over to the body, he stopped and turned around to face Lauren.

'Now, take all the time you need.' He said, becoming slightly more sympathetic than he had been previously.

'I'm ready,' she responded.

He slowly lifted the sheet and revealed the face underneath. She flinched with shock when she saw the face of her father who looked peaceful, more peaceful than she had ever seen. She felt sad and strangely elated in equal measure, she nodded, burst into tears and the mortuary assistant replaced the sheet over Tommy's face. She was led back into the waiting area. Ciara had heard their footsteps and was already back on their feet when they arrived. She reached out and hugged Lauren and then they sat down for a minute.

'Okay?' said Ciara. 'How do you feel?'

'Well, I've had better experiences!' She half smiled at Ciara. 'All in all though, I'm glad I saw him, and he looked better than I thought. Good old dad, always the pop star, even in death!'

Ciara smiled back at Lauren and led her back out of the mortuary and to the car which was waiting outside. Lauren stared out of the window all the way home. Ciara didn't try and make her converse; they would do that when they got back to the McNeill's house. For now, she would leave Lauren to gather her thoughts. The family could at least get on with the job of laying Tommy to rest.

An inquest into Tommy's death had ruled that it was an accidental death. Charlie Pike was absolved of all blame in the matter. Evidence from the taxi driver at the scene and the passing runners revealed that the driver would have had little chance of stopping. There was also evidence from the security man at Maidstone Studios that Tommy was in a hurry to find a taxi. This at least laid things to rest slightly for Natalie, Lauren and Miriam, who had concluded that Tommy was in a hurry to return to the hotel to celebrate with his friends and bandmates. Natalie never realised, however, that Tommy was rushing to see her and that he had worked out she was pregnant. Maybe that way was better for her.

27. Precious Time

The day of the funeral had arrived. It was Friday, April 17. The release of 'Forever and a Day' had gone ahead as scheduled. It had been too late to delay it, although the release of 'The Kick in My Soul,' the album, had been delayed a couple of weeks to allow Tommy to be laid to rest. The single had been played virtually non-stop on the radio and television since his death had been announced. Tommy had a certain amount of flamboyance attached to him and a certain notoriety, despite his affable personality when sober. This all contributed to a huge amount of interest in the single which had debuted at number four in the chart. It was an unusual feat and sales forecasts predicted that it would reach the number one position by the weekend. The success of the song created a wealth of mixed emotions which were felt by everyone involved in the process.

It was a very strange day for Max who drove up with Lottie to the small service being held at North East Surrey Crematorium in Morden. He parked the car in Lower Morden Lane and walked through the gates of the establishment consisting of a large cemetery and a crematorium. He held

Lottie's hand tightly as they moved towards the chapel which they could see in the distance in front of them. They were quite early as Max had overestimated the journey time, but he would prefer that to being late. The events of the past couple of weeks had really brought mortality home to him. Despite his own composition being played constantly, the only song that he could hear in his brain repeatedly was 'Precious Time,' an up-tempo Van Morrison number which focused on how short life is. They finally reached the chapel which was next to the crematorium and there was only one other person waiting outside. It was, however, a familiar one; Bernie, The Magician from the recording studio. He gave them a gentle smile and walked over to them.

'If we'd been more organized, we could have travelled up together,' said Bernie half-serious and half-joking. Max didn't know Bernie all that well, only having been to the studio on a couple of occasions to check the progress. He didn't want to make small talk but he couldn't think of anything else to say, so he said what everyone says on these occasions.

'Terrible business, I'm still getting to grips with it,' said Max.

'Yeah, I know, poor Tommy. I mean he was just getting back on his feet again, wasn't he?' agreed Bernie.

A few more people started to gather round the buildings but no one that Max recognised. Bernie pointed out a slim dark haired lady in her fifties, she was very glamorous, although her face was obscured by a huge pair of sunglasses.

'That's Polly, Tommy's ex-wife, Lauren's Mum. I hope she comes in peace, although I don't know why she shouldn't, her split with Tommy was *years* ago,' he said.

Max had read about her; she was as famous as Kate Moss, Naomi Campbell or Yasmin LeBon in the eighties, the supermodel turned mum and housewife. That was until Tommy spent most of his time out of his tree on whisky and whatever pills he could find. By the time she found the courage to leave him, she had lost all the confidence to pursue a modelling career, and ran away to France to marry a wealthy vintner. She looked pensive as she ambled slowly around the building, talking on her mobile and craning her neck to see if anyone else was arriving. Other mourners started to arrive, although Max was led to believe that there wouldn't be too many people in attendance. More people had been invited to the wake. This was part of Tommy's instructions in his will, whilst he recognised his family and friends need to grieve, he wanted the wake to be a celebration, where everyone enjoyed themselves. Max was surprised and flattered to find himself a guest at the cremation. In the distance, he could see a black hearse approaching along the long, straight road which led to the chapel. Polly immediately acknowledged the arrival of the car by heading off down the road towards it. It had been months since she had seen her daughter and she was eager to support her in her time of need. Sylvain had disapproved of Polly rushing back to England but Polly had convinced him that she needed to be there for her daughter. Eventually, the hearse came to a stop just a few yards from the crematorium. Lauren was the first to get out of the hearse, followed by Natalie and Miriam. She ran towards her mother and embraced her, shaking, as she burst into tears. Bernie wandered over towards the hearse as he was to be one of the pallbearers along with Tommy's longtime friends, Phil and Clive. They were joined by former Clown's musicians, Matt Jones, Robbie Little and Stuart Ebdon. It was ironic that Tommy had only just made his peace with the trio. They met up in London recently for a meal and relived old times. Everyone wished Tommy well on his new project and tentatively suggested the idea of working together again. Nostalgia tours were big business these days! All hope of a Clown's revival, however, was all now academic. At last, the pallbearers were ready and the gathering was invited inside the crematorium for the service. They all sat downside and eventually Tommy's coffin was placed at the front of the crematorium ready to be interned.

It wasn't a long service. It lasted just over forty minutes. Eulogies were read out by Bill Terry, Lauren and by Phil and Clive together, recalling their school days fondly. The congregation sang the final hymn, 'The Lord is My Shepherd,' and the coffin moved gradually into the cremation chamber. The congregation watched it slowly disappear, all apart from Lauren, who couldn't bear to watch. Polly gripped her hand tightly. It had been a long time since she divorced Tommy but she still felt a powerful sense of grief at this sad vision. People started to leave the building and gathered outside as they made arrangements to meet up at the wake. The press had, by and large, respected the family's request for privacy but this didn't stop a couple of the most zealous paparazzi reporters from photographing events from a respectable distance. Tommy may have died but the renewed interest in his reinvigorated career continued. The wake was to be held at a function room within the The White Cottage Hotel in Sutton. It was a small friendly local hotel, perfect for this function. The sun shone in the sky as people made their way back to the parking area and started to drive away.

The function room at the hotel was starting to fill up. A buffet had been provided and people were stood by the bar. Lauren looked on anxiously. She intended to take a lead of the situation by making a speech and proposing a toast to Tommy. She chatted to guests as they arrived, as did Natalie and Miriam. They never drifted very far from each other all through proceedings. Natalie leaned across to Lauren and began to speak above the loud mumbling of people's voices.

'How are you doing?'

'I'll be glad when today is over but otherwise not bad, you?' said Lauren.

'Yeah, kinda the same.' Said Natalie in her transatlantic tones. 'I think you've been amazing today, Lauren, a real tower of strength. We will keep in contact, won't we?'

'Of course, we will!' Lauren replied emphatically.

'Besides, I need you to help me with my career!' Lauren momentarily smiled at Natalie, she winked and squeezed her hand before greeting Bernie and Bill who had just walked through the door. She was preparing to make her speech and was feeling a little nervous. Much to her relief, Polly arrived to give her some moral support. A quick headcount told her that everyone had now arrived at the hotel. She grabbed an empty wine glass from the bar and tapped it gently with a spoon and to her surprise, it chimed quite loudly, loud enough to make everyone look her way. Polly moved through the crowd of people to stand right next to Lauren.

'Could I just have everyone's attention for just a minute, please?'

She said softly but very audibly. Her voice was very clear and she was extremely well spoken. Tommy often declared that, 'She speaks proper like what I does!' Which made Lauren chuckle every time.

'Firstly, I'd like to say thank you on behalf of myself, my grandmother and Natalie for coming today to celebrate the life of Tommy McNeill, my dad. We will all miss him so much and we are still trying to recover from the shock. As you know, he had just made a comeback to music and was really enjoying himself. The single is selling well and it looks like the album will do the same. He would have been thrilled and thanks to everyone who helped him.' She looked around at some of the faces that had been involved, Yuki, Natalie, Bill and Bernie. A tear fell from her left eye followed by a stream.

'Secondly, I know for a fact he wouldn't have wanted us here being miserable, so let me propose a toast. Please raise your glasses to Tommy McNeill, and remember him fondly with joy. Ladies and gentlemen, Tommy McNeill!'

She raised her glass and everyone repeated his name 'Tommy McNeill' in unison. Lauren stepped to one side and the room returned to its previous status quo with people resuming the conversations they were having before Lauren's speech. Bernie shuffled across to Lauren and Natalie, he smiled and praised her on her toast.

'Lovely speech, Lauren,' he said 'I really, really enjoyed working with Tommy again after all these years. It was something completely different for me. Do you think he was pleased with the record?'

'Oh, yes, I know he was,' said Lauren. 'He was thrilled to be making music again and he was looking forward to planning the next project.'

Natalie concurred. 'Yeah, he loved it. He would have loved to work with you again too Bernie.'

As she smiled at him, Natalie noticed that Bernie appeared to have a moment of epiphany. He looked across at Lauren and took at pen and notepad from his pocket. He wrote down a phone number and his name and handed it to Lauren.

'When you feel up to it, give me a call and perhaps come down to Poole for a chat! Listen though, I hope you don't mind but I'm going to hit the road now, the traffic on the M3 will be chaos if I leave it too late.'

Bernie turned on his heels and walked toward the exit on the far side of the hotel. He didn't like goodbyes on these occasions. He never knew the right thing to say. Natalie looked at Lauren knowingly.

'I'll bet he wants to work with you.' Said Natalie, smiling at Lauren, who wasn't yet allowing herself to believe that it might be the case. Just at that moment, Lauren and Natalie were approached by Max and Lottie who also looked like they were ready to depart.

'We need to make a move back home,' said Max. 'Lottie's mum has the kids and we don't want to be too late.'

'No, that's okay. I understand,' said Lauren. 'Keep in touch, won't you!'

Max promised that they would and he meant it too. The whole experience with Tommy had changed his life in so many ways. He would help Lauren and Natalie in any way he could. He smiled and waved as they watched him and Lottie leave the hotel. As they walked back to their car, Max had a distracted look on his face. Lottie was curious.

'Hey, what's on your mind?' she asked.

'Well, I've had a song in my head all day and I can't shake it off,' he replied. 'It's 'Precious Time' by Van Morrison. It's all about grabbing life by the goolies and doing what you want before it's too late. I'm going to quit my job so I can write songs.'

He smiled a broad smile as he opened the passenger door for Lottie as she climbed into the car. Lottie was frightened of the financial consequences of Max leaving his job, but he was confident – with royalties coming in from a hit single and album – that they would be fine. Max was also feeling happy enough with the new batch of songs he had written. Some of them could be just as successful in the right hands. Natalie and Bernie had already agreed to help him with this before recent tragic events occurred. He drove through Sutton and made his way back to the M3, still full of regret for what had happened to Tommy, but looking forward to a bright future.

Later in the evening, when everyone had departed the wake, Lauren and Miriam returned home. They were joined by Natalie, who couldn't face being at home on her own that night. They sat in the lounge drinking hot chocolate and discussing what the future held for them. They still didn't know the contents of Tommy's will but the solicitor promised to visit them in a couple of days. Miriam asked him to wait until the funeral was over. There was probably more money involved than they would have anticipated a couple of months ago with royalties expected from the record. Natalie shared her baby news with Lauren, who was at first shocked and surprised, but also delighted. The last thing she expected at twenty-three was a baby brother or sister. She thought about the irony of life and how it gives and takes away.

'Well, any babysitting duties. I'm up for that!' She declared feeling slightly broody herself, although she knew that would have to wait. She had a career to pursue after all! She stood up and declared herself ready for bed. After embracing Natalie and Miriam, she opened the lounge door and disappeared upstairs.

'How do you think she took it? I was worried about telling her,' said Natalie.

'Oh, she'll be fine. Don't you worry. Just make sure you look after my little grandchild.'

Natalie relaxed a little in the knowledge that Tommy's family had accepted her as one of their own. She would have to arrange a trip back to Canada to break the news to her family. Maybe she would do that in the next couple of weeks. She decided to have a look on the internet in the morning for flights to Halifax. One thing was certain, she would be booking return flights. England was home now and she wouldn't want to be anywhere else. Miriam was seriously thinking of selling her house and finding a flat in sheltered accommodation and there were plenty of nice places available. She would wait to make her decision after the reading of the will. Lauren needed a roof over her head and she didn't want to see her struggling to afford a place of her own. She was aware that Polly was staying in London for a few days and wanted to spend time with Lauren. Everything would become clearer in the coming weeks.

28. Move On Up

Three weeks had passed since the funeral and spring had well and truly arrived. 'Forever and a Day' did peak at number one for two weeks and the album, 'The Kick in My Soul,' was top ten in five countries, including number one back home in the United Kingdom. Natalie, whilst still grieving for Tommy, was boldly and stoically dealing with everything that went with managing the career of a celebrity. The will had been read and Natalie was surprised that he had updated his will very recently. It wasn't like Tommy, and he hadn't said a word to her about it. Tommy had made sure that Natalie, Lauren and Miriam were the main benefactors. Miriam commented that at her time of life, she didn't need the money, but Tommy just wanted to ensure she was well cared for. Lauren would be more than able to find herself somewhere to live and this would enable Miriam to buy a warden assisted property without having to feel guilty about Lauren being homeless. It would be all change for the McNeill's in the coming months. It was starting to be a busy time for Lauren too. She now had a collection of twenty-five songs that she had written and arranged to go and chat with Bernie next week.

Tommy had made arrangements in his will for his ashes to be scattered on the beach near Bernie's studio in Poole. He fell in love with the place and enjoyed strolling along the promenade, even though it was the middle of winter when he was recording there. This week, however, Lauren promised Natalie that she would accompany her to her twelve-week scan at St. George's Hospital in Tooting. This was where she intended to give birth. Lauren was still coming to terms with the loss of her dad but was starting to feel a little bit brighter and optimistic. One thing she *had* done was healed her relationship with her mum and Sylvain. She had promised to go to Provence and visit as soon as she could, and Lauren thought that she would probably go in June. She loved the South of France at that time of year, and as much as she called London home now, she could do with some sunshine.

Max handed in his notice with I.M.C and was placed on gardening leave, which suited him down to the ground. He spent his time in between supervising all his home improvement projects. Money had started to filter in from record sales and Max and Lottie felt secure in their house. Will rebuilt the roof which meant there would be no repeat of last year's leak. Max noted though with some irony, that none of this could have happened if he hadn't had to climb into the loft and patch up the roof tiles that night. He had been invited along with Lottie to help scatter Tommy's ashes on the beach at Canford Cliffs and he was looking forward to seeing Natalie and Lauren again. He also wanted to catch up with Bernie. Max had written some new material and wanted a second opinion before trying to present it to record companies and music publishers. Natalie also promised to help and her connections and knowledge would be vital. Max marked the date on his calendar, Sunday, May 24, next weekend. He also noted that they would meet at the Jazz Café at Sandbanks, where he and Lottie had met Tommy and Natalie months ago. It would be good to catch up with them. Natalie, Tommy and Lauren had all become good friends. He looked up at the kitchen clock and it was time to collect Arthur from school. He found Maisie in the lounge playing with some building bricks.

'Come on, Maisie, time to get ready to pick up Arthur!'

She walked along to the front door where she climbed into her buggy and Max strapped her in. They sped off down the front path and into the spring sunshine.

The weekend of the twenty fourth came quickly. Natalie and Lauren were approaching Poole on the A31 and they would be early for a change. The scan went well and baby McNeill was given a clean bill of health. Even though Natalie was in her forties, there was nothing unusual in women of that age having a baby these days. In fact, the nurse at the scan said that it was very common. It was a weight off Natalie's mind. She hadn't expected to be having a baby at this stage of her life, and if you'd told her this scenario a year ago, she would have scoffed with derision. Times had changed, however, and she was delighted to be expecting Tommy's child. They'd spent hours looking at the scan photos with Miriam who decided to stay behind today. Natalie spent hours looking on the internet at ideas for naming the baby, she already had a plan in place for this. Typical Natalie, always one step ahead.

Although Miriam's health was steadily improving, she thought that a long walk on the beach would be too much for her. If she was honest, there was a part of her that couldn't bear saying goodbye to her only son. Nobody expects their children to die before them, but aspects of Tommy's lifestyle over the years, had grimly prepared her for this eventuality. She really hadn't expected him to go the way he did. Natalie and Lauren's thoughts began to focus on the task in hand. An azure blue coloured urn was perched very carefully in a small holdall that was placed on the rear seat of Natalie's Mercedes. She joked that he would at least be able to enjoy the view there rather than being hidden away in the boot.

'I must admit,' said Lauren. 'I'm quite surprised that he opted for the beach to have his ashes scattered. I know that he loved the Thames and Richmond Park. Maybe he just fell in love with this place while he was recording the album.'

'He *did* love it here though,' said Natalie. 'He had joked about buying a place here when the album went platinum!'

The irony was not lost on either of them about the album potentially turning platinum within the next few months, as Pagoda Records was preparing to release 'Blue Sky Day' as the next single. How Tommy would have coped with all this success and fame if he was alive, was debatable. It might just have tipped him over the edge again, although Natalie did reason that the album wouldn't have been as successful, had Tommy not died. At last, they descended Evening Hill and looked for parking along Shore Road, the gateway to Sandbanks. The area was one of the most expensive real estate locations in the world. They parked the car along the main road with a view of the spectacular Poole Harbour to the right. To the left, was the turning off which led to The Jazz Café and the beach. Lauren put the money in the parking metre. It was the least she could do seeing as Natalie had driven all that way. She swiftly paid for three hours and placed the ticket on the parcel shelf, ensuring it was visible through the windscreen. Lauren grabbed the urn from the bag on the back seat. Natalie locked her car and they made their way to meet the rest of the party which included Phil, Clive, Bill Terry, Bernie, Max and Lottie. They sat on the low wall situated by the café and waited. They felt a bit self-conscious of the fact that they were in possession of the bright blue urn. They'd checked out the rules for scattering ashes on the borough council's website and there were no restrictions but it *did* say that you had to be discreet. That would be no problem, they would just find a quiet stretch of beach. It was relatively quiet for a Sunday at this time of year. There were a few people passing by with their dogs, but all in all, conditions were perfect for the occasion. It was sunny but there was a chill in the air, and everyone that passed by was wearing more than one layer. Phil and Clive were the first to join them, soon followed by Max and Lottie. Bernie appeared jogging along the seafront followed by a horrified looking Bill Terry. He had been persuaded to join Bernie on his morning jog after having a conversation with him about wanting to get fit. The rest of the party were trying to suppress a giggle. 'This is what Tommy would have wanted,' thought Natalie. He would have loved the banter, and the fact that nobody was taking things *too* seriously. This day was all about Tommy after all. He would have died happily knowing that he had produced the album that he had always aspired too, he had met the woman of his dreams and had his daughter back in his life after years apart. Natalie and Lauren were both struggling with this concept but were being brave in the face of adversity, smiling and laughing at every turn.

After walking for ten minutes westward, they reached a small cove just before the end of the peninsula. Sighted here at the end was, The Haven Hotel, and close to this was a small chain ferry which took passengers to The Isle of Purbeck and beyond. The cove, however, was quiet and peaceful and seemed like the perfect place to scatter the ashes. They all agreed that this was indeed the spot and all eyes fell upon Lauren as she held the urn in front of her.

'Right,' she said decisively. 'I'm not going to give any great speech but I'm going to scatter the ashes and will be quiet for a couple of minutes whilst I gather my thoughts.'

There was silence as Lauren took the lid off the vessel and carefully and very deliberately emptied the contents into the sea, creating a large black patch as the waves gently ebbed onto the sand. Eventually, the ashes dispersed and the water returned to its usual hue. Lauren cleared her throat and they all walked back along the shore in perfect silence. Conversation only began again when they sat down in the café deciding what they were going to drink. The conversation was now much happier and quickly turned to the future. Max announced that he was now a full-time songwriter, and that he was on gardening leave as the contract with his employers was winding down. Natalie generally announced her pregnancy and that it was Tommy's. Most people realised that they were a couple but it hadn't been announced by either of them. The coffees arrived quickly and a large plate of cakes too.

'Mmmm! Dad would have loved these,' observed Lauren. It hadn't gone unnoticed by everyone else that Natalie took the largest cream cake she could and proceeded to devour it. 'Why not,' she thought. 'I'm eating for two now.' She smiled fondly as Bill regaled the table with stories about Tommy back in the days of The Clowns. He had observed him from a distance as a fellow musician, whilst Phil and Clive were able to tell some tales from their schooldays. After a while, people started to head off home. Phil and Clive first, as they needed to be back in London, closely followed by Max and Lottie. Lauren, Natalie and Bernie were left at the table and ordered some more coffee. Bernie started to steer the subject towards the future again.

'So, Lauren, I've heard what you can do in the studio and I've been thinking. How would you like to cut some demos with me? July is looking like a clear month to me. What do you think?'

Lauren looked gobsmacked but thrilled nonetheless. Her face; a picture of someone trying to look cool, but failing hopelessly.

'Sounds good. I am going to France next month so July is perfect,' she replied.

'Okay! So, day one, I will get you to run through some of your songs on an acoustic guitar. We'll pick three of them and go from there,' said Bernie.

'I'm always here when you need to take things a step further,' added Natalie.

They talked through some potential ideas and Natalie promised to talk to Yuki about a possible record deal. Lauren missed her dad and regretted that they only had a very short time together, but she was now brimming with excitement about the future.

'I can't wait to tell Mum!' she beamed.

Bernie and Natalie looked at each other and smiled. It was good to see that she was happy, despite what had happened. Lauren was already checking train times on her mobile.

'The only thing I have to tell you, Lauren, is that I can't afford to put you up in that flashy hotel you stayed at last time! I do have a spare room for you at mine though,' said Bernie.

Lauren rolled her eyes jokingly and then looked over at Natalie.

'Did you want to make a move back home? It's been a long day and you must be tired.'

'Yeah, that's probably a good idea!' she replied.

They said their goodbyes and Bernie jogged off back down the promenade towards his house. Bill Terry walked back earlier in that direction as he had parked there. He managed to escape without running again. Bernie was convinced he could beat him there if he managed to run at top speed. 'It was all good training,' he thought.

Back in Sutton, Miriam sat in her comfy armchair and looked out of her front window. It was a view that she had been familiar with for the last forty-five years. She knew it wouldn't be easy to leave but it was time to move on to new pastures. These modern, warden-assisted flats would have everything that she needed and she would be with people her own age. Lauren, Natalie and her new grandchild would all be close at hand to visit. She picked up the pile of estate agent's details, which had been put on the table beside her, and began thumbing through them. There were plenty in Sutton itself and she had no ambitions to move somewhere else, not at her age. On the wall to her right was a large picture of a smiling

Tommy. It had been taken when he was about twenty-five and at the peak of his career. It brought back nothing but good memories. He may have had a chequered past but he had redeemed his past mistakes before he died. She looked back at the leaflets. There was no time like the present to start planning the future.

Natalie got back home just before eight in the evening, worn out and ready for a sleep. She was due to meet Yuki tomorrow. He had a proposal to for her and she was intrigued to know what it was. They were meeting at her office in The Strand and then going off for lunch. Yuki and Hikari had been amazingly supportive and whatever he was about to put to Natalie, she was sure that it would help her get through the next few months. She climbed into bed just before nine, ready to sleep, but also feeling more prepared for whatever was in store. It didn't take long until she was sound asleep.

29. Forever and a Day

Time passed quickly. The summer flew by and soon it was October. Six months since Tommy had met his tragic end. 'The Kick in My Soul' quickly became one of the biggest selling albums of the year. It earned double platinum status in the UK; gold in Australia, France, The Netherlands and Germany. It had only just been released in The United States and it was slowly climbing The Billboard 100 Album charts. It was released due to public demand. Pagoda Records, in association with Sony Music, were releasing a 'Greatest Hits' package covering Tommy's entire career beginning with and including, The Clowns. It was hoped that this would be one of the big sellers in the rush for Christmas sales. Interest in his music had never been stronger and the younger generation had been discovering his music for the first time. A television documentary on his life and work was shown to rave reviews, featuring interviews from his contemporaries. Paul Weller, Van Morrison, Boy George and Mick Hucknall had all made contributions from the UK along with US artists, Stevie Wonder and Lionel Richie. Motown founder, Berry Gordy, had also revealed that he had tried and failed to sign Tommy to his label in the late eighties. It was one of Tommy's biggest regrets but he wasn't in the right place at the time and passed up the opportunity on health grounds. The alcohol and drugs had taken their toll and Tommy was only just beginning his journey to recovery.

His death had left his dependents financially secure and able to live their lives the way they wished. The greatest gift that he could have left. Musically, his legacy had grown, as if people were only just starting to recognise just how talented he was. His silky-smooth soul voice was unique and it was remarkable how many people heard him on the radio and assumed he was black.

Lauren had been staying in Dorset. She had been working on her debut album with Bernie having produced three songs back in July. They had cultivated a sort of country-rock sound with a uniquely British feel. It sounded fresh and Lauren was certainly a natural at writing her own material. She had enlisted Max to help her and he had finished off composing several partly finished songs with immense success. He would be credited with co-writing several songs on the album. She was helping herself to breakfast in Bernie's kitchen on a grey October morning, looking at the view of the English Channel when the message came. It was from Natalie and it read as follows,

'Help :) I think... hang on, I know contractions have started! How soon can you get here? The hospital just told me to stay home until contractions are about five minutes apart. They are about every ten minutes at the moment. xx'

Lauren immediately stopped what she was doing and knocked on Bernie's door. He'd been expecting it at any time and knew that it would mean a few days off recording. He didn't mind as it would give him the opportunity to be 'creative' with what they had recorded so far. Lauren had agreed to be Natalie's birthing partner and was keen to keep her promise. It wasn't every day that you became somebody's big sister. Natalie and Lauren had both agreed, with some amusement, that Tommy would have been useless when it came to the birth. He was prone to being squeamish and hated the sight of blood. He may have passed out in the birthing suite! Bernie got moving quickly and grabbed his car keys and jumped into his car, his beloved MG. He thought that it would be better to drop her off at Bournemouth Railway Station as she could catch a more direct train to Waterloo there. Some of the trains from his local station, Parkstone, stopped at all the little stops in the New Forest. They arrived at the travel interchange as it was called, due to the proximity of the bus station, and pulled over quickly. Lauren gave him a warm hug and promised to be back in a few days. She thanked him for the lift, shut the door behind her and made her way to the ticket office which she could see across the road.

It was almost a couple of hours later that Lauren arrived at London Waterloo. She was still getting to grips with the tube but decided that she would be best taking the Northern Line to Tooting Broadway. The hospital was within walking distance of the stop and Natalie had texted to say she was in a taxi and on her way. Within twenty minutes, Lauren was walking from Tooting Broadway to St. George's hospital. She followed the signs to the maternity unit and before long, arrived in hospital. She walked over to reception and gave her name. The receptionist pointed to a seating area and informed her that a nurse would be with her shortly. About ten minutes later, a short stocky nurse appeared and introduced herself as Cindy. Lauren guessed that she was Hispanic and maybe from Central America, but her English was perfect, and she chatted with Lauren as they made their way through a maze of corridors to the birthing suite.

'Miss Mancini is fine and in great spirits,' said Cindy.

'She keeps asking if you've arrived though. She'll be pleased you're here. I think all the gas and air are sending her delirious! Contractions are only about ninety seconds apart now; it won't be too long.'

They reached a door and walked straight in. Natalie looked a little pale but otherwise happy. Lauren hugged her gently as Natalie started to tell her all the events of the last few hours.

Thomas McNeill Mancini was born at 3.27p.m. on Wednesday, October 14. He weighed in at just over seven pounds. It was a relatively straightforward birth and Thomas was passed as fit and healthy by the doctors and nurses at the maternity unit. The midwife told Natalie that if he was feeding properly, there was no reason why both mother and child couldn't go home in the morning. It was deemed a little late in the day to go home on that day. Lauren started to ring everyone she could think of to break the news. Miriam immediately called a taxi to bring her to the hospital. It hadn't been long since she moved to a sheltered home in Carshalton, not too far from Sutton. It wouldn't take her too long to get to Tooting. She hoped that the traffic wouldn't hold her back from seeing her new grandson. She was delighted and burst into tears when she heard the name. She'd already been into town today and purchased a little blue baby grow and a card. She wanted Natalie to know just how much part of the family she was and wrote some touching words in the card. She knew that little Thomas probably wouldn't remember her when he grew up, but she was keen to be photographed holding him. One day, he would know the story of his father and who he was. Thomas was lucky in that he couldn't have had any better people in his life than Natalie as his mum and Lauren as his sister. Whatever happened now, Miriam felt at peace for the first time in a long while. She stared out of the window as the taxi negotiated the busy traffic in the autumn drizzle.

The taxi arrived and Miriam slowly made her way to the maternity ward. Lauren was waiting in reception when she arrived whilst Natalie needed some privacy. Doctors were giving her a check up to make sure she was fit to go home. She passed her inspection with flying colours. Lauren held Miriam's arm and helped her along to the ward. Natalie would be free and able to receive visitors again now. They had said fifteen minutes and Lauren had been away for half an hour. Natalie was beaming as they walked around the corner and spotted her. She was sitting upright in bed holding Thomas in her arms. He had just been fed, was asleep and very content with life. Miriam sat in a chair next to Natalie's bed and Thomas was placed in her arms.

'So, welcome to the world, Thomas!' she said.

She found that she had to check herself not to call him Tommy, although the temptation was there. He dozed in her arms, occasionally opening his mouth, making little whimpering sounds.

'Ah, was that a yawn?' said Natalie. 'He seems to do that a lot!'

She opened the small gift that Miriam had bought her. It was a little on the large side at the moment but would be perfect in a couple of weeks. Natalie was touched by the sentiments in the card. She smiled and thanked Miriam for the present and the thoughts. The three ladies sat and stared in awe of Thomas. Miriam thought he looked a lot like Tommy. She didn't say anything though and babies can change so much in the first few months. Texts and phone calls wished Natalie and Thomas all the best and Natalie's family started the arrangements to fly over from Canada. Her mother, and two of her brothers at least, were going to come over. Natalie was from a large family of Italian roots. If they all came over at once, she would have nowhere to put them up. Lauren decided that she needed to go home and freshen up. She hadn't stopped since Bernie had dropped her off this morning. Since Miriam sold the house in Sutton, she had been renting a room from Natalie, but she was looking to make a more permanent home somewhere soon. She said goodbye and left Miriam, Natalie and Thomas in the ward behind her. It had been a strange year so far, a bit surreal, and she was looking forward to a break at Christmas. Polly had invited her to Provence and hopefully the album would be in the bag by then. Yuki liked what he had heard so far and promised that Pagoda Records would release it. With Natalie and her PR abilities, they couldn't go wrong. Yuki bought NM Consultants from Natalie and she now worked exclusively for him. It was an agreement that suited both parties, especially with the arrival of little Thomas, it allowed Natalie flexible hours so she had plenty of time to spend with her son. One thing that she didn't want to do was farm him out to a childminder.

Max heard the news later in the evening. He told Lottie, who immediately looked online for a gift she could send. Money wasn't a problem these days. There was no mortgage left on the house and they had built an extension on the back of the house with a studio for Max and a small office. Lottie was able to put a few more shifts in at the hospital with Max working from home full-time. He was thrilled to stay at the house. The songwriting was coming on leaps and bounds and he'd made many new contacts in the music industry. Bernie had put him in touch with some film people too and he was working on the score for an untitled indie film. Arthur and Maisie had benefitted from having their dad around a bit more and Arthur started to learn to play the guitar. Jo bought him a three-quarter size acoustic for his birthday and he didn't go anywhere without it. Max and Will's band was still not ready to start gigging although they had been back to the open mic night a few times over the summer. Time seemed to be a problem and Will had been very busy with work.

'There were obviously a few leaky roofs in Dorset. You never know what you're going to find in the attic!' He joked with Max one day.

'And just to think, none of this would have been possible without that stormy night a year ago!'

They promised themselves that they would get together over Christmas for a jam session, even if they just practiced a few cover versions and took it from there. Who knows, nothing was set in stone and Max didn't feel the need to hurry it along. He turned his attention from his own thoughts and sat next to Lottie on their sofa. They pointed and laughed at the array of baby gifts that they saw online. Max teased Lottie, knowing it would take her all evening to make a decision.

Ten miles down the road, a serious looking Bernie was hard at work in the studio. The recording sessions had gone almost too smoothly. He listened to the songs one by one and genuinely felt that they didn't need much improvement. Lauren's voice was raw and earthy; it belied her age. She had the voice of a forty-year-old at twenty-three. Lauren's songwriting was rather simplistic and her warm vocal tone produced a stunning sound. The song that excited Bernie the most was a song called 'Rainfall.' The song had started life as a simple acoustic folk song, with lyrics that were all about standing out in the rain whilst everyone was inside keeping dry. It was a song about feeling different, something Lauren had always felt. Max had taken hold of it and changed some parts of it. He changed it both lyrically and musically, not significantly, but enough to breathe some new life into it. Bernie was thinking of asking Max down to assist with the production. Max had a good ear and the fact that he was just down the road was a definite bonus. Bernie's days of travelling halfway around the world to complete projects were over. He was settled here and they would just have to come to him. He had a lengthy list of offers that he was considering. Since the release of Tommy's album, his stock was rising again in the UK. He had been largely forgotten during his Nashville years but could now pick and choose his projects, and what interested him right now, was working with Lauren. What also interested him was another cup of tea. The music had stopped so he went back upstairs to the kitchen and put the kettle on.

Lauren had returned to Natalie's at about eight in the evening, ready for a shower, something to eat and a good night's sleep. She finally got to bed at about nine and lost herself in her thoughts. She thought about her album most of the time. There was always something pertaining to music occupying her mind. One day, maybe she would meet a nice guy, set up a home and start a family, but that was years in the future. Although she was tired, she was struggling to settle down and let herself drift off to sleep. She decided to distract herself by switching on the clock radio that was next to her bed. She could set it to switch off after half an hour which would be plenty of time for her to relax. She pressed the sleep button and set the timer. Jo Whiley was on Radio 2. Lauren liked her as she had eclectic tastes, and as if to prove this point, she was playing 'Forever Lost' by The Magic Numbers. There was some chat about next year's Glastonbury, a travel bulletin and then an introduction she recognised. It was Tommy with 'Forever and a Day.' Lauren smiled as she recalled the day she recorded the harmonies on the song. At the end of the song, Jo Whiley namechecked Lauren as the backing vocalist and mentioned that she was Tommy's daughter. She felt all was well with the world as she fell asleep. Tommy would never be forgotten; he remained the main driving force in her life even though he was gone. She was determined to make a success of her recording career. She wanted everyone to know her name, Lauren Descartes McNeill.

30. Songs for The Silence

That was the end of the story as far as the characters were concerned, and as the saying goes, they all lived happily, with a touch of sorrow, ever after. That doesn't tell the whole story, however! It may or may not have grabbed your attention but all the chapter titles, barring this one, are titles of songs. This started off being a bright idea that I had at the beginning of the writing process, but it soon became a huge millstone around my neck. I wanted this story to have a brilliant soundtrack and this proved to be quite a difficult task. There were only two requirements for the song to meet the criteria. Firstly, and most importantly, the songs chosen had to possess a specific quality, and whilst that is subject to people's own taste in music, there had to be some degree of artistic credibility involved. I could at this point be accused as a music snob and I'm possibly guilty as charged, but another person and perhaps even you, the reader, might scoff at my taste. You might say chapter one? Start!? I can think of at least fifty better songs by The Jam! This would then bring us to the second requirement. The song title must be relevant to the chapter or at least reflect the content of the chapter. So, now you know where I was coming from with this! So 'Beat Surrender' or 'The Butterfly Collector' wouldn't have worked in this instance, although I could have slipped Beat Surrender in at the end just after Tommy is killed.

The other thing to say about this story is how it was conceived. I had the idea about ten years ago. I was living with my then wife and two very young children in a house larger than we could really afford. It previously belonged to a rather elderly man and the house needed renovation. Kitchens and bathrooms all needed replacing and as for the garden, it was far too big and constantly needed money to be spent on it. My thoughts kept being drawn back to my past life playing bass in a band in my late teens. We were looking to be a commercially viable band and wanted to play our own material, and much like Max Chilton, I wanted to write music. I already had three songs that I had written that the band would perform regularly at gigs, but they weren't 'A List' songs, they were fillers. I desperately wanted to provide a song to the band that would potentially be a huge hit single. So, whilst watching Nelson Mandela's seventieth birthday concert at Wembley, at a time when he was still incarcerated, I had the beginnings of a cheesy ballad! I worked on it over a few weeks and came up with a song called…yes, you've guessed it! 'Forever and a Day.' Like Max in the story, I never heard it performed by the band because we split up before I had the chance to use it. It wasn't a song that I even liked but I thought that it had better commercial appeal that anything that I had written previously. I could have imagined Marti Pellow singing it and the potential of it stayed with me.

A few years passed and as I said, I found myself with this huge mortgage. I did think about sending the song out to a few people but, of course, I never did. Being brutally honest, the song wasn't that good anyway, and I couldn't imagine anyone taking me up on it. I can still remember the chords and most of the words to this day although the tape it was recorded on ended up at the local tip in a fit of pique! More years passed and we sold the house, we got divorced and life moved on. What stayed with me was the idea of the song on the tape being recorded by someone. As the years passed, the idea of this story began to take shape. Originally, the idea would have been to have made Max the writer *and* the singer, but this seemed a bit corny so the idea of a fallen star trying to revive his career began to emerge. He needed to be a little bit of a flawed genius who had hit rock bottom. Take one step forward, Tommy McNeill!

Tommy tried to make his comeback and ironically his death made him bigger and more successful than ever. The irony wasn't lost on me that I wrote this in the year that the world lost David Bowie and Prince. Of course, I wouldn't claim that Tommy was in that bracket, but perhaps he was at a level just below that. Another thing to note about the times in which I'm writing this, is that new material by both Billy Ocean and Rick Astley is gaining tremendous airplay on the radio, Paul Young has also released his first album in twenty years. All this goes to prove that artists of yesteryear can make a comeback no matter how long it's been since their last success.

There's also a lot of other songs mentioned in the story. There's the cover versions that Tommy recorded and the ones that they jammed to at the open mic night. Most of the other songs, however, were completely fictitious, like some of the titles in Tommy's album. Nonetheless, the rest of the songs on Max's tape, like 'Never Bring Me Down,' were my old compositions from my teenage years. Some of the songs are better known than others and hopefully it will introduce the reader to some songs that they have never heard. There is a possibility they will go on to appear in your playlist. If they don't, it's unimportant. If they do, then something has been gained from the experience. I must confess that I really struggled to find a title for chapter eighteen; this one more than any of the others. I wanted something vaguely to do with the location and didn't want to use 'I Do Like to Be Beside the Seaside,' the old music hall number, not that there's anything wrong with the music hall genre! I just didn't want to be that obvious. In the end, after much use of a search engine, I found this number by Wilson Pickett. It's not one of his better-known songs and it was never released as a single but was just used as a B-side, and pleasant enough in its own way.

Anyway, I hope you have enjoyed reading this and at least enjoyed some of the songs that have been discussed in here. I have listed the chapter titles below with a little bit of information about each:

1. Start - The Jam

This was originally recorded and released in 1980 by The Jam and became their second number one single, following 'Going Underground.' It was written by Paul Weller and appeared on their album 'Sound Affects.' The riff on the song borrows heavily from The Beatle's, 'Taxman,' a George Harrison penned song from their 1966 'Revolver' LP. Chosen simply because it's the start of the story.

2. Real Wild Child (The Wild One) - Iggy Pop

I wanted a song to represent Tommy McNeill and his glittering past, so I chose this. The song, which was covered by Iggy Pop on his 'Blah, Blah, Blah' album of 1986, has an interesting history. It was originally released in 1958 by Australian singer, Johnny O' Keefe. It's title back then was 'Wild One.' It was covered by various people over the years before Pop's version, including Buddy Holly and Jerry Lee Lewis. The album ended up being Iggy Pop's most successful solo work to date. This chapter was another hard one to find a title for, and so early in the story too! I quickly realised the task that I had let myself in for.

3. Don't Look Back in Anger – Oasis

Probably the best known and most iconic song ever performed by Oasis. This was released in 1996 at the height of the Britpop era and was taken from their huge selling album, (What's the Story) Morning Glory. It was released a good decade after events in this chapter took place but it fits the subject matter perfectly.

4. The End – The Doors
A full twelve-minute epic which featured on The Doors' eponymous first album in 1967. The song is not one of their best-known numbers, especially when compared to 'Riders On the Storm' and 'Light My Fire,' but signifies the end of a relationship or even an era.

5. The Beginning of a Great Adventure – Lou Reed
Released in 1989, I can wax lyrical about Lou Reed's 'New York' album, although truthfully, it's been a long time since I've listened to it. This is quite a quirky, jazzy song and I couldn't think of a better song to signify the beginning of Tommy's and Natalie's relationship. The song is not really about a new relationship at all, but rather about Lou Reed's relationship with his then wife. It does, however, hint at what is to come for the characters in the book.

6. Four Seasons in One Day – Crowded House
There was always going to be something by Crowded House in here. Their music is always enduring and has a sort of timeless quality, making it just as relevant in the present age. This song was apparently written about the Australian city of Melbourne and its changeable weather conditions. I think, however, that it's a metaphor, dealing with the changing moods of a person, people or a general situation. Coincidentally, this chapter could also have been called 'My Ever Changing Moods'. I stuck with this title so that I could shoehorn both songs in as they are both classics.

7. Station to Station – David Bowie
Shortly before I had finished writing the sixth chapter, David Bowie's death was announced. Nobody knew about his illness, or at least very few people were aware, only his closest friends and family. It was easy then to select one of his songs for this chapter. Especially as Lauren was travelling by Eurostar from Avignon to St. Pancras.

8. On The Road Again - Canned Heat
Recorded in 1967 and released the following year, this was Canned Heat's best known song. They were another interesting band with an intriguing history and this song is probably featured on the soundtrack of many 'road' movies.

9. A Sort of Homecoming – U2
I'm not short of an opinion or two when it comes to music and what I'm about to say may be controversial but… I'm going to say that U2's album, 'The Unforgettable Fire,' released in 1984, is far superior to 1987's, 'The Joshua Tree'. This view is, I realise, flying in the face of critical acclaim but I have my reasons. 'The Joshua Tree' to me, just sounds like an attempt to sell to the American market, whereas 'The Unforgettable Fire' is subtler and more experimental. The opening track of this album is 'A Sort of Homecoming,' a beautiful way to interpret a long journey home.

10. Come Together – The Beatles
This was the chapter where Tommy and Lauren were reunited and Natalie became involved in a relationship with Tommy.

The McNeill family had finally *become* a family, so this Beatles number was the first one to enter my mind.

11. Magic – Coldplay

There were a few songs with 'magic' in the title, but none that I really had any intention of mentioning on here. This song is from Coldplay's 2014 album, 'Ghost Stories,' and is significant for me as it reminds me of a particular day in my life - but that's another story!

12. Time for Action – Secret Affair

This song takes me right back to my teenage years! We would regularly attend parties and discos at church halls and youth clubs. There were two songs that always got requested by all the lads in attendance. This song and 'Gangsters' by The Specials. I'm not sure why but they had a cult following. Originally released and recorded in 1979, 'Time for Action' is a call to arms, figuratively speaking at least. It is steeped in the mod revival culture of the late seventies and early eighties.

13. One Day Like This – Elbow

Probably one of my favorite songs of all time, this depicts the type of harmony that was displayed in this chapter, following Tommy and Lauren's first meeting after twenty years. The lush string arrangement and Guy Garvey's strong and warm vocal really help the melody shine through.

14. Beginning to See the Light – The Velvet Underground

Lou Reed makes another appearance here, albeit at the helm of his old band. This is a fun up-tempo number and not very representative of their back catalogue, which can be dark and mysterious, to say the least!

15. Do They Know It's Christmas – Band Aid

The inclusion of Band Aid's multi-million selling single is self-explanatory and I tried (and failed!) to choose something a little less obvious. I suppose it reminds me of teenage Christmas parties and brings a smile to my face, however, reluctant I am to admit it.

16. With A Little Help From My Friends – The Beatles

Beatle time again! I could have chosen other versions of this song or indeed other songs. There is, however, something about the fact that they allowed Ringo, the odd lead vocal here and there, that makes me chuckle. It's probably not Lennon and McCartney's finest but demonstrates Tommy's friends helping him back to form.

17. Heart of The City – Nick Lowe

Originally recorded by Nick Lowe for his album 'Pure Pop for Now People' in 1978. It was subsequently covered by Dr Feelgood and The Strypes, the latter version being released quite recently. I think they still play it in their live set to this day. If you haven't heard this before, I recommend The Strypes version.

18. Down by The Sea – Wilson Pickett
Like I said earlier on, this isn't Wilson Pickett's best-known work. His most celebrated song of course is, 'In the Midnight Hour,' which has been covered by just about everyone! Including bands that I myself have been in. He's also well known for 'Mustang Sally,' which he covered. If you've ever seen the film, 'The Commitments,' then you will be more than familiar with it.

19. In Between Days – The Cure
Well it had to be, didn't it? Everyone in the story was waiting to see what was going to happen, especially Max, who probably had the most to lose in this situation. This is another song hand-picked from my youth and the many parties I went to back then. There was always plenty of Robert Smith lookalikes dancing away to this when it was played.

20. Senses Working Overtime – XTC
I have probably overstated it in the story but the genius that is Bernie, or the Magician, comes to the fore in this chapter. He seemed to simply pluck ideas from everything that he could see, hear, smell, touch and taste. In the words of the song, his senses were truly working overtime at this point.

21. When the Sun Goes Down – The Arctic Monkeys
Apologies if you are familiar with The Arctic Monkeys' number one single from 2006. You probably presumed that Tommy was going to go looking for prostitutes in Sheffield rather than rambling in The Cairngorms. It was either this number or Level 42's, The Sun Goes Down (Living It Up) and

actually, I was torn between them for a little while. They are two very different songs but both would have aptly represented Tommy trying to find his way back to base in the dark.

22. 10/10 – Paolo Nutini

Or Ten out of Ten! Well, it's my story, and I wasn't about to give Tommy poor reviews for his comeback. This was one of my favourite tracks from Nutini's 'Sunny Side Up' album and brings back fond memories. It had to be used for this chapter. It's a bright, optimistic and happy song although it really has nothing to do with record company meetings.

23. The Message – Grandmaster Flash and the Furious Five

This song came back into my mind recently. I was on a night out, there was a DJ and I suddenly had the urge to hear it. I think I did the DJ a favour too. The dance floor filled up quite quickly after that. I've no idea who Grandmaster Flash is, or was. I also haven't a clue why his five were so furious. This chapter is where Tommy is playing the publicity game so 'The Message' fitted in nicely.

24. The King of Rock N' Roll – Prefab Sprout

A fantastically witty lyric in this song and it probably doesn't really fit with the content in the story. By this stage, Tommy was back to his former self and not the sad figure that the song suggests. At last, he arrived back in the big time. His duet with Jools Holland was the pinnacle of his resurgence whilst he was still alive. It was an impeccable performance and one that would live in the memory of all his old fans for many years.

25. Talking Heads – Road to Nowhere

Unfortunately, Tommy's dream was about to be shattered, not that he would have known anything about it. His impulsive attempt to get back to Natalie in London resulted in his untimely death. It's probably slightly corny but Talking Heads' quirky song, 'Road to Nowhere', from their 1985 album 'Little Creatures' just had to be the title.

26. Big Sleep – Simple Minds

A great song from one of my favourite albums. 'New Gold Dream' was released in 1982 and was their breakthrough album in the UK. It's quite a sad song but the chapter deals with Tommy's death. This really is the only song that I could have used here.

27. Precious Time – Van Morrison

This is a lovely uplifting song but probably not one of his best known. It's a timely reminder that life is short and is there to be enjoyed. A lesson for all of us. It's not surprising that Max can't help but think of it on the day of Tommy's funeral.

28. Move On Up – Curtis Mayfield

I think the original purpose of Curtis Mayfield's 1970 classic, 'Move On Up,' was to represent Tommy's moving on to another place. I think, however, I wanted to inject some optimism after all that melancholy in the previous two chapters! I was torn between the two versions that I am aware of. The Jam included it on their final single, 'The Beat Surrender' EP. It's a creditable attempt but I had to plump for the original on this one. Well, it's not very often that a cover version betters the first version.

29. Forever and a Day

There *was* really a song with this title, nowhere near as good as the one in the story but it *did* exist. Thankfully, all evidence of its existence has now been destroyed. Now I feel I can lay it to rest nearly thirty years on from the time it was written. One thing I will say, it only seems like five minutes ago!